Can't Explain

Can't Explain

A frightening tale of
Parental Alienation Syndrome

LUKE MATTHEWS
JULIE BURKHARDT

THE CHOIR PRESS

ISBN 978-1-909300-17-0

Published by The Choir Press

Contents

Acknowledgements

First we would like to express our sincere gratitude to all those that found the courage to tell us of their own experiences of parental alienation, enabling the forceful injection of realism into this novel. We would like to give particular recognition to those brave enough to admit they have been actively involved (whether intentionally or not) in the alienation role for whatever reason, helping to dispel the view that Parental Alienation Syndrome (PAS) is a myth. To those alienated parents who found the internal strength to graphically describe the anguish and torment to which they have been subjected, we express our sympathies and wish you well in repairing your relationships with your children.

We would like to acknowledge the False Allegation Support Organisation (FASO) for their good work in supporting those that have been falsely accused of child abuse.

We would like to acknowledge the good work and research being done by various other professionals and organisations, including the Families Need Fathers and Fathers for Justice groups, that help to publicise the dangers and potentially permanently damaging consequences of PAS.

Finally we would like to thank all friends and family for their advice, encouragement and support with regard to the publication of this novel.

Luke Matthews
Julie Burkhardt

Prologue

Paul Nelson sat bolt upright in bed. He couldn't sleep. His mind was racing after receiving his daughter's devastating letter earlier that day. How could a nine-year-old child bear so much intense hatred and spite towards their father? He just could not explain it. It was so unjustified. He knew he was not perfect, but who is? He kept going over and over past events in his head, frantically looking for a reason. He stretched his memory right back to his own essentially happy childhood, desperately looking for clues.

Paul grew up in the sleepy village of Lipston with his parents, alongside his elder brother. His mother had trained as a nurse caring for the elderly, although the majority of her time was spent bringing up the two boys. Occasionally, she would supplement the family income with various agency jobs. His father had spent most of his working life building up his own window-cleaning firm, providing a highly valued service to the surrounding villages. He was now retired, but kept himself busy doing voluntary work with various organisations within the community.

Paul left secondary school in the summer of 1983. He had his whole life ahead of him and was excited. He had recently passed his driving test, successfully gained an apprenticeship with a construction company and was madly in love with his first girlfriend. Alas, like many teenage romances, this eventually ran its course and he was most upset when she called time on their relationship. Deep down he knew it was the right thing, but he was still heartbroken. Little did he realise then the full magnitude of heartbreak.

Fortunately for Paul it wasn't too long before he got over his first love and started to take pleasure in his new single status. He appreciated being carefree with no serious responsibilities, especially now he had some money in his pocket allowing him to rent a small but comfortable flat. He liked a drink with the boys, playing pub league Sunday morning football and taking girls out, although he was keen to avoid anything too serious. He had a passion for music and spent many evenings watching live bands, not getting home until the early hours of the morning. Like many youngsters in their early twenties, he liked to socialise and arguably frittered away too much of his earnings on frivolous activities, but he did not have a malicious bone in his body. People would comment, 'What you see is what you get with Paul.' He was never sure whether to take this as a compliment or insult, but it was meant as a compliment. Ultimately they regarded him as a young man with integrity, trustworthy and not afraid to speak up for his beliefs. Overall he was having a great time and engaged in some wonderful experiences. Occasionally there would be one or two embarrassing ones he'd rather forget, but regardless, he considered them experiences just the same.

Alongside the socialising, Paul remained for the most part focused on his job and its associated training. He recalled the glorious summer's day when he received the results from his Architectural Design course. He was elated. He had passed with flying colours! He was the first person ever in his family to obtain a higher education qualification. It wasn't that his family were too dim to go to college or university; it was more to do with the fact that they did not come from that sort of social environment. Although they were not poor, their roots were in a working-class background and a higher education was not really financially viable without some sort of help or support.

Paul was truly overjoyed with his exam result. Of most significance to him was that his days and nights of studying were over. He had studied for his apprenticeship part-time, sponsored by his employers. It had been hard work, but he felt extremely privileged to be bringing home a wage whilst his company paid for his education. To him the job was far more enjoyable than the associated study, supported by the fact that he would remain in the same profession for a further thirty years, carving out a successful career. The thought of continuing his studies in the USA or in a sunnier climate somewhere did cross his mind fleetingly, but these ideas soon faded away to nothing when he thought of all the fun he would be missing out on at home.

One of the main things that kept him sane during his intensive periods of study was playing the saxophone. He wasn't all that good, but his sax was always his trusty friend. He could always find a tune to suit his mood and escape into another world. He had previously promised himself that once he had completed his apprenticeship, he would buy himself a top-quality instrument, something he had dreamt of since his very early teens, but could never afford. Well, now was the time. He drove to the music store in the town and bought the most expensive saxophone in the shop. For the next two months, he and the instrument were inseparable. 'Who needs a girlfriend when you can play the sax?' he would joke with friends and colleagues.

The following Sunday lunchtime, whilst enjoying a drink with his football team-mates, Paul excitedly mentioned that he was thinking of starting a jazz-funk band. He had not realised one of his colleagues was an accomplished keyboard player. That same evening they got together and had a bit of a jam session. They had a great time and vowed to do the same again the next week.

It wasn't long before others noticed the emotional high they were on and shared in their infectious enthusiasm. Other budding musicians from the local area wanted a piece of the action and within a few weeks they had formed a tight little ensemble. Saturday afternoons had now changed forever, being faithfully devoted to rehearsing in an old barn that a local farmer had kindly let them hire for a minimal fee. After one such rehearsal (and a few beers), they pondered over the idea of doing a live gig in front of a real audience. Were they up to the challenge? Naturally the beer started talking: of course they were good enough. They could do Wembley Stadium!

It is from this point forward that the unjust and tragic story within this book unfolds. It starts with the all too sad, but familiar story of a couple in their mid-twenties falling in love, getting married, starting a family and then running into matrimonial difficulties, eventually leading to divorce. The territory that may not be so familiar is that of 'Parental Alienation Syndrome', an evolving phenomenon, first reported by doctors, psychiatrists and other professionals in the USA in the 1980s.

When Paul first noted that his relationship with his nine-year-old daughter Kara was faltering, he started to keep a journal of all the strange occurrences that kept happening. The journal starts from the point at which he strongly suspected his ex-wife, Phoenix, was a little imbalanced and 'poisoning' Kara's mind against him. It catalogues the next seven years, highlighting Phoenix's increasingly weird and sometimes disturbing behaviour. It continues right up until Kara was permanently detached from him and his family, through no fault of his own, supported, incredibly by the UK legal system. It exemplifies the systematic manner in which a child can easily be manipulated and 'brainwashed' into believing a previously cherished parent should be extricated from their life forever. It describes the associated mental cruelty and emotional bullying an alienated parent goes through. It depicts the anguish and terror of facing false accusations of child abuse and how Paul and his long-term partner desperately struggled to save their reputations and livelihoods. There was even a spell when he was envisaging a jail sentence. Most shocking and disturbing was the apparent negligence and biased nature of supposedly family-friendly organisations such as Social Services and the Children and Family Court Advisory and Support Service (CAFCASS), which unscrupulously influenced the UK Family Courts. Not only was such an injustice allowed to happen, but it appeared to be actively encouraged and praised by the judge!

Paul's problems, and ultimately Kara's, were rooted in the subject of Parental Alienation Syndrome (PAS). Social Services, CAFCASS and the UK Family Courts appeared reluctant to recognise or fully understand this phenomenon and there are many that believe this whole scenario is something that needs urgent and drastic reform in the UK.

As well as highlighting the consequences of PAS, this story draws attention to early warning signals of its ugly reality in an attempt to help others avoid the same pitfalls that Paul and his daughter could not. It also gives a snapshot of the working practices of organisations such as Social Services and CAFCASS, and presents views on how the systems and working practices within these organisations could be improved.

It is difficult to understand the exact nature and full extent of the torment that alienated parents endure. Those that have been through such anguish understandably find it difficult to talk about their experiences and it becomes all too easy for overseeing authorities to just brush aside concerns raised, giving them low priority. As a consequence, systems are slow to change and the problems continue. However, all men and women involved in raising children, or just thinking of starting a family, need to be aware of how easily they could find themselves in such terrible circumstances.

Disclaimer

All characters mentioned within this book are fictitious and have been created to exemplify how Parental Alienation Syndrome can destroy family relationships. The characters are not intended to represent anyone alive today, or deceased.

Chapter 1

Pre-marital relationship

- ✧ Paul meets Phoenix
- ✧ Getting to know Phoenix's family and past history
- ✧ Paul proposes

On Sunday morning, Paul thought long and hard about the previous night's conversation he had shared with his fellow band members following their rehearsal. Although he recognised they had all been in high spirits, he remained persuaded that they should at least try and play one gig, possibly at a party or a nearby club. On behalf of the band he compiled a set list and it wasn't long before they were practising these songs religiously. News soon spread about their intentions and friends and family would drop by the barn, curious to see and hear how they were progressing. He knew those first rehearsals sounded pretty awful, but everyone was thoroughly enjoying themselves and they were getting no end of support from friends and loved ones.

As the winter arrived, so did the band's first live gig. It was to be held at Lipston Village Hall. They were excited and nervous at the same time. They wanted it to go well, not just for themselves, but because a lot of their friends and families would be present.

Fortunately it did go well and a hugely enjoyable time was had by all. The gig had attracted people from outside the village and additionally raised a fair amount of cash for charity. The Parish Council were also impressed, not so much because of the quality of the music, but more because the gig had also raised some much-needed funds to go towards the upkeep of the village hall. As a result, the band was booked to play again three months later.

These two gigs boosted the band's confidence no end and they started playing at other venues. This soon became a significant part of Paul's social life and the band built up quite a following that would regularly come and support them (and also try to drink the venues dry!). There was a group of girls that would invariably turn up at these gigs. One in particular, with cropped, bleach-blonde hair, regularly caught his eye. A couple of times he ended up chatting with this girl, who he subsequently discovered was called Phoenix. They shared similar interests in music, although her taste was a bit too poppy for his liking. Nevertheless, there was definitely some common ground with a couple of their favourite artists.

Phoenix worked in the nearby town as a secretary for a local firm and one night they agreed to meet after work and go to a concert. One thing led to another and they soon became good friends, going out regularly. They enjoyed their time together and an inevitable closeness built between them. One evening after a gig, Phoenix stayed over at Paul's, and although they had not planned it, it was then that their relationship became intimate. Rather than forging a stronger bond between them however, they both felt a bit let down and the next morning there was an air of embarrassment between them. Their friendship cooled off somewhat after that and two weeks later Paul found out from a friend that she was dating another guy. At this point, Paul reluctantly admitted that their friendship had now cooled to zero. He decided to immerse himself in his saxophone playing and Sunday morning football. He had a number of friends, both male and female, with whom he liked to go out and socialise. He had no serious girlfriend, but for the time being he was happy that way.

One evening about six months later, without warning, Phoenix turned up at Paul's flat. He hesitantly invited her in for coffee. He was wary of her since he was not impressed with the way their relationship had ended. She explained how she had driven round to his flat late at night a couple of times that past month, but had not mustered the courage to ring the doorbell. Instead she had parked outside and waited for about an hour, staring up at his bedroom window before driving off. Paul found this a bit weird, but he relaxed a little once they got chatting. He opened a bottle of wine, after which the conversation started to flow more easily.

'Why did you go so cold on me before when we were going out?' he asked her outright.

She didn't really give an answer, but explained how her latest liaison had gone very sour, to the point of being abusive. Paul didn't like to push too hard as to the exact nature of the abuse, but he was rather taken aback when she described being locked in a room and having money and possessions stolen. She also implied some physical abuse may have taken place. He let the subject drop at this point as he did not want to cause her unnecessary distress.

'Are you seeing anyone now?' Phoenix asked.

'No, not at the moment,' he replied.

'Would you like to try again?'

Being a softy, he replied, 'Why not?' with a shrug of his shoulders.

This time their relationship went from strength to strength and within months they had bought a cosy little cottage with wonderful views across acres of farmland. Paul particularly started to enjoy the convivial relationship he now shared with Phoenix's mother and stepfather. At first he had considered them rather over-flamboyant characters for his liking, too full of their own self-importance and always craving attention. These potential barriers to friendship were soon easily overcome, however, by the fact that they all shared a deep passion for jazz music. They weren't conventional in-law material. They were more like friends. They would invite him and Phoenix over to share in rather raucous evenings, alcohol being in noticeable abundance and every now and then they produced the odd spliff. On more than one occasion they had intimated that they were part of the 'swingers' fraternity, but Paul was not sure whether to take them seriously or not. He wondered if it was a throwback to their adolescence, being part of the 'make love and peace' psychedelic era of the 1960s. Phoenix would notably distance herself from these events and air her disapproval. These evenings did not happen often, but they did appeal to Paul's more adventurous, curious and easy-going nature. Phoenix on the other hand was far less relaxed and would remark how her mother and stepfather appeared to go out of their way to embarrass her. Paul recognised that virtually all offspring say their parents embarrass them at some point, but he did notice that something appeared to run a little deeper with Phoenix.

As time went on, Paul got to learn more about Phoenix's past and family history. Phoenix was the result of a night of passion between two youngsters in their late teens. A baby was clearly not intended at this time, but they did the so-called decent thing and got married. When Phoenix was born, the young parents continued with the pretence of marriage, but times were tough and they were not fully equipped for the hard work a young child entails. Phoenix's father would suffer from bouts of depression, which were made worse by his wife's obvious wandering eye. Although he was aware of his wife's dalliances during the six years of marriage that followed, it finally came to a head when he caught her in bed with another man for the second time in as many months. This finally pushed him over the edge and he packed his bags and left. Phoenix obviously raised questions with her mother as to where and why her father had gone, but these questions were not satisfactorily answered. Instead she was introduced to the man who became her stepfather.

As Phoenix approached fourteen, she inadvertently found out via a friend of her mother's that her natural father had initially travelled to Ireland looking for work. Shortly after arrival, he had apparently spent some considerable time hospitalised in a psychiatric ward. Although Phoenix was content living with her mother and stepfather, hearing this news sparked an urge in her to trace her natural father's whereabouts and contact him. After two weeks of investigation, she got the tragic news that he had died six months earlier in a mining accident. This was an obvious blow for her, but on the outside she appeared to cope relatively well and continued to live with her mother and stepfather for the next few years.

Now when alone with Paul, Phoenix would often relay how her mother and stepfather had never praised her for any of her achievements when growing up and consequently she never felt good enough for them. When Paul was first told of these incidents, he was both surprised and saddened. He wondered if such experiences would have left any long-term scars.

Putting these issues to one side, this was indeed a very happy time for them both. As well as enjoying activities together, they had their own independent careers and hobbies. He continued to play saxophone and football, whilst she enrolled on an Open University course, studying different periods of history. They would regularly meet up with friends and family, go to various events and enjoy meals out. There were a few minor hiccups; for example she was noticeably not keen on him going out without her, but he believed this to be typical of any normal male–female relationship. Sometimes he did sense that he was possibly losing some of the warm companionship he used to share with his friends and family, but he put that down to now being part of a couple.

There were a few occasions, however, that did give him a little more cause for concern. The first was when Phoenix had a top-of-the-range jacuzzi hot tub installed in the garden, without consulting him at all. Another was when she bought him a brand new saxophone, again totally out of the blue, without his knowledge. Now, a number of people might think that these were lovely gestures, but he was not a lover of surprises of such an extravagant nature and Phoenix was aware of this fact. He was also conscious that they did not have money to burn. Despite this, she had taken a considerable sum of money from their joint bank account to pay for these luxuries without his knowledge or consent.

He was not a control freak, but a feeling that everything was being done for him was becoming increasingly frequent. The importance of his opinion appeared to be diminishing over matters that should really concern them both. He never did say anything to her outright, for he did not want to upset her, particularly since she had obviously gone to a lot of effort. In hindsight, he wondered if he should have recognised these strange acts of extravagance as early signs of abnormal behaviour. Perhaps if he had been more forceful at times he could have avoided the dark, horrific times that were ahead of him.

Overall, he considered himself very fortunate. He had a good job, a nice house, a steady relationship and he enjoyed his hobbies. Occasionally people would ask him when he was going to get married. He had never been a fan of marriage, but pressure from others started mounting. The pressure was not from Phoenix, or their respective families, but more from other married couples. They would say things like, 'Don't you think you owe it to Phoenix to get married?' He noticed that these people were not necessarily happy in their own relationships, but were likely trying to self-validate their own decision to get married. He wondered if they now had regrets, but there was no way they could possibly admit it to themselves or the outside world. Instead they were trying to convince themselves how wonderful their own lives were and that others should follow their example.

Regardless of his own perceptions, it had planted a seed in his mind that perhaps he should ask Phoenix to marry him.

Paul proposed six years after he and Phoenix originally moved in together. She kept him waiting until the evening for an answer.

The answer was 'Yes'.

Chapter 2

Marital relationship

✧ The wedding
✧ Moving house
✧ A baby girl, Kara

Paul and Phoenix were married a year later in Scotland. The ceremony was held in a converted castle. It was hidden away in fifteen acres of woodland and provided the most romantic of settings. They were joined by their respective sets of parents. Sadly for Paul, other members of his family and friends were not able to join them due to the logistics involved, not to mention the expense. On the positive side, it suited Phoenix's request for a quiet affair since she came from a very small family and did not want the guest list to be heavily weighted in favour of the groom. The setting was idyllic, with every luxury a person could want.

On the day of the wedding, however, Paul experienced a feeling that an ever-increasing distance was growing between himself and his friends and family. It wasn't helped by the events of the previous evening when he had noticed something was obviously troubling his father, but he had been unable to get to the bottom of it. The distant feeling with its associated sadness became particularly apparent at the end of the ceremony. Paul looked around. There was hardly anyone there and it felt cheerless. Normally he liked quiet private gatherings, yet for some reason, this did not feel right.

Following their return home, they had a wedding reception to which all their friends and family were invited. Although everyone was there, once again Paul found the same sad feeling lurking in the background. Everything seemed a bit false and he felt that the congratulations did not come across as very heartfelt. He resigned himself to thinking that this must be normal when you get married and he should now be focusing all his energies on his new wife. As far as he was concerned, they were going to be happy for the rest of their lives.

For the next year or so, they were indeed very happy; at least he thought so. To add to their delight, shortly after the wedding they excitedly announced they were expecting their first child. Secretly Paul was hoping for a daughter, although he would have been happy with either a boy or a girl. As with most expectant parents, his main wish was that their child would be healthy. At the same time they made plans to move to a bigger house to accommodate them all.

Phoenix enjoyed the idea of being a career woman and was insistent that she did not want to be a stay-at-home mum. In the past she had always been rather disparaging of women who had given up work to look after their children. She could see no reason why a woman should not be able to do both and over the past few months had converted Paul to her point of view.

They took out a large mortgage and bought a wonderful house with a garden, easily able to accommodate them and their expected arrival. Things were shaping up very nicely and as fate would have it, they found a suitable nanny who lived right next door to their new address.

Once they had moved their belongings into their new home, they started getting the nursery ready. Everything continued to work out splendidly. The only downside was the recent news that due to cutbacks in the construction industry, compulsory redundancies were going to be made at the building firm where Paul worked.

Phoenix worked right up until a week before her due date and within days they were rewarded with a lovely baby girl, beautiful in every way. Paul loved her the minute he saw her and his natural protective paternal instinct kicked in. They named her Kara. Paul was so proud and very much the doting father, as his friends and family would testify. He tried to be careful not to fall into the trap of boring everyone senseless with photos and anecdotes as is common with new parents, but it did prove difficult, particularly when broody females were around.

The next three months were exhausting for them both, as any parent will understand. Paul carried on working at the construction firm whilst Phoenix did the lion's share of looking after Kara. He arranged for a home help to assist Phoenix with the domestic chores during the day. When he returned home from work in the evenings, they would share the responsibility of looking after Kara before collapsing into bed. They took it in turns to do the night feeds. It would have been nice to think of these as special bonding times, but in reality they were absolutely shattered, acting more on autopilot than anything else. Regardless, they loved having Kara around.

Paul could sense that Phoenix's attentions were understandably now fully diverted to their daughter rather than him. Friends of his had previously warned him that this was common for new mums. Although he missed the close loving companionship he had previously shared with his wife, having Kara around was consolation enough at this time.

Chapter 3

Difficulties in marriage

- ✧ Back to work
- ✧ Bad atmospheres
- ✧ Paul's fling

When Kara was three months old, Phoenix went back to work as originally planned, but she did not seem happy with this arrangement now, despite having found a wonderful nanny. Nonetheless, considering the unforeseen forces that were stacking up against them, Paul and Phoenix did a fine job of keeping everything on track for the next eighteen months. They made sure that wherever possible, they set time aside for Kara so that they could take her out at the weekends and be there for her in the evenings. Regrettably this could not always happen, for there were occasions when their careers necessitated one of them working away from home.

As with most first-time parents, they weren't fully prepared for just how much their lives were going to change. Paul had to give up his Sunday morning football and Phoenix put her studies on hold. As consolation, however, for every luxury they might have lost, the love they obviously shared for Kara more than compensated.

Paul always looked forward to coming home from work to see Kara. She would excitedly greet him with a smile, beaming from ear to ear. She always had a smile for her dad and they would laugh and play together whenever they got the chance. He would take her to the local park to play on the swings. She would come down the slide whilst he sat at the bottom, pretending to get in the way. He purposely would not move until the very last moment, just before she bounced into him. He had never heard a little girl laugh so hard. Occasionally Phoenix would accompany them and join in the merriment.

On Kara's second birthday, Paul presented her with a small

drum in the hope that one day she would share his passion for playing music. She beat nine shades of hell out of it, but it was wonderful music to him all the same. He loved spending time with her and missed her terribly if he had to go away for a few days on a business trip.

Unfortunately, underlying all the great times Paul had with his daughter, things were getting a little strained concerning his relationship with Phoenix. The humour they used to share was becoming non-existent. Anything he laughed at just seemed to annoy her, whilst the things she found funny, he considered weirdly banal. They both continued to work extremely hard and found little time for each other. On the occasions that they were together, there was invariably an atmosphere between them and they found it increasingly difficult to communicate without it turning into an argument. He felt he was constantly being pushed away.

'I want to give up work,' Phoenix tearfully stated one day.

Paul tried to be supportive, but he was concerned because of their financial commitments. 'We could sell the house,' he suggested.

Phoenix was not happy with this suggestion, or any other options he tried to put forward. He felt in an impossible situation.

Things just got worse between them from this point onwards. He got the impression that Phoenix would disagree with whatever he said or did, just for the sheer hell of it.

'I'm leaving you,' she announced on one occasion, totally out of the blue. Another time she just yelled 'I hate you', repeatedly, directly at him.

He felt rejected and used. He wondered if she was suffering from some sort of depression. He noted that she was neglecting to take pride in her appearance. To make matters worse, visits from friends and family had become more infrequent and he and Phoenix were not making an effort to see them either.

Although Paul was fortunate enough to keep his job, it did come with a lot more responsibility and necessitated working longer hours with more travel. On the plus side, the large

11

corporation that had taken over his firm was acutely aware of how the latest cutbacks had demoralised the workforce and was now desperately trying to elevate the mood amongst its employees, making it a more enjoyable place to work. As a consequence, there was a significantly heightened level of camaraderie. All remaining staff had been through the same unpleasant and unsettling experience, but were now being made to feel special as 'the Chosen Ones' to take the new business forward. Occasionally Paul would meet up with his work colleagues after a long day to help unwind.

Regrettably, at the same time, Phoenix was becoming increasingly fractious and then without warning accused him of having an affair! This he obviously denied since it was completely untrue, but he could see their relationship continuing to seriously deteriorate.

As the year was coming to an end, their relationship descended to another new low point. It's a well-known saying that 'Christmas can make or break a relationship'. Well, this relationship was very much at breaking point. Trying to manage their respective careers whilst looking after a toddler meant they were continually exhausted and they made the fatal mistake of letting their relationship suffer. The only thing that kept them going was looking forward to seeing Kara. There was one occasion when Kara sat between them on the sofa when they were arguing. She put her tiny hands on their knees.

'Please stop shouting,' she said, looking up at each of them.

Paul and Phoenix went silent. Paul picked Kara up and gave her a massive hug, trying to reassure her that everything was okay. At the same time he gave Phoenix a very dirty look.

Over the next six months, Paul continued to occasionally stop off after work and have a quick drink with colleagues to help relax. He even started to attend some work social events and joined the work football team as a further means to de-stress. This was something he would not normally have entertained, for he was a believer in keeping work and social life separate. Nevertheless he kept it up and became friendly with a group of people, some slightly older and some slightly younger than himself. At the time, he felt he was giving himself and Phoenix some much-needed breathing space. In reality, however, it caused them to drift further apart and lead more and more separate lives.

There was one individual in this group with whom Paul became particularly friendly. She was an attractive, yet seemingly troubled woman called Pippa. She was a couple of years older than him, yet did not look it. Frequently they would chat and as they became more familiar, they shared some of the difficult times they had each been through in their lives. He enjoyed talking to Pippa. She took his mind off troubles at home. They shared the same sense of humour and came from similar backgrounds. Absolutely nothing happened on a physical level between them, but people were soon making idle gossip and it was not long before unfair accusations started being bandied about.

Having become good friends, they decided to ignore the accusations for the rubbish they were. They even joked, 'Let's give them something to really talk about,' taking a line from the famous Bonnie Raitt song, and engaged in some playful banter and flirting.

Quietly to himself, Paul felt very flattered that people thought a good-looking woman would be interested in him. It was certainly a relief from the unwelcome atmosphere he was getting at home and he was enjoying himself. He considered himself strong and mature enough to handle any situation that might develop. Behaving in this fashion was a big mistake, however, for it just brought him and Pippa closer together. Some people were even encouraging him to take advantage of his position, expressing opinions ranging from 'Opportunities like this don't come along every day' to more sleazy comments such as 'She's well up for it'. Looking back, he considered it likely that unhelpful comments such as these contributed to his downfall. He desperately needed emotional support and sound advice. Unfortunately his family and true friends were not fully aware of the emotional turmoil he was going through, since he was too embarrassed to ever raise the subject. He did try talking

13

to Phoenix about it, but she was not particularly interested, saying, 'I've got more important issues of my own.'

One hot summer's evening, Paul went for the customary drink with work colleagues to celebrate someone or other's birthday. Pippa was there and they got chatting as usual. They both had one too many drinks to drive, so they decided to do the 'sensible' thing and share a cab back to their respective homes. He offered to escort her back to her apartment as it was on his route, and since she was without her car, he offered to pick her up the next morning on his way to work. Neither of them would later claim to recall exactly how it happened, but they shared a lingering kiss just before she got out of the taxi to go to her front door.

As the taxi pulled away, Pippa rather drunkenly waved at Paul, but he did not look back. He felt guilty and wanted to forget what had just happened.

The following morning, Paul drove to Pippa's apartment as planned. He was a little nervous, for although he had been tipsy the night before, he could clearly remember the kiss in the cab. As he walked up to the front door, he felt an air of embarrassment. He rang the intercom and the door opened automatically. He naively went in when invited and walked up the staircase. As he got to the top, Pippa greeted him half-dressed, having just got out of the shower. He couldn't deny she looked good.

'Come with me,' she whispered. She smiled mischievously and firmly took him by the hand. She led him to her bedroom, where she kissed him passionately and had obviously planned for things to go further. Paul had not experienced such a rush of excitement for a long while and a feral passion arose within him. He fully succumbed to the temptations on offer and for the next five whole minutes they were lovers.

Immediately afterwards, Paul was immersed in remorse and shame. He knew he had behaved badly and felt dreadful. He got dressed and suggested they get off to work otherwise they would be late. During the journey he apologised profusely.

'I'm so sorry, I should never have let things get this far. I'm a married man.'

Pippa agreed and admitted that although she had no regrets about what had happened, they should put a stop to anything further developing.

Paul had no rational explanation for his regrettable and out of character behaviour, but rather pathetically put it down to external pressures and a possible mid-life crisis. He had never behaved like this before and vowed to never behave like it again.

The following days at home were torture. He could sense Phoenix knew something was wrong. He wanted to confess, but he was not sure what to do for the best. Part of him felt guilty and ashamed, but another part of him felt justified considering the poor treatment he had received from Phoenix over the last year. He couldn't remember the last time they had been affectionate.

He kept asking himself the same questions. What would be gained by telling Phoenix? As long I make sure it never happens again, would that be okay? Can I be sure it won't happen again? Is there a part of me that wants it to happen again? Have I fallen for Pippa? What about Kara? She means everything to me. I need to make sure she is protected from this mess.

He knew it was a tired cliché frequently associated with men of a certain age, but it was true: he was very confused.

The decision about whether to tell Phoenix was soon taken away from him. A so-called friend of Phoenix's was only too happy to let her know that she had seen Paul passionately kissing another woman in a taxi.

When he arrived home from work that evening, Phoenix angrily confronted him, screaming, punching and throwing things at him. She then backed away.

'You're dirty, don't come near me. I want nothing more to do with you. I want you out of our lives forever.' She threatened he would never see Kara again.

He tried to placate her as best he could, for he could understand her anger. The rage continued for another half an hour before he finally managed to calm her down. They agreed to talk rationally once they had found a neighbour to take care of Kara.

Once Kara was out of earshot, he confessed to everything. Phoenix's initial rage turned to stunned silence and then they both got tearful. She looked utterly devastated and he had never felt such a low-life. Although their relationship had not been going well over the last few months, he would never have meant to hurt her, or anyone. They hugged each other for about five minutes and then mutually agreed it would be best if he left the house for the next few nights to give each of them some time to think. He intended this to be two or three nights whilst he cleared his head.

Leaving Kara that evening was one of the hardest things he had ever had to do, even if it was only intended for a short period of time. How do you explain to a three-year-old how much you love them, but that you have to leave? He did his best, but the puzzled look Kara gave him was something he found emotionally very painful and something that would haunt him for the rest of his life.

Chapter 4

Separation

✧ Paul moves out
✧ Counselling
✧ The divorce
✧ Involving solicitors

That first evening Paul drove to his brother's house. Paul's brother and his wife were already aware of the situation since Phoenix had wasted no time telephoning round Paul's family, enlightening them about his confession. He was not looking forward to providing an explanation. He was struggling to understand what had happened himself. His brother and sister-in-law were predictably upset and concerned when he arrived.

Over the next four hours he relayed his version of events. They had not realised just how unhappy he had been. Although still upset by his actions, they wished he had said something to them earlier.

Paul did not go to bed that night. His mind was racing and there was no way he could sleep. He spent the time pacing round and round his brother's garden. A couple of times nerves got the better of him and he vomited. He had heard of the expression 'worried sick', but this was the first time he had personally experienced it.

As daylight broke he set off for work. He knew he had to keep going for Kara's sake, but there were numerous times when he thought it would just be easier to end it all. As he was driving down the empty motorway, he contemplated how easy it would be to simply plough into the central reservation. He felt terrible and blamed himself totally. He wondered if he was going a little mad, perhaps suffering a breakdown. He felt incapable of making any good decisions. He knew he had let Kara down badly, but was not sure what he could do about it.

Over the next few days he continued to feel physically sick and the whole state of affairs had him utterly bewildered, particularly as to why he had acted so out of character (or at least he considered it to be so). He even made arrangements to see professional life counsellors to try and unearth some sort of explanation. He was riddled with guilt, for he knew it was as a result of his actions that his relationship with Phoenix had entered this latest tumultuous phase.

It was becoming clear who he could really count on as friends. His true friends remained non-judgemental and were prepared to listen to his side of the story. Some he had once regarded as friends immediately stereotyped him as a complete bastard and simply abandoned him. Others appeared to revel in witnessing the emotional pain he was suffering, pronouncing, 'Serves him right' and 'What did he expect?'

Phoenix made it clear he was not welcome back at their home. He went along with this on the agreement he could still come over and visit Kara, something he was keen to impress upon Phoenix.

During that first week he stayed overnight at different homes of his true friends. Although they were kind enough to make up a bed and support him where they could, he continued his pattern of sleepless nights, pacing the gardens. To make matters worse he was now chain-smoking. He tried his best not to be an imposition and spent a lot of time at the office, working late into the evening or starting very early in the morning. His office had become a second home and he was making good use of the office washroom facilities.

Despite spending so much time at work, his productivity was extremely poor and he found it difficult to concentrate on anything work-related. Kara was on his mind the whole time and he missed her terribly. Every little job seemed a big upheaval. Even brushing his teeth was a major ordeal.

At the end of that week, Paul visited a couple of old friends who had invited him round to dinner, for they were concerned about his welfare. This couple had been in a steady relationship for the past three years and seeing them together reminded him of the good times he had once shared with Phoenix. They could see he was in a terrible state, arguably deranged. They invited him to stay with them for as long as he liked. He wasn't sure why, but it was that evening he started to calm down and he got his first night's sleep.

During the second week after his confession, Phoenix filed for divorce, asserting that she did not want Paul to be a part of her life any more. She immediately reverted to using her maiden name for both herself and Kara. Paul considered she had now taken on an incredibly hostile and vengeful quality that he had not witnessed in her before, in a perfect personification of the established phrase 'Hell hath no fury like a woman scorned'. There was one ugly scene in particular where she had arranged for them both to meet with the local garage to sort out the joint finance payments on the car. He found her incredibly obnoxious, shouting and generally running him down in front of everyone. It made the staff noticeably uncomfortable. After she left, he apologised for her behaviour. Had he now seen her true colours?

She made it clear that there would be no chance of reconciliation and re-asserted that he was not welcome at what used to be their family home. He tried explaining that he could understand her anger and would not oppose a divorce if that was what she truly wanted, but he did not consider this course of action to be in Kara's best interests. He was naturally deeply concerned about Kara's future and did not want to jeopardise the good father–daughter relationship they shared. Regardless, Phoenix charged ahead and instructed solicitors to act on her behalf. Paul felt a little intimidated, for he had never had to deal with solicitors before. He was also rather naive when it came to the law and his legal rights as a father.

They mutually agreed that for the short term it would be best if he more formally moved out of the family residence. He was reasonably content to do this with the understanding he could keep in contact with Kara.

Over the next month Paul resorted to the predictable alcohol and cigarettes as a crutch, but he also took the positive steps of continuing with his counselling sessions and thoroughly researching his predicament, carefully weighing up his options.

The counsellor listened to his sorry story and advised that for now he stay away from Phoenix, giving them both some breathing space. She warned him that in her experience, women of Phoenix's nature were unlikely to be forgiving and he should give serious thought as to what had driven him to behave like this in the first place. She was not making excuses for him, but did suggest that his out of character behaviour could possibly have been a delayed reaction to the number of stressors he had recently been under, such as getting married, moving house, starting a family and the threat of job redundancy all at the same time. His deteriorating relationship with Phoenix could have been the final straw. The counsellor suggested that in most cases, an extra-marital episode is a symptom of marriage breakdown and not the cause. Pippa was simply a catalyst to the inevitable.

He pondered on this theory and agreed there might be something in it. It didn't take away his feelings of guilt or shame, but any rational explanation was welcome.

With respect to the legal aspects, he decided he would handle his own affairs and did not need a solicitor. He felt solicitors were expensive and could possibly lead to further hostility. He was pretty sure he and Phoenix could settle this amicably. He was not after much; he simply wanted to continue his good relationship with Kara. He did not want to be a 'runaway' or absent father. He could not comprehend how anyone could abandon their own child.

Bearing in mind the friendly relationship Paul had shared with Phoenix's mother and stepfather, he felt he owed them an explanation of his intentions and made a point of speaking to Phoenix's stepfather, apologising for letting everyone down.

'You shouldn't have got caught,' her stepfather replied. Was he serious? 'I'll have to break all contact with you now,' he continued, 'otherwise Phoenix and her mother will make my life a misery.'

'I understand,' Paul responded with a heavy heart.

Paul saw Phoenix's stepfather only once after that, quite by chance about a year later at Heathrow airport. They started chatting reasonably amiably and he told Paul about his impending relocation to France and how he and Phoenix's mother wanted to escape from everyone back in the UK. Paul was taken aback, but did not say anything.

As they shook hands to say goodbye, Phoenix's stepfather's demeanour rapidly changed. He leant in close towards Paul, purposefully invading his personal space, trying to intimidate him.

'You're gonna wish you had never been born,' he spat viciously in his ear. He then walked off as if nothing had happened.

Paul was understandably a little stunned. He had noticed a spiteful, childish and arguably cowardly streak in this man a few times before, but he had never been on the receiving end of it. What a peculiar way to say goodbye! He did not realise then that these would be the last words he would hear Phoenix's stepfather say.

The friendship that had existed between Paul and Pippa very rapidly dwindled to nothing. Feelings of guilt swiftly extinguished any sparks of passion that might have existed. She had no time for him whilst he was feeling sorry for himself, licking his wounds. There was never a proper relationship of any sort. Working together was initially awkward. They both requested transfers to other departments. She took a post working abroad whereas he continued at the same base.

Five months after Paul had left the family home, he and Phoenix were officially divorced. The divorce hearing was held at the High Court. He had no idea why Phoenix wanted it to be held at the High Court, as opposed to the Family Court, other than maybe to humiliate him further. If that was the case, it did not work since he did not turn up. He considered there to be no point in him being there. What is the point of contesting a divorce when someone wants to divorce you?

Paul remained extremely embarrassed by the whole saga. Phoenix on the other hand took it very badly, and forgiveness was never on her agenda. He considered it a regrettable one-off skirmish, whereas she constantly referred to the episode as a full-blown affair and would throw it in his face at every opportunity.

The original invite from Paul's old friends was supposedly for dinner, but somehow he ended up staying there for the next seven months. These friends were very good to him, sympathetic to his predicament and supporting him as he desperately tried to get his life back on track. On alternate Sundays he would bring Kara back to their house, or take her out to various places where they would have fun together. Sometimes his friends would join them. He focused his efforts on fostering his relationship with Kara and holding on to his job. His goal was to purchase a suitable property where Kara could spend quality time with him. He considered it vital that he work towards some sort of stability in his life for her sake.

Throughout this period, many of his friends and family conveyed their sympathies, remarking how sorry they were for what had happened. Surprising him, a number also mentioned how they had never felt he and Phoenix had been right for each other. He initially struggled with this revelation, but as time passed he started to recognise that they were probably right. He hoped that as Kara grew older she would somehow understand and learn from the mistakes he and Phoenix had made in order to avoid going through similar regrettable events herself. This did not mean that he and Phoenix had not had their good times. They most certainly had, but it was a shame that the good times had come to an end. Little did he realise then that her inability to forgive would lead to callous and spiteful revenge.

Chapter 5

Contact with Kara

- ✧ Paul and Phoenix get their own places
- ✧ Contact arrangements agreed
- ✧ Paul meets Jenna
- ✧ Kara meets Jenna
- ✧ Time with Kara
- ✧ Phoenix's concerning behaviour

The family house was sold about five months after their separation and Paul agreed with Phoenix that she could keep the majority of the proceeds from the sale. Additionally he arranged for a regular standing order from his bank account to her account, to ensure Kara was adequately provided for on an on-going basis. All negotiations at this point were via Phoenix's solicitor, since she refused to talk to him directly. It was further agreed that he could continue to have Kara on alternate Sundays until he was able to find a property of his own, at which time the situation would be reviewed. In between these Sundays, Paul made sure he telephoned Kara at least once a week.

Phoenix temporarily moved into the penthouse suite of a luxury apartment block in the heart of town, but then moved over 60 miles away, making simple regular contact between Paul and Kara more difficult. She had chosen to reside in a large farmhouse with five bedrooms, despite there only being the two of them. She had also purchased a flashy Rolex watch and made a point of showing Paul the authentication certificate at the earliest opportunity. He was not jealous, for he had never had time for people who liked to show off, but he was curious as to where she was getting her money from and why she was choosing to spend it in a reckless fashion. His main concern, however, was for Kara. As long as she was being properly looked after, he was happy.

Around the same time, he moved into a place of his own, a modest two-bedroom apartment next to the local park that suited his needs perfectly. He immediately started decorating the spare room so that Kara could come and stay.

Although he had an open invitation to stay longer with his friends, it was the sale of his joint residence with Phoenix that allowed Paul to afford a deposit to put down on a place of his own. His goal was to provide a welcoming home environment with space for Kara to play, giving them both some much-needed stability. It also boosted his confidence, proving that he was ready to stand on his own two feet again.

After much wrangling back and forth over the next three months, Paul finally managed to reach an agreement with Phoenix (again via her solicitor, since she still refused to have direct contact with him) that Kara could come and stay for a trial weekend. Assuming everything went satisfactorily, the plan was for this to happen on a more regular basis, typically every other weekend. A regular monthly maintenance fee was agreed and Paul signed a settlement, instigated by Phoenix, that neither of them would have any financial holding on the other going forward.

With respect to the agreed contact and maintenance fee arrangements, Paul kept the solicitor's letters with the terms written down, but nothing was officially signed. He was pleased they had managed to settle on a reasonably informal arrange-ment with some degree of flexibility, hoping that all the hostility experienced since their break-up would now come to an end. He was also chuffed that he had not had to bear the expense of a solicitor. Why spend money on a solicitor when it could go to Kara? In hindsight, he realised this could have been yet one more mistake.

A year after his separation from Phoenix, Paul had the incredibly good fortune of meeting his new partner, Jenna. They were introduced to each other by a mutual friend. Jenna was strikingly beautiful, with long raven-black hair and olive skin. Although 100 per cent an 'English rose', she could easily have been mistaken to be of Hispanic origin. She had been a professional ballerina in her younger days, and as a consequence of her rigorous training, moved with remarkable poise, grace and elegance. She had performed in various productions around the world but had now retired from the professional arena to run her own dance school. She shared Paul's intense passion for music and it was not long before she was teaching him to dance. They got on very well from the start and the following year, despite being a little wary, she moved in with him. Over the next few months, Paul slowly introduced Kara to Jenna and they formed a good relationship, Kara happily accepting her as a permanent fixture.

Everything appeared to be going wonderfully, apart from one unpleasant episode when Kara was four. Paul, Jenna and Kara were travelling to see friends for lunch. Paul parked up outside a flower shop to buy some flowers. Whilst Kara and Jenna were alone in the car, Kara leant over to Jenna and with a hateful tone in her voice said, 'My mummy told me she could beat you up if she wanted to.' When Paul got back in the car he could sense Jenna was upset about something, but Kara acted as if nothing had happened.

Jenna told Paul about the episode later that evening, after returning from taking Kara back to her mother's house. Jenna explained how hurt she had been and found it difficult to believe a child could make her feel so upset. They had been getting on so well up until then. Where had this venom suddenly come from?

Paul and Jenna were naturally concerned. They concluded it was probably a symptom of Kara's age and how she naturally would like to see her parents back together again. They agreed to keep an eye on the situation. Paul suggested that Phoenix might be resentful that he had settled down with a new partner. In comparison, her life had been rather turbulent.

Apart from the flower shop episode, arrangements continued to run reasonably smoothly. Kara would stay for at least one weekend every month, but more often than not every other weekend, as per the agreement, and Paul would talk to her at least once a week on the phone. On one occasion, Kara even asked if she could call Jenna 'mum'. Both Paul and Jenna delicately suggested that it would be best if she continued to refer to her as Jenna, since Jenna could never replace her real mum. This did not mean Jenna loved her any less, but it would avoid confusion. This seemingly placated Kara.

Paul tried to make the best use of the limited time he and Kara had together, taking her out or participating in activities around the home. She particularly enjoyed helping to bake cakes, making models, watching films (especially Disney), playing board games and reading bedtime stories. If Paul had to go out alone for the evening (which was rare), Kara would very happily play with Jenna. Jenna had a wealth of experience keeping children entertained, having regularly looked after her numerous nephews and nieces who all loved her company. Kara and Jenna would spend time sewing dolls' clothes or costumes. They also made birthday and Father's Day cards for Paul, since Phoenix would never provide any such thing on Kara's behalf. This was despite him always making sure Kara had something to give Phoenix for Mother's Day or her birthday. Enjoyable outings included the cinema, the theatre, the swimming pool, zoos, adventure parks and visits to friends and family. They were also lucky enough to go on some wonderful holidays, which included Paul's extended family. They all loved having Kara around and she loved playing games with her young cousins. All the family showered affection on Kara and they could see the obvious bond she shared with Paul. They were like any other normal loving family.

With regard to weekend visits, Phoenix and Paul reached an understanding that he would pick Kara up on a Saturday morning around 9am and drop her back home late Sunday afternoon, around 5pm. They agreed to telephone in advance if either of them needed to change these times for any reason. Paul was reasonably happy to go along with these arrangements and followed them pretty much to the letter. He felt he could not risk upsetting Phoenix, who he considered a little unbalanced following their break-up, for fear she would make his access to Kara awkward. The main drawback from his point of view was that he never got to see Kara on Christmas Day or her birthday, because Phoenix maintained that this did not fit in with her plans. As a substitute, he and his family would arrange special family get-togethers as near as possible to these dates, so they could all celebrate with Kara together. Although this was not ideal, it was the best Phoenix would allow and he felt he had to go along with her stipulations, for it was better than nothing. He did try to ring Kara on special occasions such as her birthday, but this had to be on Phoenix's strict terms and sometimes she would block it, which he found a little galling to say the least! If Phoenix was trying to hurt him, she had succeeded.

Despite the concern and frustration regarding Phoenix's behaviour, the informal contact and maintenance arrangements continued to function reasonably well. There would be occasions when Phoenix would make things difficult by changing plans at the last minute, or be extremely antagonistic when speaking on the phone, but overall Paul and Jenna considered they coped with it admirably. They flatly refused to be drawn into any petty arguments or recriminations, although there were times when they admitted they would have really liked to have let rip at Phoenix. There was no way, however, that they were going to let a spiteful woman upset or come between them.

There was one fracas in particular during the run-up to Christmas when Paul let it slip that he and Jenna were not exchanging Christmas gifts that year.

'Why's that?' enquired Phoenix.

'If I'm honest, we have everything we need, so we decided to donate the money we would have used to the local children's hospice instead.'

Phoenix hit the roof, going into an intense rage.

'If you have money to give away, you should be giving it to me and Kara,' she cursed at him.

Paul was dumbstruck. He had not witnessed such a lack of generosity in her before. In his eyes she was already leading an overly lavish lifestyle and he was paying very generously for Kara's maintenance. Perhaps he had not explained himself properly. There was no way he would intentionally see Kara go without. He wasn't denying Kara a Christmas present. This was simply a small gesture by Jenna and himself, giving something back to those so much less fortunate than them.

'Perhaps she's on some sort of medication,' he suggested to Jenna when he got off the phone. 'If not, perhaps she needs some.'

On another occasion, Phoenix telephoned Paul at work and seemingly tried to turn him against Jenna.

'Are you aware that Jenna slapped Kara during her last visit?'

Fortunately he knew this to be completely untrue, not just because Jenna would never contemplate doing such a thing, but because she had not even been at home that weekend. Was this a desperate and spiteful attempt to try and cause a rift between him and Jenna? He was becoming increasingly of the opinion that Phoenix begrudged him for having settled down with a loving partner, whereas she herself appeared to have difficulties maintaining any of her relationships.

Whenever Phoenix rang and Jenna happened to pick up the phone, Phoenix was always incredibly short and rude, simply ordering, 'Get Paul', talking to her as if she was worthless. This understandably upset Jenna, for she always made an effort to be extremely polite and pleasant to everyone. Paul explained on several occasions that she should not take Phoenix's conduct personally. 'Phoenix appears to treat most people in this manner, particularly my friends and family,' he would say. 'That is of course unless she wants something, in which case she is extraordinarily capable of transforming her persona into an awfully sickly sweet and overbearingly pleasant nature.'

Those that knew Phoenix well, and had similar experience of being on the receiving end of her unpleasant manner, made no bones about telling him how they also found her metamorphosis into the sugary act quite stomach-turning.

The weekend after Phoenix's claim, when Paul went to collect Kara, he purposely asked Phoenix in Kara's presence about the supposed slapping incident.

'What's all this about Jenna giving Kara a slap, then?' He

made a point of asking the question gently, so as not to upset Kara. 'You do know that Jenna was not even there that weekend?'

Phoenix dismissed his questioning as unimportant now and did not want to talk about it. Paul looked at her in disbelief, but nonetheless was grateful to avoid confrontation, especially in front of Kara.

Kara would often tell Paul how she looked forward to her visits. He was always thrilled to see her and he loved having her around at the weekends. As any father of a young daughter will know, there is a strong paternal bond. He wondered if the bond he shared with his daughter had been made even stronger by the fact that he could not always be physically around for her. He never told anyone, but there were times when, driving home after dropping her off, he had to pull over because he could not see for the tears welling up in his eyes.

He really missed her and wished he could be there more for her.

Chapter 6

Issues with contact

✧ Phoenix's increasing animosity towards Paul and his family
✧ A worrying pattern emerging – 'parental alienation'?
✧ A change in Kara's behaviour
✧ The start of the journal
✧ Kara's devastating letter
✧ Next steps for Paul
✧ Weekly letters
✧ Phoenix's abscondment

Over the next four to five years, Phoenix's attitude towards Paul did not mellow – in fact, if anything, it was more the reverse. He found her gradually becoming more and more anti-social and she flatly refused to have anything to do with his family. When he or his parents tried to arrange a visit to see Kara, their phone calls were rarely acknowledged, and Phoenix never made any effort to take Kara to see them. He found this increasing animosity strange, since as far as he was concerned, neither he nor his family had done anything to deserve this level of hostility.

Paul had another sleepless night fretting about Kara. He lay awake tossing and turning with all sorts of thoughts going through his head. Unfortunately nights such as this were becoming more common. Looking on the positive side, they did give him time to try and fathom where this increased animosity was coming from and what, if anything, he could do about it.

He dwelled on how difficult Phoenix had made his life over the last six years. It even crossed his mind that perhaps she had been purposely trying to erode him from Kara's life. If it had been done slowly, over a period of years, perhaps he hadn't noticed it happening. He was now seriously wondering if this had been her intention all along.

A sudden rush of panic went through him and he sat bolt upright. He had a flashback to when they had first split up and how she had viciously screamed at him, 'I don't want you in our lives any more.' At the time he had put this down to her understandable rage and anger. He had been confident that once the dust had settled, she would see the obvious benefits in Kara having free access to her father. However, six years on, perhaps she had not moved on at all. He got out of bed and collated a list of examples of how she had tried to push him out of Kara's life. The list included:

+ Immediately after their separation, Phoenix had reverted to using her maiden name as her surname for both herself and Kara. He could understand this for Phoenix, but not Kara. Kara should continue to take his surname, as recorded on her birth certificate.

+ At the earliest opportunity, she had moved a considerable distance away, making simple regular contact between Kara and him awkward.

+ She had made it increasingly difficult for him to contact Kara. Despite him phoning up to three times a week, he would be lucky if the phone was actually answered once. He would ring the mobile and landline, leaving messages, but Phoenix rarely returned his calls.

+ She always undermined him in front of Kara. She constantly made out that his views were unimportant or wrong. He could not recall her ever saying 'Sorry' in her whole life with any sincerity. She never accepted blame for anything. Incredible as it sounded, he had several witnesses who would back this up. Was it a consequence of low self-esteem from her childhood experiences? He really did not want Kara to end up going the same way.

+ She would change contact arrangements at the last minute, making life awkward for him and Jenna.

Although these things in isolation hadn't seemed overly significant at the time, they did cause him irritation. The fact that
Phoenix would change plans as to when Kara could come and
stay at the eleventh hour, meant that he and Jenna had to be very
careful about making definitive plans for their own weekends.
Regrettably, they felt they had no choice but to go along with her
if they wanted Kara to come and visit. Occasionally they would
discuss the issues they were having with Phoenix between themselves. They agreed they would not retaliate, but would rise
above the vengeful nonsense. They wondered if she got some
sort of kick out of being difficult and unpleasant, or was she just
plain ignorant? Regardless, they considered it to be ultimately
her problem. As events unfolded, however, they later found out
to their despair that this was not true.

Whilst awake, Paul continued to reflect on the past six years,
recalling incidents that had been strangely inexplicable at the
time, but were now collectively painting a very unsettling
picture. Particular noteworthy incidents were:

✦ Whenever he or his family bought presents for Kara, she
  would let it slip that Phoenix had told her they were
  second-rate to anything that her family bought. He did
  not let this get to him too much, but one year was particularly upsetting when he bought Kara a large cuddly teddy
  bear (she was five at the time) wearing a T-shirt with the
  message, 'Daddy loves Kara' emblazoned on the front in
  large letters. He was hopeful that this would remind her he
  was never far away. On her next visit to his house, she
  brought the teddy bear with her and he noticed the T-shirt
  had been forcefully ripped and the word 'Daddy' had been
  scribbled out. Fortunately he was able to buy a replace-
  ment T-shirt and Jenna helped with the repair, but sadly
  he agreed with Kara that it would probably be safer for
  teddy to stay at his house from now on.

✦ He and his family were always made to feel second best.
  Phoenix would not agree to Kara visiting or staying with

them over the Christmas period or her birthday. Any telephone contact he or his family tried to make with Kara on such days was strongly discouraged and effectively blocked.

✦ Shortly after he and Phoenix separated, her parents moved to France. On a couple of occasions he asked Phoenix for their new address and telephone number, so he could contact Kara on occasions when he knew she would be staying with them. Phoenix always refused this request, saying things like, 'It would not be convenient.' He found this particularly upsetting on Christmas Day and Kara's birthdays, when she appeared to make ultra-sure he did not get any contact with Kara. He was now questioning whether Phoenix had purposely orchestrated this, so she could say to Kara, 'Your father never bothers to contact you on these special days.' Kara was certainly never encouraged to ring him on Christmas Day, his birthday or Father's Day.

✦ He was always expected to do the travelling when Kara visited, picking her up and taking her back home. This would amount to well over 200 miles in a weekend. When he went to collect Kara and rang the doorbell, the door was rarely answered on time and he was made to wait for up to ten minutes, even if it was pouring with rain. Phoenix never offered to help with the journeys, claiming the whole situation was entirely of his own doing and as such he should pay the consequences. He did not want to make matters any worse than they were, so he did not challenge Phoenix, but went along with her childish notions in an attempt to keep the peace.

✦ For the last six years, Phoenix had cut off all contact with his family (Kara's paternal grandparents and Paul's brother and family) and never returned any of their calls.

✦ He had noticed Kara becoming a little reluctant even from the age of three to share information with him about activities she had been doing, whether at home or at school. This became much more noticeable as she got older and he got the impression she had been instructed by her mother to be secretive and not tell him anything.

✦ Phoenix rang Paul the evening before one of Kara's planned weekend visits to say that Kara was unwell and would not be visiting that weekend. He was naturally concerned and, despite Phoenix's protests, drove down to see Kara the following day. Kara was playing in the front garden and appeared fine. Was it a very quick recovery, or had Phoenix made the illness up?

✦ Not once did Phoenix arrange for Kara to send him a Father's Day card. Jenna and his family were so appalled that they used to buy the Father's Day cards themselves so Kara had something to give to him. Sometimes they would sit and make them with her. In contrast, when he was with Kara, he would always either encourage her to make or buy a Mother's Day card and present for her mum.

✦ Paul, Jenna and Kara were all invited to his brother's wedding. Kara was asked if she would like to be bridesmaid. She was only five and ever so excited, really looking forward to it. Paul told Phoenix about it and they reached agreement that Kara could stay with him the weekend in question. Regrettably, Phoenix rang a couple of nights before the ceremony to inform him that she and Kara had decided to go and visit her parents in France that weekend, so Kara would not be able to attend the wedding.

✦ Up until Kara was about six, whenever Paul went to pick her up, Phoenix always dressed her scruffily, in ill-fitting clothes. This got so bad that Jenna purchased a complete spare wardrobe so Kara could change when she arrived at their house. They wondered if Phoenix did this on purpose to insinuate to Kara that their house was dirty, which was certainly not the case. Alternatively, was it her way of hinting she wanted more maintenance money?

✦ He recalled a pair of soft, pink ballet shoes that Jenna had given Kara, intended for her to wear when she attended Jenna's dance school. Kara was ever so proud of them and wanted to take them home to show her mum, like any other excited little girl. On her following visit however, they came back a very washed-out grey instead of the bright pink they were originally. There was no doubt in Jenna's mind that Phoenix had done this intentionally out of spite.

✦ During one particular visit when Kara was about six, she remarked that her mum had said to her, 'Your father does not provide anything for us.' Paul tried to explain softly to Kara that this was not true and gently introduced the concept of maintenance payments. Kara revealed she was aware of this, but her mum had said, 'The money your father provides is not enough.' Paul inwardly found this most annoying, since he knew that the voluntary payments he was making were far more than any Child Support Agency calculation would compute.

✦ When Kara went on holiday with him, Phoenix demanded that he make sure Kara ring her at least once a day, which he did. It was as if he and his family could not be trusted. Phoenix never co-operated by putting a reciprocal arrangement in place. He never once got a phone call or even as much as a postcard when Kara was on vacation with Phoenix, despite his repeated requests.

✦ Whilst on holiday in Cornwall with Paul and his extended family, Kara angrily told him out of the blue, 'You walked out on us,' referring to herself and Phoenix. She was about seven at the time. Not only was this not true (he and Phoenix had mutually agreed it would be best if he was the one to leave the family home), it was something he considered had connivingly been planted in Kara's mind.

✦ From the age of eight upwards, Kara would bring a mobile phone with her when she came to visit. Phoenix and Kara would constantly text each other during this time. It soon became apparent that this mobile phone was not for emergencies, but more for Phoenix to get an update on Kara's activities on an hourly basis and talk in some sort of coded language. Although Paul found this rather irksome (he had never been a fan of mobile phones), he accepted it was probably a bit of a novelty for Kara. To him, the whole scenario was a rather pathetic show that Phoenix had nothing better to do. On the odd occasion he tried texting Kara on her mobile when she was with Phoenix, he either got no reply or a very short and rather hurtful response back.

✦ At about the same time, Kara started bringing a camera with her on visits. He didn't think too much about it at the time, since most children liked to play with cameras, but he did consider it unusual that she was taking photographs of every room in the house. Jenna remarked that this was not normal. 'Kara appears to be on some sort of private detective mission for her mother,' she joked. In hindsight, they would realise this was probably not too far from the truth.

✦ Although it pained him to say it, he and Jenna had started to notice an underlying slyness in Kara's behaviour once she had reached the age of about nine, but they had put this down to her age and were hopeful she would grow out of it.

Looking at all these incidents together, Paul could see a disturbing pattern had definitely emerged. He started to realise that ignoring Phoenix's behaviour had been a huge mistake. He should have taken each of these individual incidents as a warning signal. Had he been too much of a pushover, not wanting to rock any boats? Had Phoenix cruelly and without moral conscience taken advantage of his easy-going nature? Had he been overly naive and simply buried his head in the sand?

'It's more likely you simply couldn't believe someone could be so nasty as to purposely orchestrate these events,' Jenna suggested, trying to be supportive.

Following Kara's ninth birthday, Paul and Jenna noticed a major change in her behaviour. She was becoming increasingly distant and evasive on the phone, accompanied with excuses as to why she did not want to come and visit. Paul questioned Phoenix about this directly.

'Kara has a very hectic social life, so she's unlikely to want to stay weekends with you any more,' she explained.

Although extremely disappointed, he accepted this and suggested that instead he visit Kara after school or at the weekend. He could then take her out for tea or lunch and Phoenix could join them if she wished.

'No, thank you,' replied Phoenix indignantly.

'Whatever,' said Paul. 'Whatever Kara prefers, I'll be happy to go along with.'

Sadly he only saw Kara twice between June and September of that year, due to Kara saying she was not available.

One fateful Wednesday evening of that September, during one of their weekly telephone calls, Kara was once again being very evasive when he tried to arrange to see her. He was getting very tired of being put off whatever day he suggested, even if way in the future.

'I'll be down to see you on Saturday,' he blurted out in exasperation. He was totally gobsmacked by the very strong objection she made to this, so he asked to speak to her mum to try and find out what was going on.

'Leave it with me,' said Phoenix, 'I'll talk to Kara.' She promised she would sort it out and ring him back.

Paul was getting increasingly concerned and decided it would be wise to keep a diary of all significant happenings from this point forward. It was this diary that evolved into 'Paul's Journal'.

Two days later, Phoenix returned Paul's call around 9pm.

'Kara doesn't want to see you any more,' she bluntly informed him.

'Why?' he asked in disbelief.

'Because you have been a bad father, never turned up when you said you were going to and didn't phone when you said you were going to.'

He was crushed. He tried to reason with her, protesting that they both knew this was not true, but Phoenix hung up. He poured himself a large whisky and decided he would give her a ten-minute cooling-off period before calling back to try and rescue the situation.

Phoenix answered the phone and once again harshly told him, 'Kara does not want to see you and considers everything is entirely your fault.'

'But you know that's not true,' he protested. 'Please, can't you help set her straight?'

'I don't want to interfere with Kara's wishes,' she replied curtly.

In desperation he tried to convince her that the three of them should meet up in the presence of a therapist or counsellor. Phoenix eventually conceded this was a possible way forward, so he offered to start making some arrangements.

Paul considered this typical of their recent phone calls. She claimed she was not bitter about their break-up, but the way she behaved clearly indicated to the contrary. There were times when she would not even agree to disagree! When things got personal, she would blame him for everything. He would sarcastically say, 'Well, I suppose none of this is your fault.' She would then hang up. Typically, after about ten minutes, he would call back to try and remedy the situation. Tonight's phone call was no different in that respect.

Paul tried hard to find suitable professionals that could help with the situation. Unfortunately he could only find services that were located a considerable distance from each of them. He telephoned Phoenix a couple of days later, and to his surprise, she picked up the phone.

'I've not had much luck finding a suitable counselling service,' he informed her.

'I might know of someone who may be able to help,' Phoenix replied. 'I'll contact them and get back to you in a couple of days.'

He thanked her and then asked, 'Can I talk to Kara?'

'Kara doesn't want to speak with you right now,' she replied. 'She has made up her mind that she will only speak with you through a mediator.'

He was distraught and dumbfounded. Where had Kara got this term 'mediator' from?

After four very long days, Phoenix had still not telephoned. He considered this ironic bearing in mind this was the offence of which he was being accused. In reality, it was she who was guilty of this felony. He decided to ring her and ask if she had made any progress. She surprised him by again picking up the phone.

'I've made some initial enquiries with respect to mediation,' she informed him, 'and I've also seen a therapist. I plan to follow it up next week with a view to making an appointment. Don't call me; I'll phone you once I have some news.'

Before they ended the call, Paul asked, 'Can I speak with Kara?'

'I've already told you, Kara doesn't want to speak to you,' she replied.

Another five days passed and Phoenix had still not telephoned. He could bear the waiting no longer and rang her number.

'I've made some more enquiries, but not yet successfully booked any appointments,' she informed him. 'I'm doing what I can.'

He offered to try again to find suitable services, but she

insisted they use her contacts, to which he felt he had no choice but to agree, for fear she would not show up otherwise.

'I'll call you again tomorrow to see how things have progressed,' he informed her. This clearly antagonised Phoenix.

'Just leave it with me and I'll call you once I've sorted it out,' she retorted angrily.

'Can I speak with Kara?' he asked again.

'She still doesn't want to talk to you,' Phoenix replied. 'It would be best if you left us alone for now.'

Yet another three days passed and Phoenix still had not telephoned Paul. He was getting very frustrated. He could not understand why she was behaving in this fashion. He feared he was fighting a losing battle.

On a more positive note, his sister-in-law had managed to speak with Kara on the phone. She had dropped into the conversation that Paul was missing her very much and was upset that she would not talk to him. She tried to reassure Kara that they all loved her and they would love to hear from her at any time. Kara just clammed up when Paul's name was mentioned and was reluctant to say anything.

Over the next week or so, Paul continually tried to call Phoenix to see if there had been any developments, but repeatedly got no answer. He continually left messages on her answer phone asking her to call him back, but they were all ignored. He thought about driving to Phoenix's house and talking to her face to face, but did not want to risk an ugly confrontation in front of Kara.

Two weeks after Phoenix had said she would call, Paul finally managed to make contact when he rang her number. To his surprise and delight, it was Kara who picked up the phone.

'How are you?' he asked in a soft voice, so as not to alarm her.

'Fine,' she replied.

Although she said she was fine, he sensed that she was a little shaken speaking to him, despite him trying to be as gentle as he could. She then passed the phone to Phoenix. Paul enquired about the therapy sessions.

'Kara and I went last week,' Phoenix informed him.

'What? Why didn't you let me know about it?' he exclaimed.

'Because you were not invited,' she replied.

He was desperately trying to hide his frustration, but could not hide his disappointment.

'Don't you think it would have been better if I had been there? I would have liked to have been present,' he protested. 'If there are any future sessions coming up, please make sure you invite me. You know I will never give up on Kara and I'll always be there for her.'

'Kara is fully aware of this,' Phoenix informed him, 'but her mind is currently made up that she doesn't want anything to do with you or your family at this time. For now it would be best if you stopped calling.'

Paul was understandably finding this whole episode very hurtful and deep down did not believe it had originated from a nine-year-old child. He reflected on the very loving father–daughter relationship he and Kara had previously shared. He searched his soul trying to find a reason for this change. He knew the reasons Phoenix had given were untrue. His mind was filled with all sorts of questions. Why should a child be denied the love of a caring father just because her parents don't love each other any more? Why couldn't he get this message across to Phoenix? He believed he and Phoenix should be presenting a united front for Kara, convincing her of the benefits of access to both her parents' love, rather than letting her, or possibly encouraging her to, embark on some misguided mission to cut one parent from her life. All Phoenix appeared to say was, 'It's what Kara wants.'

He tried to rationalise the situation. Why did Kara want this? Was this really what she wanted? Was it possible that Kara's behaviour was a result of Phoenix brainwashing her? He wondered if Phoenix was revelling in all this, enjoying witnessing his suffering. Perhaps she felt it gave her a power over him which appealed to her bitter and twisted persona. Even if she was not encouraging the situation, she was certainly not being effective in putting it right. What could he do about it without making matters worse? For the moment, he decided to wait and see if there was any progress as a result of the therapy session that Phoenix had spoken about.

Paul never did learn the outcome of any therapy sessions. He kept trying to contact Phoenix, but she never picked up the phone or responded to any messages he left on her voicemail.

On the Friday of the following week, Paul arrived home from work to an empty house and found a recorded delivery package left on the side. Jenna had obviously taken delivery of it for him. He didn't often get packages of this type, so he was intrigued. He opened it up and found it contained a two-page handwritten letter from Kara with an accompanying CD. He was absolutely delighted and sat down in the lounge to read it with an air of excitement. Perhaps she has recorded some of her favourite songs for me to listen to, or perhaps it's a DVD of her starring in the latest school production, he thought to himself.

As he read the first few lines, however, his excitement turned to pure horror. Part of him wanted to stop reading it, but he knew he would have to keep going to the end. He forced himself to keep going and once he had finished it, he put it down, then got up and poured himself a large whisky.

After downing a couple of glugs, he picked the letter up again and read it through once more. The letter reiterated virtually word for word the same account Phoenix had previously given him on the phone. In summary, it stated that Kara did not want anything to do with him or his family at this time in her life. It accused him of not loving her, ignoring her wishes and controlling her, and alleged he did not turn up on time to pick her up for pre-arranged visits. It finished by demanding that he not get in contact with her or her mother.

The whole letter had a cruel and spiteful tone, clearly written by someone who felt very angry. He studied it carefully. It appeared to be in Kara's handwriting. He felt utterly devastated. He knew the statements in the letter were untrue. Why was she feeling like this? Why was a girl her age writing such a letter? Why was her mind filled with all this nonsense? Where had she got it from? It was very easy to jump to the obvious conclusion that Phoenix had been a big influence in its authorship, but would she really sink so low? What could he do to rectify the situation? He felt totally helpless.

Paul finished his whisky and poured another. He looked at the CD that had come with the letter and mentally prepared himself for what it might contain. He reluctantly put it in the CD player and pressed the PLAY button. Some very dramatic orchestral music started followed by an angry woman singing, sounding like a cat in pain. It was a desperately sad, bitter and angry song called, 'Don't Waste My Time' and contained lyrics such as 'You destroyed my love' and 'You make me sick'. It was obviously meant to reinforce the points made in the letter and upset him further. He was heartbroken, but did not know whether to laugh or cry. The whole thing was so ludicrous and over-the-top that it was difficult to take seriously. He was really starting to worry that Kara had become a victim of her mother's psychological problems. How else could a girl of her age be experiencing such strong adult emotions?

Paul didn't sleep that night, wondering what he should do. Despite being embarrassed, he showed Kara's letter to Jenna, close friends and family. They were all shocked and outraged, sharing his concern that these were not the words of a normal nine-year-old girl. They knew the accusations against him were completely untrue, and were of the collective opinion that Phoenix had been a strong influence in the letter's content. They were incensed she could get away with this selfish and arguably psychotic behaviour and ultimately felt sorry for Kara. Why should Kara lose out on the love of a father because of the pettiness and bitterness of her mother? Their advice ranged from stopping maintenance payments, to getting Social Services involved, to taking legal action. These thoughts had already crossed Paul's mind, but he was concerned that these options would not help the situation, but rather aggravate it further.

Paul was very downbeat. Despite all his efforts, Kara was now allegedly accusing him of being a bad father. Was Phoenix encouraging her to feel this way? He knew he was not perfect and acknowledged he had made mistakes, but no more than a lot of fathers. Phoenix had also made her fair share of mistakes, but so far had refused to acknowledge any of them. He continued to believe they should be working together to help Kara through this difficult period, helping her understand she had two parents who loved her very much. This was going to be near impossible with Phoenix's current attitude. He was not sure what to do for the best. Kara had made it clear she wanted no contact with him or his family and Phoenix was going to support her in this ill-advised crusade. Where or who could he turn to? He had no contact details for Phoenix's parents since they had moved to France and he was not sure of the response he would get even if he did manage to make contact. He decided that Kara's school would probably be the best starting point.

The next week turned out to be very eventful. On the Tuesday and the Friday he met with the headmistress of Kara's school. On the second occasion they were joined by Kara's class teacher. Paul informed them how he and Phoenix had separated seven years ago and up until the last six months, he and Kara had shared a good father–daughter relationship. He relayed how Kara used to stay alternate weekends and how he would telephone her at least once a week. It was over the last six months that Kara had turned distant and then he had received her letter.

They informed him that Kara and Phoenix had been into the school and had met with them both. Kara's teacher was a trainee student counsellor. They had been under the misapprehension that Kara was going to talk to them about her father and how her relationship with him could be improved. They were shocked when they heard what she actually had to say. 'I don't want to see my father again, ever!' Kara had told them.

Despite questioning, they could not understand where this was coming from. They had tried to point out to her that she should not burn any bridges. 'Write a letter to your father, describing how you feel,' they had advised.

Paul showed the headmistress the letter he had received. She studied it for a short while.

'I didn't expect her to have been so harsh,' she remarked, and she offered it to Kara's teacher to read. Kara's class teacher said she did not want to read the letter. Paul noticed she looked upset and very embarrassed. They obviously realised how hurtful it must have been for him to receive such a communication.

Paul expressed his two main concerns.

'First I would like confirmation of Kara's general wellbeing and how she is doing at school. Secondly, I would like to know if there is any way you can help me maintain some sort of contact with my daughter.'

With respect to Kara's general welfare, they were able to put his mind at ease. They confirmed the accounts that Kara used to give him. She was at the top of her class in most subjects and her schoolwork had not suffered any setbacks. This came as a welcome relief to Paul and although he considered Phoenix to have psychological problems, he did not believe she would deliberately do anything detrimental to Kara's education. With respect to maintaining some sort of contact with Kara, they reluctantly informed him that the school's hands were tied somewhat, but they would be very happy to send him reports and details of Open Evenings and other such events. Paul expressed his sincere gratitude.

'I'll make every effort to be there,' he replied.

They suggested he continue to go along with Kara's request for space for now and write her a letter. The headmistress suggested he also send a letter to Phoenix, explaining his intention of writing to Kara.

'It's not unusual for children to go through these phases,' she advised, 'although Kara does seem rather young.'

'I'm wary that Phoenix could have played an instrumental part in all of this, as a means of getting back at me for our break-up,' he admitted.

'The school has to be non-judgemental in these cases,' the headmistress replied, 'but it is a possibility.'

Paul left that Friday having agreed with the headmistress that the school would keep him updated on Kara's progress.

Additionally, the school would take advantage of any opportunity that might arise to rectify the regrettable situation that had arisen. In the meantime, it was a matter of waiting for Kara to come round, hopefully sooner rather than later.

That evening Paul reflected on the good times he and Kara had shared together over the years and recorded them in his journal. He fondly remembered when she was little and how they would go to the theatre to see shows such as 'Joseph and the Amazing Technicolor Dreamcoat', 'Peter Pan' and 'The Lion King'. She loved them and would sing along to all the songs. He wondered if she had these same memories. He also recalled taking her to adventure theme parks, fun fairs and zoos. On many of these occasions they were joined by friends and family. They were all fun days and Kara clearly enjoyed herself. He proudly remembered how brave she was, asking to go on some of the bigger rides with him. He loved all the little notes he used to get where she would draw him pictures and declare how much she loved her dad. A number of them were still stuck on her bedroom wall at his home, alongside many photographs of them playing together.

Although it was not always easy to find common ground for a father and young daughter, he thought they did remarkably well. They used to bake cakes, play games, go to the park and play on the swings, go swimming, go shopping with Kara's birthday or Christmas money, celebrate Halloween and bonfire night and get involved in all sorts of other such enjoyable activities. They had been on wonderful holidays with his extended family and all the family had very fond memories of the fun they had together, as many photographs would testify. He was acutely aware that the last holiday with Kara had been when she was eight years old, about one year prior to receiving this upsetting letter. They had both had a wonderful time and Kara had been so excited about it for ages. How had things changed so dramatically and so quickly?

The next day Paul read an article in one of the national newspapers about a parliamentary minister. The article discussed how his former partner had turned very bitter and vowed to get him out of her life for good, denying him access to their child. The child was only three. She was attempting to blackmail him, threatening that if he attempted to contact them, she would make his public life very difficult and ensure he lost his job. It did not make pleasant reading, but Paul found some consolation in being reminded that he was not the only man dealing with a very bitter woman. He wondered how many other men were going through similar circumstances. He considered that this minister may have been in a slightly more favourable position than himself, in that the public could more easily see that the minister and his child were the 'true victims'. Paul still had an uphill battle in front of him in that respect.

Paul took the school's advice and the following week mailed a short letter to Phoenix with a special letter for Kara enclosed.

To my dearest Kara,

Since receiving your letter I have felt so very sad about how you feel. I have always loved you and I continue to think about you every day, hoping you are well and enjoying yourself. I've always looked forward to seeing you and enjoyed having you around. All my family say the same.

Although I don't understand where your recent feelings have come from, I will go along with your wishes and give you some space. Please understand though that I will always be there for you should you need me, no matter what.

Please don't let it be too long before you want to contact me again. Until then, I sincerely wish you well in everything you do.

All my Love,

Dad, x

Additionally he wrote to the headmistress in an attempt to ensure Kara received the letter.

Paul spoke to Jenna that evening and opened up to her.

'Is it possible I might have said something derogatory about her mother which Kara overheard and this is what has sparked her behaviour towards me? If only she had mentioned something earlier to me about how she was feeling, perhaps I might have been able to turn things around.'

He started to question if Kara had tried to tell him, but he had not picked it up. He became very self-critical, blaming himself for this latest turn of events.

Jenna quickly leapt to his defence.

'You have done absolutely nothing to deserve this treatment. It's others who should be ashamed of themselves for allowing this awful predicament to develop. At best, your ex-wife has been totally ineffectual in helping to resolve this situation; at worst she has likely encouraged it. If the latter is true, then she makes me feel ashamed to be a woman.'

That week Paul and Jenna spent a lot of time talking over the latest developments. Jenna had been his rock throughout and he was not sure how he would have coped without her support. They remarked on how this time last year they had shared a great relationship with Kara and how the three of them had been looking forward to going on holiday together. What had happened since then? One possibility they considered was the break-up of Phoenix and her boyfriend at the time, Garth. Kara was supposed to be going abroad on holiday with them. Paul had signed a consent form in preparation for Kara's travels. However, this holiday had never actually materialised. Kara had mentioned how Phoenix and Garth had argued over payments for the trip and how this, on top of a number of other unpleasant events, had led to their unfriendly break-up. From what Paul could gather, this did sound a rather acrimonious split, particularly when Kara remarked that her mum had told her, 'Garth's name is never to be mentioned again.'

Paul reflected on how Phoenix had never had a long-term relationship with any man apart from him. She claimed that other men had treated her extremely badly, for example locking her in a room or stealing from her and dumping her miles away from her home. On one occasion she even alleged she had been attacked as a teenager, insinuating she had been physically abused. She had never reported it to the police for fear of not being believed. Paul had not been sure whether to believe her or not at the time.

Regardless, he had been conscious not to mention it during their relationship, for he did not want to bring back bad memories.

He was now questioning the reliability and relevance of these allegations. Had she made them up? Was it possible that she had some sort of psychological problem when it came to men? Was this rubbing off on Kara? Had he become a substitute target for their hatred and frustrations with all men? At any rate, both he and Jenna knew of women who had been through similar traumatic experiences, but they had still turned out to be very kind, caring, thoughtful individuals.

'You can make excuses for people's bad behaviour, but some people just seem to revel in it,' Jenna compellingly pointed out to him.

Paul wondered if Phoenix's mother and stepfather were aware of how desperate the situation had become between him and Kara. Surely they would have some feelings on the matter? Since their move to France, it was possible that they knew nothing of what had been happening. Unfortunately he had no contact details for them. Could he get them somehow?

He carried out a search on the internet. About twenty possible matches came up, with phone numbers and addresses disclosed. He decided to ring each telephone number in turn. As fortune would have it, on dialling the first one, he recognised his ex-mother-in-law's voice immediately. He was taken by surprise.

'Hello,' she said about four or five times. Paul did not know what to say and no words came out. After about ten seconds, she hung up.

Once Paul had calmed down, he savoured the satisfaction and full significance of having found this address. He could now send birthday and Christmas cards to Kara via Phoenix's parents. He also had contact point in addition to the school in case of emergency.

Since Christmas was approaching, Paul took the opportunity to mail Phoenix's parents a Christmas card with a letter inside. He wished them well and summarised his predicament with Kara. He expressed his concern that Kara was going through a tough time. He enclosed a Christmas card and letter for Kara together with some gift vouchers, since he guessed they would be seeing Kara over the Christmas period. He explained that he had bought some other presents for her throughout the year, but was not sure how to get them to her, or even if she would want them at the moment. He politely asked if they could present the vouchers to her at an appropriate time and reassure her that 'her dad loves her'. Finally he asked if they could possibly mail a photo of her to him and provided a telephone number where he could be contacted on Christmas Day, should Kara wish to speak to him.

Paul did not hear anything from Kara at all over the Christmas period. He was surprised that Phoenix's parents had not tried to make contact in response to his letter. Perhaps they had not receive it. He remained hopeful that something would transpire before the end of the year. He was aware that his side of the family had mailed presents and cards directly to Kara's house, but no one knew if she had received them or not.

Unbeknown to him at the time, his mum and dad had mailed a Christmas card to Phoenix with a letter inside. They expressed their sadness at not seeing Kara and their bewilderment at the devastating letter Paul had received. They had personal experience of the efforts their son had gone to over the years to make sure they all got to see Kara.

In mid-January, Paul received an acknowledgement letter from Phoenix for Kara's Christmas presents. Although he found it had her usual belittling tone, it did wish him, Jenna and his family a happy Christmas and New Year and thanked him on Kara's behalf for the gifts. He consideredit to be a bit late, but nevertheless, it did give him greater confidence that Kara had actually received her presents. Dare he think that things could be looking up? He suspected Phoenix's stepfather may have had some influence in her writing this letter. Rather oddly, it did include the statement, 'Don't contact my mother or stepfather again'. This seemed a very strange request, but for the sake of keeping the peace he thought it best to go along with her wishes and trust that anything he sent to Kara would indeed get through.

During January, Paul continued to trawl the internet, desperately trying to find good advice on what to do next. He came across one really good website called ParentLine, a national charity that dealt with the types of issues that he was experiencing. He rang the helpline and they were very understanding of his dilemma.

'You have probably done all you can for the moment,' their representative suggested. 'The best course of action will likely be to allow Kara a cooling-off period before sending another letter. However, a potential problem may be that Kara is not receiving your letters. Perhaps they are being intercepted?'

Paul didn't really believe Phoenix would be so malicious as to behave in this way, but nonetheless it was an unpleasant thought that lurked at the back of his mind. ParentLine agreed that his journal was an excellent way of ensuring that Kara found out the truth one day, should circumstances ever sink to that level. For now they would send him copies of their leaflets, which gave advice on how children should be strongly encouraged to remain in contact with both their parents. They suggested he and Phoenix read them together.

The leaflets arrived mid-February and Paul telephoned Phoenix to tell her about them. She seemed most put out.

'I am well aware of this organisation and I don't need reminding of the principles outlined in their leaflets, especially from you,' she replied. 'I talked Kara through it all about four years ago, thank you very much.'

Paul found this a little unbelievable. Kara would only have been about five at the time and he was not sure this organisation had even existed then. On a more positive note, as their conversation continued, Phoenix did soften a little and thanked him for the thought, becoming surprisingly pleasant on the phone. He decided to take advantage of her unusually co-operative mood.

'Would you mind if I ring occasionally to enquire how Kara is?' he asked.

'That shouldn't be a problem, as long as it's after 8pm, after she has gone to bed,' Phoenix replied.

'Please pass my love on to her and let her know I am always thinking of her.'

'I can do that,' she responded.

'Is there anything else I can do to help?' asked Paul.

'It would be best if you backed off, just for a little while longer and we can see how things go.'

'Is the time right to send another letter to Kara?'

'No, absolutely not,' Phoenix replied very firmly.

The following week Paul telephoned Phoenix at 8:30pm to find out how Kara was keeping. After some introductory pleasantries (although Paul found this was not easy with Phoenix's attitude), he tried to get some more information.

'How is Kara?' he asked.

'Fine,' replied Phoenix.

'Is there an Open Evening coming up at the school?'

'The school doesn't have Open Evenings; it has pre-arranged consultations,' she replied. He found this a little strange, since the headmistress had told him something different.

'In that case I'll arrange an appointment with the headmistress.'

'Just ring her, don't visit,' responded Phoenix brusquely.

'What would Kara like for her birthday this year?' he enquired.

'She's not likely to want anything from you.'

The conversation continued in this stilted manner for a couple of minutes before they agreed it would be best if he sent some gift vouchers.

'Has Kara any new hobbies or interests?'

'Nothing new.'

After further prompting, however, Phoenix did inform him that Kara had joined the school's five-a-side football team and the team had recently won a quarter-final match in the school cup. He thought this was great news.

'Can you please let Kara know I telephoned?' he asked, hoping to appeal to her better nature.

Phoenix was very reluctant to do so.

'Kara has become paranoid about answering the phone in

case it's you ringing. If you absolutely must contact her, now might be a better time to write her a letter.'

Paul conceded that this would probably be best for now. He just hoped Kara got to see the letters he was sending and Phoenix wasn't throwing them in the bin.

'Also, if you must ring in future, make it much later in the evening, around ten o'clock. That way Kara will be in bed and your phone call won't upset her. You must appreciate she's older now and doesn't go to bed at 8:30 any more.'

Paul felt that whatever he did was wrong in Phoenix's eyes. It was only a few days ago that she had told him that Kara went to bed at 8pm!

'Is there a particular night that Kara goes out?' he asked.

'Kara doesn't go out – she stays in most nights with me, her mum.'

He considered this also contradicted earlier statements she had made. About six months ago she had told him Kara was always out when he was trying to organise visits. Regardless, at least this latest telephoning arrangement gave him some way of keeping up to date with Kara's welfare.

'I'll ring again next week,' he informed her. Phoenix was not happy with this at all.

'You must leave at least six weeks before ringing again,' she insisted.

He tried reasoning with her for the best part of five minutes, but it was to no avail. At least she had agreed he could ring.

After Paul put the phone down, he reflected on how strained the conversation with Phoenix had been. Was she intentionally trying to keep him out of Kara's life as much as possible? Would she really be that wicked or was he getting paranoid? She had been very reluctant to let him know of Kara's hobbies and interests. Was it possible that she would stoop so low as to purposely poison Kara against him? He got the feeling that she liked to dig the knife in, saying such things as 'Kara is growing up so fast' and 'Kara is doing extremely well', knowing that he was not there to share directly in the joy of these experiences.

That night he wrote Kara a short letter, expressing how

much he missed her and how he hoped she would get in contact with him soon. He mailed it to her the following day.

A month later, Paul had still not received any sort of reply to his letter. He didn't even have confirmation from Phoenix of whether Kara had received it. He held Phoenix responsible for the lack of reply. If the situation was reversed and Kara was living with him, he knew he would try his utmost to make sure Kara replied to any letters her mother had sent. If he seriously could not get Kara to reply, then at the very least he would reply on her behalf. It was only good manners. Phoenix appeared to have had a bypass where these aspects of common courtesy were concerned.

Unfortunately he could see no option other than to put his trust in her for the time being, for fear of making matters worse. At least he could console himself that the school had agreed to notify him of anything that warranted his attention. He had not heard anything to date, so he felt some degree of comfort that Kara must be doing okay.

After he talked to Jenna one evening about how he was coping with missing Kara, she once again assured him that keeping his journal was a good idea. She remarked how in her experience, many children wanted questions answered when they got older and this would be an excellent way of ensuring Kara got to see her father's side of the story. He requested that if anything should ever happen to him, she present Kara with it at a suitable opportunity.

'Of course,' Jenna replied.

Inwardly he was hoping that Kara would never have to see the journal. He still hoped everything would be sorted in the near future, but he had to admit there had not been much sign of progress over the last six months.

Since Christmas, he had spoken with many different people, trying to get some ideas as to what to do for the best. He had tried to keep in contact with Kara by phone and letter, but he did not seem to be getting anywhere. He was not sure if he could trust Phoenix, so the only way he could reassure himself about Kara's welfare was via the school.

At the end of May, Paul returned from a business trip to find a letter from Kara's school. They informed him that Kara was taking part in the school's end of year concert, playing the cello, a 'virtuoso' performance. They gave him a number to ring if he wanted tickets. He was absolutely thrilled, yet flabbergasted at the same time. Why hadn't Phoenix let him know about Kara's obvious musical ability? For now he decided to concentrate on the positive aspects of this news, considering it an excellent way of building bridges with Kara, although he was unsure of how to approach her. She had not spoken to him directly for six months and he did not want to cause her distress.

He decided to send her a birthday card, for her tenth birthday was fast approaching. He enclosed a letter saying how much he would love to see the show and asked if she would have any objection to him coming to the concert. Additionally he included some gift vouchers. He would have dearly loved to telephone her on her birthday, but Phoenix had previously warned him off, telling him that the time was not right and he should not risk upsetting Kara on her birthday of all days. He settled on chasing up the birthday card with a phone call the following week.

A week after sending the card, Paul tried to ring Phoenix as he had planned. Predictably he could not get through. He left a message politely asking, 'Please call back.' As usual she didn't respond, so he spent the rest of the week repeatedly trying until he eventually got an answer. Phoenix was reasonably pleasant on the phone.

'Kara has received your birthday card and letter,' she informed him. 'She asked me to read it to her. Maybe you will get a "thank you" note, but who knows? She remains adamant that she doesn't want contact with you and definitely does not want you present at the school concert. She's refused to perform if you are there.'

Paul was stunned and bitterly disappointed. He tried reasoning with Phoenix, but in the end he once again reluctantly agreed to go along with Kara's alleged wishes.

Phoenix attempted to reassure him that over the last six months she had made good progress with Kara.

'If you can give us space for just a little while longer,' she urged, 'I'm confident I can talk Kara round.'

Paul was getting tired of her empty promises, but felt he had no other option to pursue at this time.

'I'll ring the school and thank the headmistress for the offer of tickets, even though I won't be attending on this occasion,' he replied.

Phoenix seemed insulted.

'I don't mean to sound callous, but the school couldn't care less about you,' she replied.

Paul firmly pointed out that when he had visited the school, they had expressed concern about this whole situation and obviously realised how important it was for a child to have regular contact with their father.

'Whatever,' Phoenix responded.

'How is Kara?'

'She's fine,' Phoenix replied offhandedly.

This consoled Paul a little, but not much, bearing in mind Phoenix's tone of voice.

'I'll ring again in the not too distant future, just to ensure Kara is okay.'

'That will not be necessary,' replied Phoenix. 'I've made it clear to Kara that she is free to ring you whenever she wants, should she feel the need.'

At least this last remark sounded sort of good news to Paul.

Paul rang the headmistress the following day to express his thanks for the offer of tickets, but regretfully informed her that following a discussion with Kara's mother, sadly they had established the time was not yet right for him to come to the show.

'I understand,' she replied.

'Will the school photos and reports be out soon?' enquired Paul.

'Yes, they are to be sent out shortly. There is also a school Open Evening coming up which you are most welcome to attend.'

'Thanks, I'll definitely be there,' replied Paul.

Two weeks later Paul was delighted to receive a card from Kara thanking him for the birthday card and the present he had sent. Although the message was somewhat curt, it did appear a fantastic step in the right direction. He knew he still had a long way to go to rebuild bridges, but at least there appeared a glimmer of light at the end of the tunnel. Conversely, that same week he was saddened he did not receive a Father's Day card. He supposed he should have expected it, for Phoenix had never encouraged Kara to send him birthday cards or Father's Day cards since she had been three years old.

Paul rang Phoenix that evening in the hope he could express his gratitude to Kara. He wanted to personally thank her for the card she had sent to him. Additionally he wanted to let Phoenix know that he would be going to the school Open Evening the following night after work. As usual he got no reply, so instead he left a message with his intentions on her answer phone.

As planned, Paul went to the school Open Evening. As he walked into the main hall, the headmistress greeted him. Paul noticed there were some children in the hall, which he had not expected.

'Is Kara here?' he asked.

'No, I don't think so,' she replied, then proceeded to escort Paul to Kara's classroom, where her teacher was conversing with other parents. On the way, the headmistress noticed that Kara was indeed in the hall, playing the cello with a small orchestra. Paul caught her eye, but was not sure if she recognised him. At first he did not recognise her. Her hair had grown much longer, but she looked well. It really hit home how despite his efforts, it had been almost a year since he had last seen her.

They decided to walk round the other way to see Kara's teacher. The teacher confirmed Kara was doing well in all subjects, but noticeably excelling in mathematics and drama.

'What about her general social skills?' Paul asked.

'She's pretty much the same as any other ten-year-old girl in that she blows hot and cold over who she does and doesn't like on a day-to-day basis. She can be very competitive and there are times I have noticed she lacks confidence, but I don't believe there is anything significant to worry about.'

Paul looked around the classroom and noticed a poem on the wall that had been reviewed by Kara. It was about an orphan boy looking for his family, trying to discover his roots. He wondered if there was any relevance in Kara choosing this piece of work to review.

On leaving the classroom, he found himself in a corridor behind the school orchestra. He was able to see the young musicians through the window, but they could not see him since they were facing the other way. Kara was still playing the cello and the orchestra was playing 'Over the Rainbow'. He had this incredible urge to walk up and say 'Hello', but he was not sure if this would be a wise move. He stood and listened to a couple of tunes and then the orchestra took a break.

At that moment he decided to seize the opportunity and approach Kara. Surely this would be better than leaving without saying anything? For all he knew, she might have been dying for him to say something. He slowly made his way over and crouched down in front of her.

'Hello, how are you?' he said in as friendly a voice as he could. He gently took her hand. 'It's lovely to see you,' he added.

He registered a look of absolute terror and anguish on her face. She hastily backed away from him and ran up to another man.

'Paul's here!' she yelled.

Paul was amazed and horrified at this reaction. He assumed this man to be a teacher.

'Go and sit back with the orchestra,' the man instructed her.

Paul went over and introduced himself.

'Hi, I'm Kara's father. Is everything okay?'

'Kara's a bit upset that you're here whilst her mum isn't,' he replied. He went on to explain that he was not a teacher, but a friend of Phoenix's, and was looking after Kara until Phoenix arrived. 'Phoenix has been unavoidably detained and isn't likely to be here for another half hour or so,' he added.

'I'm about to leave now,' Paul informed him, 'but could you please tell Kara her father is very proud of her?'

'No problem,' he replied.

As Paul turned to leave, he thought he would have one more try at making things better with Kara. He turned around and approached the same man.

'Would you mind asking Kara if she wants to say either "Hello" or "Goodbye" to her dad?'

The man (who Paul later found out was called Ross) appeared to consider this a most reasonable request and went over to Kara. Paul watched Kara's reaction as he asked her the question. It was obvious Kara did not even think about it.

'No,' she hastily replied, shaking her head vigorously, still looking upset.

The man looked across at Paul, shrugged his shoulders and shook his head. At this point Paul dejectedly left the school hall and headed for home.

During the drive home, he mulled over the evening's events and tried to analyse what had happened. On the positive side, he had seen Kara and found out directly from her teachers and the headmistress that she was okay in herself and doing rather well at school. Her studies were going well and she was continuing to play the cello. On the negative side, it was clear that she still did not want to see or talk to him for whatever reason. Just seeing him caused her extreme distress. What was that about? It substantiated his fears that her head must be full of all sorts of nonsense, but where had it come from? Sadly he conceded that any joyous reunion was still some time off.

Jenna could clearly see Paul was upset when he got home. Once he told her what had happened she became angry. She hated to see him upset in this way and she knew he did not deserve this treatment. She reminded him of the number of children in her dance school that didn't have a father for all sorts of reasons, including tragic examples where the father had sadly passed away. All these children would love a chance to be with their dads, but regrettably some would never get it. Jenna was convinced that Phoenix was using Kara to punish him for the breakdown of their marriage. She called it 'woman's intuition'. She offered to ring Phoenix and go and see her, talk to her woman to woman, face to face. Paul considered this a very generous and thoughtful offer, but suggested they wait a little while to see if there was any fallout from the Open Evening.

He felt a mix of emotions that evening, including sadness, bitterness, anger and resentment. He felt so sorry for Kara in that she had lost so much time knowing her father. The feelings of bitterness, anger and resentment were for Phoenix, since he held her personally responsible for allowing this awful situation to develop, maybe even orchestrating it.

The following day, Phoenix rang Paul. For the first five minutes she just shouted at him whilst he tried to calm her down and make sense of what she was saying.

'How could you be so irresponsible?' she ranted. 'What possessed you to turn up at the school?'

Paul finally lost his cool.

'You've poisoned our daughter against me,' he angrily accused her. Phoenix retaliated by simply hanging up.

He considered this typical and went out into the garden for a cigarette. He had not smoked for the last six months, but she was driving him back to his undesirable habit. He had kept an old pack stashed away for such emergencies. He had just lit it up when the phone rang again. He was in two minds whether to pick it up, since he anticipated it would be Phoenix and he was very tired of arguing. However, he was glad he did. It was indeed Phoenix, but this time her nature was much more pleasant. They managed an adult and productive conversation, covering all sorts of ground.

'I can assure you that I have not been poisoning Kara's mind against you and I am as concerned as you are that our behaviours could upset Kara long-term,' she explained. 'Kara is not a man-hater and one day wants to get married and have children. I am aware that she could easily go against me if she thought I was intentionally poisoning her against you. She does not hate you; she just doesn't want contact with you at the moment.'

'But why?' asked Paul. 'It makes no sense.'

'I can't give a rational explanation,' replied Phoenix. 'She did once say that she felt a bit left out of things during her last couple of visits. Perhaps that's the reason.' There was a slight pause before Phoenix went on to add, 'Kara was left extremely embarrassed by the Open Evening episode and did not want to go to school the next day. She holds you totally responsible. She asked me to make this telephone call to you and wants me to get your guarantee that you will not turn up there again. She feels the school is her territory.'

'I didn't know she was going to be there,' Paul protested. 'I only turned up with her best interests at heart, to try and show support. Surely you understand that?'

Phoenix appeared to understand and agreed, 'I'll relate this back to Kara.'

'Okay, in future I will only visit the school when I can be sure Kara is not there,' Paul conceded. 'I'll write to Kara in about two to three weeks' time and apologise to her for the whole Open Evening episode. I'll make sure she knows that if I plan on attending occasions like that again, she knows about it beforehand. You do know that I left a message on your answer phone stating my intentions of attending on this occasion, don't you?'

'No, I don't know. I never got it,' Phoenix replied. He did not know whether to believe her or not. 'The "thank you" card you received from Kara for her birthday present was all her own doing, with no influence from me,' she continued. They agreed that this appeared a huge step in the right direction. Phoenix was quick to point out however, 'You've probably put things back now, though, by turning up at the school Open Evening.'

As usual, Paul felt in a no-win situation. He once again tried to make it clear to her that he was only trying to act in Kara's best interests.

'You know I'll make myself available at any time should Kara ever want to talk over a cup of tea, a burger or anything,' he assured her, 'either with or without you present.'

Finally they spoke about their marriage break-up and sadly came to the realisation that they had not been in full possession of all the facts at the time. They came to the conclusion that others around them had made matters much worse with idle and malicious gossip.

Overall this call was probably one of their most valuable and civilised conversations in a very long time. They recognised that they had both grown up over the last seven years since their break-up. They acknowledged there was still a long way to go to put the Kara situation right, but Paul did come away with the feeling that things were moving in the right direction. He was optimistic that Phoenix was trying in her own way. Jenna was not so sure, but did not want to dampen his spirits.

The following weekend, Paul mailed a letter to Kara with a small lucky horseshoe enclosed. He apologised for surprising her at the school Open Evening. He also congratulated her on her fine cello playing and all the positive remarks her teachers had made about her school work. He let her know how proud she had made him and expressed his love on behalf of himself and his family.

Paul continued to keep in touch with the school. Shortly after the Open Evening, he telephoned the headmistress to relay recent events and his subsequent efforts to smooth things over with Kara. It was then he found out something quite alarming. The headmistress informed him that Phoenix had been to visit and had requested that the school stop letting Paul know about school events such as Open Evenings in the future! In response, the school had pointed out to her that they had a legal obligation to inform Kara's father of such events and if Phoenix wanted this stopped, she would have to get a Court Order.

Paul considered he and the headmistress now understood each other very well and additionally he now had some proof that Phoenix was indeed contributing to the breakdown of his relationship with Kara. Once again he was not sure what he could do about it, but it was certainly more evidence to mull over on those sleepless nights.

The headmistress apologised on behalf of the school for not having contacted Paul directly, but the school had incorrectly assumed that Phoenix was passing on messages. Paul explained that this was not happening. They agreed he would be a direct point of contact from now on with respect to future correspondence.

'A school photo should now be on its way to you, along with a DVD of Kara in the end of year concert,' she added as some consolation.

In early August, Paul and Jenna went to the New Forest for a short break. Whilst there, he read a letter sent to a national newspaper by a father in a similar predicament to him. The advice given was to contact Families Need Fathers. It quoted, 'Families need fathers, otherwise the children are likely to grow up feeling sad and confused.' This did not surprise Paul at all.

When he returned home, he logged on to the Families Need Fathers website. He noted to his disappointment that this organisation appeared to be very much geared to litigation. He did not want his own situation to end up in court. His last conversation with Phoenix had been quite positive and he felt that invoking litigation at this point would only make matters worse. Nonetheless, he rang their helpline to see if they had other suggestions to offer.

He could not get through to the offices of Families Need Fathers, since they were only open in the evening. Instead, he decided to ring Social Services to see what they had to offer. He spoke directly to one of their representatives.

'For the next couple of months, why don't you try increasing the frequency of writing to Kara?' the representative suggested. 'Alternatively, perhaps you and Phoenix, and even Kara if she is agreeable, could go to RELATE-type counselling.'

Paul explained how he had tried something similar before, but Phoenix had purposefully arranged the sessions without him in attendance.

'If Phoenix will not go to counselling as a family unit, then perhaps the only option open is to take it through the courts,' the representative advised.

Paul had another sleepless night, thinking long and hard about the advice from Social Services. He recognised that going to court was a viable option, but he was anxious that pursuing this route would only push Kara further away from him. On top of that, it could be very costly and he was not sure of the chances of success. He decided for the short term to increase the frequency of letters he sent to Kara as Social Services had initially suggested.

The following evening, Paul tried phoning Phoenix to let her know about his intentions of writing letters to Kara on a weekly basis. Furthermore he now intended to telephone Phoenix on a fortnightly basis for a progress update.

As usual he could not get through, so he left these sentiments on her answer phone and politely asked her to get back to him. He decided to keep a record (and copies where possible) of all the letters and cards he sent from this date forward, in case Kara was not getting to see them.

During October, Paul and Jenna spent a weekend in the Cotswolds. They spent time cycling around the small villages and did some early Christmas shopping in the quaint little shops. He sent Kara a postcard. It was particularly at times like these that he thought of her and missed her most. He could not help feeling hard done by. He knew his contribution to his marriage breakdown was wrong, but he felt he was paying an overly large price and Kara was unnecessarily suffering too, even if she did not realise it at the moment. Fortunately he had Jenna by his side, who continued to be a tremendous support.

On their return home, they found the DVD of the school concert had been delivered. Paul excitedly watched it that night. It was first-class and it brought a lump to his throat when he saw Kara on stage playing the cello so brilliantly.

'Perhaps she takes after me,' he proudly professed to Jenna, a little tongue-in-cheek. He was really pleased to see this DVD, although at the same time he was annoyed that Phoenix had never had the decency to tell him about its availability, nor that Kara was such a star in it.

In the run-up to Christmas, Paul continued to be very busy at work. This included an ever-increasing amount of travel, which meant he was not at home as often as he would have liked. Fortunately, he had managed to purchase all Kara's

Christmas presents beforehand, but he was not sure how he would deliver them. He would have loved to give them to her personally, but she would probably not want that and he was sure Phoenix would block it anyway. He decided to ring Phoenix to see how the land lay, assuming she answered the phone.

The following evening, Paul telephoned Phoenix and she did indeed answer. It had been a good couple of months since they had last spoken to each other, despite his efforts.

'Is Kara receiving her weekly letters?' he asked, after the usual stilted introductory pleasantries. 'Is she enjoying them?'

'Of course she's receiving them,' replied Phoenix in an indignant manner. 'She's even using some of the gifts you enclosed.'

This raised Paul's hopes and he relayed his idea of personally delivering some Christmas presents.

'I'd dearly love to see Kara, even if only for five minutes,' he added.

'We'll probably be out,' replied Phoenix. He had not even proposed a date at this point!

'Perhaps you could offer an evening when you are likely to be in and I'll come then,' Paul suggested, trying not to sound too mocking. As usual, he found her to be her unco-operative self.

'I'll speak with Kara to see if I can persuade her to see you,' she replied huffily.

'Thank you,' replied Paul, but he did not get his hopes up. Phoenix had so far been very ineffective when it had come to repairing his relationship with his daughter and he had little confidence that anything would be different this time.

'I'll ring again next week to arrange a date,' he said, before they exchanged goodbyes.

During that week Kara's school photo arrived. Paul was delighted with it and put it in a frame where it took pride of place on his sideboard. He also ordered extra copies for his family.

As Christmas approached, a number of his friends and

family asked if there had been any improvement in his situation with Kara. None of them could believe Phoenix had let it drag on this long or that she had failed to persuade Kara to have a change of heart, for Kara's own sake. Kara was losing so much: not just a father, but the love and companionship of a whole part of her family. They suggested that a silver lining to this black cloud might be that she did not realise just how much she was missing out on at the moment, bearing in mind she was still quite young. However, no one would be able to blame her for feeling very bitter towards her mother as she got older, once she was away from her influence.

In Paul's letter to Kara that week, he explained how much he would love to see her and that he had some Christmas presents for her. 'I'll ring your mum during the week to arrange the best time to deliver them,' he wrote.

The following week he telephoned Phoenix as planned.

'Kara has received your letter,' she informed him, 'but has decided that she doesn't want to see you. However, I am prepared to meet with you somewhere neutral so you can hand over your gifts.'

Paul felt most crestfallen that Kara did not want to see him, even if only for five minutes. He resigned himself to meeting just with Phoenix the following day at a coffee shop, local to where she lived. At least he had found a route of getting the presents to Kara.

Coincidentally Paul's brother rang later that same evening and enquired as to his intentions with respect to Kara's Christmas presents. Paul explained the arrangements he had just made with Phoenix.

'Would it be okay if we accompanied you?' his brother asked, referring to himself and his wife. 'You never know, Kara might change her mind about meeting up and we'd both love to see her.'

'I don't think that's likely,' Paul replied, 'but I'd love to have you both along for moral support anyway. We need to be careful that we don't make Phoenix feel intimidated though. You know what she's like; she may not turn up if she feels outnumbered. Mind you, having another woman along might help things go more smoothly. I'll pick you up on my way through tomorrow.'

The following morning, Paul, his brother and his sister-in-law met with Phoenix in her local coffee shop. The two women sat down at a table whilst Paul and his brother bought the drinks. Whilst waiting in the queue, they looked across and noticed the two women were conversing quite normally. In fact, Paul considered it suspiciously pleasant.

'How is Kara doing?' his sister-in-law asked politely.

Phoenix was surprisingly forthcoming with information.

'Kara's doing well, both at home and school.'

'Why is it that Kara doesn't want to see Paul or the family any more?'

'Kara has put it all in a letter,' replied Phoenix.

'I saw the letter. A lot of the information in it was simply not true.'

'Kara was desperate to see more of Paul when she was younger, but he didn't make sufficient time,' explained Phoenix.

His sister-in-law let the subject drop at this point. She had personally witnessed how Paul used to go out of his way to see as much of Kara as he could, picking her up and taking her back home at weekends. She knew from personal experience that Phoenix used to make his life difficult. Phoenix would not let the family see Kara at Christmas and made it clear that they were not welcome to see Kara on her birthday.

'Kara doesn't like Jenna,' Phoenix unexpectedly threw into the conversation.

Paul's sister-in-law found this very odd and it further aroused her suspicion that Phoenix was on some sort of vengeful mission, but she did not retaliate.

'We would like to ring Kara on Christmas Day to pass on our best wishes. Can we have a phone number?' she asked.

Paul and his brother returned to the table at this point and handed out the drinks.

'We'll be spending the day at my boyfriend's mum's house,

so a phone call will not be welcome,' Phoenix replied. She then started gushing about her new boyfriend, revealing how she had met him in the spring of that year and how she was hoping for many more children. Paul and his companions were unsure what to make of all this, for they found this sudden change in the topic of conversation inappropriate and a little bizarre. As Paul listened, however, he was hopeful that this new relationship might lead to a mellowing in Phoenix's behaviour. 'Perhaps you could ring Boxing Day,' suggested Phoenix. 'We should be back home by then.'

Once they had concluded their conversation, Paul and his sister-in-law handed over the presents they had brought with them. They all wished each other a merry Christmas and bade their farewells.

On the journey home, Paul and his brother reflected on how things had gone. Paul admitted that although he had found the meeting awkward, overall it had been more pleasant than he had anticipated, to which all three of them agreed. Paul's sister-in-law added how she had always found it difficult to forge a close bond with Phoenix, despite trying many times over the years.

'I get the impression that she looks down on me and has always been jealous of how well I get on with your family, especially my good relationship with Jenna,' she explained.

A few days after the visit to see Phoenix, Paul's sister-in-law apprehensively relayed back to Jenna Phoenix's proclamation that Kara did not like her. She genuinely did not mean to upset Jenna, but Jenna was understandably hurt and upset, for she had always tried to do her best for Kara. When Kara was a little child, Jenna was always there for her, but as Kara grew older, she used to purposely stay in the background, because she felt Kara wanted more of Paul's attention. All the family recognised how good Jenna was with children. This was also borne out by the pupils of Jenna's dance school. They all loved her dearly. Thankfully, Jenna was not down for too long. Paul's sister-in-law reminded her that Phoenix was likely still a very bitter woman, acting in a spiteful, child-like fashion.

On Boxing Day, Paul rang Kara to wish her a happy Christmas, as had been agreed with Phoenix at their last meeting. Disappointingly Kara would not come to the phone. He asked Phoenix to pass on his love and best wishes to her. The whole situation made him wonder how Phoenix was bringing Kara up. Surely at the very least she could have persuaded Kara to come to the phone to express thanks for her presents. He sincerely hoped Phoenix's influence would not cause Kara to grow into a spoilt, ungrateful adult.

Later that evening he found out that his sister-in-law and his parents had also tried ringing during the day, but they had got no answer.

Paul had continued to make entries in his journal over the past months, but it was at times like these he felt a particular need to write something, so he could feel close to Kara.

26 December

Once again, I want Kara to know that I don't really blame her for any of this mess. I can only conclude that Phoenix has instilled these beliefs in her so she knows no different. I only hope that as Kara grows older, she will understand what really happened.

He had continued writing weekly letters to Kara since August of that year, despite getting no reply. He was obviously disappointed not to have received anything, but there was no way he was giving up on his ten-year-old daughter, who he considered had been unfairly influenced by her mother.

One morning in February, Jenna brought the post in and there was a package from Kara. Paul opened it and found three 'Thank you for my Christmas presents' cards. One was for him and Jenna, one for his mum and dad, and one for his brother and sister-in-law. Although the messages were very short and did not say much apart from 'Thank you', he found it really heart-warming to at least have received something. He wondered if he had been a bit hard on Phoenix. Perhaps she had been trying to make Kara write these letters and it was Kara herself who had been resistant. Regardless, he was delighted to receive them and felt it was a step in the right direction.

He wrote a letter back to Kara that day thanking her for the cards, letting her know how thrilled all the family would be to receive them.

Throughout March and April, he continued to write and send his weekly letters, but still got no response. Once May arrived, he decided to ring Phoenix for an update on how things were progressing. The following month would be Kara's birthday and he wanted to arrange delivery of her birthday presents. She would be eleven and he sadly acknowledged that he had not seen her for the best part of eighteen months.

As usual he found it very difficult to contact Phoenix. He would leave messages on her answer phone, but she would never return his calls. After three days of constantly ringing, she eventually picked up.

'I've not returned your calls because I lost your phone number,' she explained.

Paul didn't believe her. Funny how she managed to find his number when she wanted something. Stupid bitch!

After a short chat, Phoenix informed him, 'Kara has passed her 11-plus exam.'

Paul was delighted. He also managed to draw out of her that Kara had secured a place at the local secondary school which was held in high regard, although he noted Phoenix had been very reluctant to pass on this piece of information.

'How is Kara in herself?' he enquired.

'She's fine, but she still doesn't want to see or talk to you.'

He explained that he had some birthday presents he would like to give to Kara.

'Perhaps we can meet at the same coffee shop we did before, you know, where we met last Christmas,' he suggested. 'It would also be a good opportunity to talk face to face about Kara.'

Phoenix was noticeably reluctant.

'Just post the presents,' she replied. Once again, he found she was being difficult.

'That would be very impractical,' he explained. 'I've got

presents from all the family.' Despite her inexplicable lack of co-operation, he did finally manage to persuade her to meet with him in a couple of days.

The following afternoon, Phoenix left a rather unintelligible message on Paul's answer phone.

'I've changed my mind about meeting up. I don't want to see you,' she informed him.

When Paul got in from work and replayed the message, he immediately rang her back to find out what was going on. Phoenix answered and confirmed the message. He tried reasoning with her, but his attempts were futile.

'If you must deliver the presents, you can leave them in the front yard. I'll leave an empty dustbin behind the oak tree and you can put them in there,' she finally conceded.

Paul made further entries in his journal that evening, one of which was:

I continue to get the feeling that Phoenix is a little imbalanced and a bit of a 'control freak'. At least I should get a chance to deliver the presents. Throughout all of this I know I have to stay focused on Kara's wellbeing and not let Phoenix's selfish behaviour get me down.

On a summer's evening in June, true to her word, Phoenix had indeed left an empty plastic dustbin in the front yard so he could drop off the presents from him and his family. Once he had off-loaded the gifts, he knocked on the front door just in case Phoenix happened to be in and would care to greet him like a normal human being. There was predictably no answer.

He made a special note in his journal on Kara's birthday.

Today is Kara's eleventh birthday. I would love to talk to her, but I know Phoenix will only say, 'Kara does not want to speak to you'. Perhaps Kara will ring me if she wants to talk, once she has opened her presents. I hope she likes them.

Kara's eleventh birthday came and went and he received no acknowledgement for the gifts.

By late July, Paul had still not heard anything from Kara. He rang her school and spoke to the school office. The secretary told him that Kara was doing well as far as she was aware.

'She has passed her 11-plus exam and has secured a place at the local secondary school. She will be starting in September. I'll ask Kara's class teacher to ring you back with any further information if you like?'

Kara's teacher did ring back and confirmed she was doing fine. This at least was some comfort. She also informed him that a recent school photo had been taken and that the school would mail out an order form.

A week later the form arrived with a copy of Kara's end of year report. It confirmed all the good things the school had been saying. Paul left a message on Phoenix's answer phone, asking her to pass on his congratulations to Kara.

At the end of July, Paul and Jenna got the fantastic opportunity to stay with friends in a remote part of Sri Lanka. They would get their board and lodgings paid in exchange for carrying out some voluntary work. They just needed to find their flight money.

Paul had travelled to Asia a couple of times before on business, but he had never been to Sri Lanka or experienced the culture. He and Jenna were really looking forward to it.

Prior to their trip, he wrote in one of his weekly letters to Kara, 'We have been offered the wonderful opportunity to visit isolated parts of Sri Lanka. I will continue to write on a weekly basis, but I have a feeling delivery of my letters will be a little erratic since the postal service is not as developed as in the UK. I've been told that it can take over six weeks for a card to arrive back in the UK from where we are going. I'll be thinking of you all the time though. Hopefully one day we can visit these places together.'

Paul and Jenna spent almost a whole month away and they fell in love with the place, vowing to return. They experienced beautiful deserted beaches, rich mangrove forests, mouth-watering native cuisine, a vast array of wildlife including sloth bears, monkeys, crocodiles (and snakes!), but best of all they enjoyed meeting the local people. There was little sign of material wealth, but instead they personally witnessed how their riches came from other, far more significant spiritual attributes. Everyone was so friendly and all bore the most welcoming, beaming smiles.

They made many new friends and felt most honoured to be invited to join the indigenous communities within the hot, steamy jungle. They found it fascinating and inspiring to see the extraordinary farming and crafting skills that had been passed down from generation to generation and relished the opportunity to teach English and dance in the remote schools. They regarded it as a well-earned break from the materialistic, pretentious trappings commonly experienced in the western world. It was certainly opportune relief from all the petty unpleasantness they had experienced from Phoenix of late. Above all, it was a timely reminder of the important things in life and helped them put everything back in perspective.

Paul sent Kara six postcards while away and gathered numerous mementos he hoped to personally present to her in the not too distant future.

Paul had now been writing letters and postcards to Kara on a weekly basis for over a year. He had kept copies wherever possible. He would write of things he had been up to and discuss general news. He would always add how he and the family missed her and how they would love to hear from her when she felt ready. He would typically include small gifts such as cuddly toys, gift vouchers, dress jewellery, photographs and stationery for school. On one occasion he sent a book written by a ten-year-old girl. The book described how this young girl had coped with her own parents' divorce. Paul hoped it would bring some comfort to Kara.

A typical letter is reproduced below.

Hi Kara,

Well it looks like the first days of summer arrived this week. All the gardens look so colourful, the trees are getting their leaves back and walking through the countryside can be great fun. I hope you are getting the chance to get out and about.

I was working in Paris last week and whilst there, I bought you this cello-shaped brooch (enclosed). Are you still playing with the orchestra? What's your favourite piece? Who's your favourite composer? It would be great to hear from you, if only just a couple of lines in a letter.

Jenna and I found out this week that we will be looking after a friend's dog next month. He is a 12 month old black Labrador called Harry and although very friendly, he is also very strong, lively and mischievous. However he is ever so adorable. Do you still like dogs?

I hope all is going well for you and you are enjoying all your hobbies.

All the family send their love,

    Miss you lots,

      Love Dad, x

Despite sending these letters, he never did get a reply. Periodically he would telephone Phoenix and ask if Kara was receiving them. 'Of course,' Phoenix would reply. One time she added, 'Kara doesn't always read them straight away, but puts them to one side to read at a later date when she feels ready. Other times she asks me to read them to her.' Paul found this a little strange, but he was hopeful that at least Kara knew he was thinking of her. 'Things are moving in the right direction,' Phoenix continued to persuade him. 'You will be hearing from Kara shortly.'

In reality this never happened.

On his return from Sri Lanka, Paul's thoughts turned to Kara and how she would be starting at her new school the following week. He tried to ring her on Phoenix's land-line, for he desperately wanted to wish her the best of luck and let her know he was thinking of her. To his surprise, the number registered as unobtainable. He tried ringing Phoenix's mobile, but got a message saying, 'The owner is unavailable.' He tried directory enquiries only to be told, 'The name does not match the address given.'

Knowing how unco-operative Phoenix could be at times, this raised awful suspicions in his mind. Could they possibly have moved without telling him? Had Kara received any of his correspondence? He started to get very concerned.

That evening Paul drove to Phoenix's address to confront her directly. Her car was not there. On consulting a neighbour who was standing outside, he was shocked to discover that Phoenix had moved out six weeks earlier! Phoenix had obviously not bothered to let him or his family know. He sat back in the car and recalled all the times she had tried to convince him she was making progress with Kara. 'Just give me a little more time and space,' she used to say.

He was now feeling extremely foolish for having believed her and his fury built as the full consequences of this latest incredibly selfish act sank in. He had always tried to be as accommodating as possible, acting in Kara's best interests, and this was how Phoenix repaid him. What a bitch! She must still be a very bitter, twisted woman, he concluded, and is likely heading for a loony bin.

What disturbed him most was that he now had no contact address or telephone number for Kara.

Chapter 7

Cessation of contact

◇ Contacting the school, lawyers
◇ Views of friends and family

On discovering Phoenix's apparent abscondment, Paul contacted Kara's new school and requested an appointment to see someone in authority at the earliest opportunity. An appointment was arranged for the following day, which happened to be the first day of the autumn term, with Kara's head of year.

Paul and Jenna went to see him together and explained the situation. He was pleasant, helpful and sympathetic to their plight, but made it clear that the school would not want to act as a go-between. He agreed to confirm Paul's legal entitlements and make sure they were fulfilled. As a minimum the school would forward on school reports and details of any Open Evenings, but he would need to check about school photographs and whether Paul could be listed as a 'next of kin'. Paul asked if he could have Kara's home address and telephone number.

'I'm afraid the school is not at liberty to pass on this type of information,' the head of year explained, 'but I will let Phoenix know that you are asking for it. If it's still not forthcoming, I suggest you consult Citizens Advice or Social Services. As some consolation, I can tell you that Kara did show up at school this morning and I have had no reports of her not settling in. I can assure you that she will be well looked after. Perhaps you would like a tour of the school?'

Paul and Jenna took him up on his offer, being conscious not to take up too much of his time, for he was obviously busy. The building itself did appear very impressive. Jenna pointed out to Paul the well-equipped music studio, which he found most encouraging.

Following the tour, they expressed their thanks and the head of year wished them the best of luck.

Paul felt a little better after having visited the school, but was in rather a quandary as to what to do next. Having seemingly exhausted other options, he decided to leave text messages for Phoenix and Kara using the last mobile numbers he had for them. He typed the words, 'Please forward on your new home mailing address.' He would have spoken to them directly, but when he tapped in the numbers, all he got was an anonymous voice saying, 'Answer phone service is not available.'

That evening Paul spoke to friends and family about these latest developments. They were all appalled, yet not overly surprised by Phoenix's latest stunts. They put it to him that although he had constantly tried to do the right thing by keeping things amicable, he had been far too lenient. She had taken full advantage of his easy-going nature, to the detriment of any relationship between Kara and himself. What she was doing was not only damaging to Kara, but possibly also illegal. One proposal was to stop the standing order for child mainte-nance from his bank account, to see if that provoked any response.

The following day Paul contacted his work's Legal Advice Department and explained his situation to a representative. Once again he found the receiver of his news, who happened to be a woman, very understanding of his position and sympa-thetic to his circumstances. It made him wonder how common an issue this was within the UK. He asked a number of questions and got some useful responses.

'Is there anything I can do to stop my ex-wife cutting me out of my daughter's life?'

'It's a good idea to contact the school as you already have done,' she advised. 'Make sure you exercise all your parental rights and responsibilities, such as getting school reports, attending Open Evenings and getting general progress updates. Additionally, you could ring the local county court and ask for an application for a defined Contact Order. Whilst the order is being finalised, in the interim the judge will most likely encourage contact. A couple of stumbling blocks will be firstly that you have not got a contact address for Phoenix, which will make delivery of the Court Order more awkward, but there are ways around that. Secondly, you need to be careful that any action you take does not aggravate the situation further.'

'What is a Contact Order exactly and how do I get Phoenix's address?' he asked.

'A Contact Order is an order requiring the parent with which the child lives to allow the child to visit or stay with the non-resident parent, or at least have some form of contact, for example by telephone. The first step would be to petition the court to grant you a Contact Order for Kara. It would be helpful if you could supply an address for Kara, but it's not mandatory. You're not the only one who's not in possession of his ex-spouse's address! The court will track her down and then hopefully an amicable arrangement can be worked out. With respect to getting the address yourself, you could hire a private detective.'

The idea of getting a private detective did not appeal to Paul. He did not want to get accused of stalking to add to his woes.

'Is Phoenix breaking the law by denying me Kara's address and telephone number?'

'No, she's not committing a criminal offence as such. However, you should contact Social Services. They will most likely encourage her to provide you with contact details. Alternatively, they may encourage you to take it through the courts as we have just discussed.'

'What would happen if I cancelled the standing order for child maintenance? Could I agree to put the money to one side, ready to mail on once I have an address?'

'Nothing would happen in the short term. This would be a good tactic to try and provoke some sort of response from your ex-wife.'

'Do you consider the amount I am voluntarily paying is sufficient?'

'That's a difficult one to answer, but I can confirm that based on your salary, you are providing significantly more than the basic Child Support Agency recommendation.'

'Can I be listed as an emergency contact for the school?'

'Yes, this should not be an issue. You and your ex-wife have equal parental responsibility. The only difference between you is that she already has custody, albeit agreed informally.'

'Am I entitled to school photos?'

'Yes, absolutely, as part of your parental rights.'

After further discussion, Paul concluded that an appropriate way forward would be to contact Social Services, explain his predicament and ask for their recommendation. He would also cancel the child maintenance standing order forthwith to try and provoke some reaction from Phoenix. If an address was subsequently forthcoming, he would then send future mainte-nance payments by cheque in the post.

Before applying to the court for a defined Contact Order, he would wait for a response to these courses of action (assuming there was one). He agreed he needed to be careful that any action he took did not aggravate the situation further.

Paul cancelled the monthly standing order from his bank the following day. For all he knew this money was funding drugs or something equally damaging. Instead he would put cheques aside, ready to mail on once he had a forwarding address. He also had some presents that he had brought back from Sri Lanka. He had no idea if post was being forwarded on to Kara from her old address. The fact that nobody had let him know, despite his efforts, strongly suggested to him that even if mail was being forwarded, no one was appreciative of the letters he had been sending, or at least that was the message Phoenix was trying to convey.

The following week, the head of Kara's school year tele-phoned Paul. He was pleased to hear Paul had taken legal advice and passed on the following useful information.

'I can confirm that you are entitled to receive photographs and these should be arriving in the next few weeks. We have spoken with Phoenix and conveyed to her that you want a contact address for Kara. Unfortunately she does not want to pass it on to you, but she did say Kara has your phone number and address should she wish to contact you.'

From this information Paul could only conclude that Phoenix had purposely chosen not to give him any contact details for Kara. Phoenix obviously wanted everything on her terms.

'Phoenix has informed us that Kara knows you are writing to her on a weekly basis,' the head continued, 'and she has your letters. However, we only have Phoenix's word for this. Apparently Kara has left them currently unopened.'

'Can't you talk to Kara directly?' asked Paul.

'We don't want to do that at the moment, bearing in mind she has just started at the school. We don't want to cause her unnecessary distress. Also, I must stress to you that the school does not want to be acting as go-between. We will endeavour, however, to ensure fair play wherever possible.'

'I'm considering contacting Social Services and taking it to court to get a Contact Order,' Paul informed him.

'That sounds a good idea. I suggest you try the Children & Parents central clearing number for Social Services, but please be warned they do get overloaded and they may not be able to do much.'

'What about my request for being listed as next of kin in event of an emergency?'

'We respect your right to be listed as a contact number, but Phoenix has made it clear to us she does not want you listed. The reason she gave was that if you turned up in an emergency situation, it might distress Kara further. We have had an opportunity to speak to Kara, albeit in the presence of Phoenix, and she has additionally requested you are not listed.'

Paul was astounded.

'There's absolutely no reason why Kara should feel this way,' he protested. 'She was never mistreated as a child, only loved very much by both parents and their respective families.'

'Do you know that Phoenix has a new partner now?' the head asked. 'Do you think this could possibly be an influencing factor?'

Paul did not know what to say. It could be a possibility.

After lengthy discussion and despite Paul's reluctance, it was agreed he would not be listed as a next of kin day-to-day contact number, but would be contacted in case of extreme emergency.

'My main concern is that problems are being stored up for the future,' the head concluded.

This was a statement with which Paul fully concurred.

There was now little doubt in Paul's mind that it had been Phoenix's intention all along to try and destroy his relationship with his daughter. For now it appeared she had succeeded. The only rational explanation he had for Kara treating him in this fashion was that Phoenix had poisoned her mind against him. Was his ex-wife still so full of hatred that she was blinkered to the damage being done to their daughter? Was she really that bitter and twisted? She appeared to be going to extreme lengths to hurt him as much as possible. Did she not realise that in the long term it would be Kara that suffered?

On a more positive note, the head did mention that Kara appeared to be settling in well at the school and seemed happy in herself. Additionally, he had invited Paul to contact the school at any time, should he feel the need.

Paul felt very down during the course of that week. It was heart-wrenching to hear Kara felt this way about him (or at least that was the message that had been portrayed in the presence of her mother). He decided it best to go along with Kara's wishes for now and not attempt to make contact, although he still believed she had been heavily influenced by Phoenix. He would review the situation over the Christmas break. This would give Kara a whole term to settle in to her new school and if matters had not improved, he would then pursue the court route. At the back of his mind, he was still hopeful for a joyous reconciliation, but even with his enduring optimism, he had to admit this was looking less and less likely. He remained committed to keeping his journal up to date, not just for his own sake, but to ensure Kara had a chance to see his side of the story when she was older, should she wish. He was determined that she would understand that he had never, ever abandoned her.

Kara, if you ever get to read this, I want you to know that I don't blame you for any of the awful situations we have had to endure. I have loved you, and will always love you whatever happens. In hindsight, I can now empathise with how difficult and confusing it must have been for you when you were younger, especially if you had to hear bad things said about me by your mother. I completely understand that you could not go against your mother's wishes at a young age, even if you were so inclined. If only I had been aware of your mother's cruel and selfish intentions back then, perhaps things would have worked out differently.

Regardless, a father's love is unconditional. If I never get the chance to speak to you again, please don't make the same mistakes as your mum and I should you have children. Please remember that there are two sides to every story and nobody is perfect.

Everyone makes mistakes in life and when this happens, the best thing is to be open and honest, sincerely apologise and try to repair any damage. Make sure you learn from any mistakes you make, since you will end up the better person and others will respect you for it. Remember, those around you will also make mistakes, but if they are genuinely sorry, then have the goodness within your heart to forgive them. There will be times in life when you will not get your own way and at the time it may seem unfair, but give way graciously. Remember that you may not always understand something at the time, or why it has happened, but as you get older, along comes experience and wisdom. Things should then become clearer.

The following day Paul e-mailed the head of year, thanking him for his time and support in keeping him updated on Kara's welfare. He also brought to his attention that although he did not think Phoenix would intentionally hurt Kara, he believed she had unfairly influenced her and would not hesitate in manipulating the truth to suit her own purposes. The head replied straight away, acknowledging his comments and confirming such lines of communication were open. He would update his staff with their discussions.

Over the next few weeks, Paul resigned himself to the fact

that there was not much point in writing his weekly letters to Kara. He had no address to send them to and she would probably not be appreciative anyway. Regardless, she remained on his mind virtually all the time.

Friends and family continued to call, asking if there had been any improvement in the situation. They were all disgusted at Phoenix's conduct, accusing her of being an unfit mother and setting a dreadful example. She had abused his trust and taken advantage at every opportunity to undermine his father–daughter relationship, intentionally creating a rift between them.

He thought back to the days when he and Phoenix were happy together. Even then she had a knack of creating rifts between him and his loved ones. Describing these sentiments in his journal helped to defuse his frustration and he added a message for Kara.

Kara, I only hope that as you get older, you will come to realise the selfish way your mother has behaved and you do not repeat these mistakes with any children of your own.

Paul's dad's birthday fell in the following week. His family usually met up at times like these and this was no exception. These were cheerful occasions, the only downside being that Kara had not been in attendance for the last few years. Although they had grown accustomed to her not being there, they still found it disappointing. Sadly Paul's dad (Kara's granddad) did not receive a call or a card from Kara.

Paul could understand why he himself was on the receiving end of Phoenix's spite, but why was she taking it out on his family too? His family had nothing to do with their marriage break-up. It seemed so unfair, not just on him and his family, but Kara was missing out too. His mum regularly asked how he was coping and this occasion was no different.

'I feel sad and hurt by the whole state of affairs,' he explained, 'but I suppose overall I am okay. The worst part is I feel guilty for letting Kara down.'

'How can you think that? Please don't say that,' his mum replied, expressing her concern. 'You have done all you can to try and salvage your relationship with Kara. You have done so much more than a lot of other fathers in your position. Phoenix has been a thorn in your side the whole time. Since your break-up, you have done absolutely nothing to feel ashamed or guilty about.' This did make Paul feel a little better. It was good to know he had his mum's support. He knew she must be missing her granddaughter too. 'Don't worry unduly if Phoenix doesn't get in touch and give you an address. It's time you focused your energies on your own life and stopped letting that silly woman stress you out. She is a sad, bitter woman that can't let go. I have a strong feeling that all will work itself out in the end, but not until Kara is well away from her influence, which unfortunately is some time off yet. For now, focus on the great relationship you have with Jenna.'

By early December, over two months after the abscondment, Paul had still not heard anything from Phoenix. He could only assume that she would rather sacrifice his maintenance money than give him a contact address for his own daughter. Perhaps she did not need it and was being financially supported by the new man in her life. Looking on the bright side, it gave him a chance to get on with his own life, although he still fretted about Kara every day, hoping all was well. At least he could draw some comfort knowing that she had his address and telephone number should she want to make contact with him at any time.

The next week he rang Kara's school and enquired as to the whereabouts of the school photographs he had ordered.

'You should have received them by now,' they informed him. 'Let us make some calls and see if we can track them down.'

They called back later that afternoon. 'The supplier thinks the photos may have got lost in the post.'

This all sounded a little suspicious to Paul and he wondered if Phoenix had anything to do with them going astray. He remembered how something similar had happened the previous year, but he had thought nothing of it at the time.

Perhaps they had been sent to Phoenix's address and she could not be bothered to forward them on. He contacted the suppliers himself and explained the situation.

'We'll send some new ones right away,' they replied.

He wondered if perhaps he was getting a little paranoid and mentioned it to Jenna.

'No, not at all,' she responded. 'You shouldn't trust that woman any more.'

By mid-December, at the end of Kara's first term, her school report arrived along with the school photographs. The report showed she was doing well, which appeased Paul's concern somewhat. He rang his family to let them know the good news and mailed on copies of the photographs. He had been thinking about Kara even more than usual during the run-up to Christmas. Although he felt very sad that she wanted nothing to do with him, he was slowly coming to terms with it. He missed buying her presents and taking her to the pantomime, though he recognised she was probably too old for this now. He was hopeful that the following year would see some sort of breakthrough.

Over the Christmas period, Paul remained in close contact with his friends and family. They knew he missed Kara and would naturally enquire how things were going and offer their support. This would be his third Christmas without any contact. The more he spoke about his dilemma, the more friends and family would remind him how spitefully Phoenix had treated him over the years, even whilst they were married. They spoke of other peripheral events, which although they had not seemed overly strange at the time, now bore particular relevance to his situation. Everyone remained appalled that Phoenix still refused to give him Kara's address. Friends of his who had gone through marital break-ups of their own involving children all considered Phoenix's behaviour unnecessarily wicked and abhorrently selfish. Those who knew her parents were surprised they had not tried to intervene somehow, to help remedy the situation.

'They probably don't know how bad things have become,' one suggested.

Paul conceded this was a possibility. He would keep typically his chin up and say things like, 'I'm looking to the future' and 'I'm sure things will work out long term'.

His friends would typically agree, adding sentiments such as, 'As Kara grows older, she will want to take a more balanced view and work out for herself what really happened.'

Chapter 8

Taking action

◇ New year, new strategy
◇ Decisive action taken

It was the start of another year and Paul was hopeful it would bring better fortune concerning his relationship with Kara. He and Jenna had a pretty good Christmas, enjoying quality time with family and friends. Once again, however, it was tinged with sadness that neither Paul nor his family heard anything from Kara.

Over the holiday period, Kara had constantly been in his thoughts and he had come to a stark realisation. Although she did not want contact with him presently, if the current situation continued, she might think that he did not care, or he didn't want her to get in touch with him. He had to somehow make sure that Kara did not think along these lines. If Phoenix continued to refuse to give him an address, then it would be impossible for him to write to Kara and let her know his feelings. This realisation was the final straw that pushed him into taking some serious action. He was now convinced Phoenix had no intention of helping him to rescue his relationship with Kara, despite her earlier promises. If anything, she was encouraging Kara to distance herself from him.

The first week of January, Paul started trawling through a wealth of information on the internet, looking for sound advice. First he rang FamilyLinePlus. They could not do much and advised he contact Families Need Fathers. Families Need Fathers advised he contact Parent Mediation Helpline, who in turn advised he contact the Citizens Advice Bureau. The Citizens Advice Bureau was closed.

The first three bodies were very sympathetic to his plight and understood how hurtful and hopeless his situation must feel. They tried to help in their own way, recommending their own websites, but all agreed that his circumstances were difficult since he did not have the co-operation of his ex-wife. They suggested that the only remaining course of action might be to take it through the courts to get a Contact Order, but pointed out that this could aggravate Phoenix and Kara, possibly making the situation even worse.

He contacted Social Services and they gave him the same advice. They also suggested he ring Families Forever. Their number was permanently engaged, but he managed to get through the following day. They were most helpful. They also advised he apply to the court for a Contact Order. They explained that there had been precedent lately of the courts coming down hard on mothers who had been manipulating circumstances such as his for their own benefit. They agreed to send him some information through the post.

That afternoon Paul went to the Citizens Advice Bureau (CAB). They suggested three options:

✦ Contact the school and ask if they would be prepared to forward on Christmas and birthday cards.

✦ Try tracking Phoenix down using the internet, for example by looking at businesses where she may be working.

✦ If the above do not give satisfactory results, then go down the Contact Order route. They agreed that this route could inflame the situation further initially, but this would likely be only temporary.

The Citizens Advice Bureau fully empathised with his predicament and pointed out how short-sighted Phoenix's actions had been. They were of the opinion that if the poisoning of Kara's mind was so deep that Kara herself contested any future contact with him, then the court would be able to see through Phoenix's manipulation. That being the case, the court would recommend some sort of contact, even if initially restricted to letters. The alternative would be to sit back and wait in the hope Kara eventually came around. The problem with waiting would be that Kara might think he did not care and once she reached eighteen and left school, he would have lost all opportunity to have some sort of contact.

Paul thought long and hard about the advice he had been given from the various bodies. He really did not want to take it through the courts unless it was absolutely necessary. He would explore the alternatives given to him first, but he accepted that using the courts might now be his only viable option. If Kara still did not want contact, at least the court could ensure he had an address to which to send Christmas and birthday cards. If she chose not to open them, then that would be her choice. Unfortunately, there was still the possibility that Phoenix could intercept anything he sent.

The following day, Paul rang the head of year at Kara's school. He wished him a happy new year and expressed his thanks for the copy of Kara's end of term report and photographs. He also informed him that regrettably Phoenix had still not provided a contact address or telephone number for Kara.

'Would the school be prepared to pass on very occasional notes to Kara, such as Christmas and birthday cards?' he enquired. 'Just to make sure she knew her father was thinking of her and she was welcome to contact me anytime?'

The head sounded amenable to his suggestion.

'That sounds perfectly reasonable. I will give it some thought,' he replied.

Paul decided to wait for a firm reply before taking any further action. If the school was amenable to passing on cards, then he would hang fire on the court route. If not, then he would pursue the Contact Order immediately.

He continued to record all the latest developments, details of his life and how he was feeling in his journal.

With all the activity associated with trying to get access to Kara, I have neglected to mention that over Christmas we were looking after a pet lizard, named Izzie. She goes back tomorrow.

The reason I mention this is that when Kara used to come and stay she used to love animals. I don't know if this is still the case or not. Once Kara stopped visiting, I used to write letters enclosing pictures of the various animals we had staying with us. This is obviously something I cannot do at the moment since I do not have an address for her. It's heartbreaking.

Hopefully this will be the year when this all gets sorted out.

Paul spoke to his own father that night about the latest developments. He was taken aback when his father mentioned that despite all his efforts, he had struggled to get along with Phoenix ever since he had known her.

'Your mum feels the same way,' he went on to say. 'Phoenix always gave us the impression we were not good enough for her. There were times when you would leave the room and Phoenix would be quite rude to your mother, but we didn't feel comfortable saying anything to you about it, in case you thought we were stirring up trouble.'

At first Paul was upset and a little annoyed that they had never told him this before, but after a while he started to empathise. He felt sorry that his parents and the rest of his family had been treated in such a fashion.

On the Wednesday of the following week, quite out of the blue, Paul got a letter from the Child Support Agency stating that Phoenix had applied for child maintenance from him. He rang the CSA that same morning to inform them he had no issue with paying the money, but he would like a forwarding address so he could mail a cheque.

'I am afraid we are not at liberty to provide an address,' they informed him.

Paul explained the issues he was experiencing with his ex-wife and that he was quite willing to restart the maintenance payments, but he wanted a contact address for Kara so he could send birthday and Christmas cards.

'That sounds reasonable,' replied the representative. 'We will ring your ex-wife and inform her of this on your behalf.'

The CSA rang him back later that afternoon.

'I am afraid we can't help you. We have spoken with Phoenix, but unfortunately she is adamant she wants no contact with you whatsoever. You will have to take it to court as a separate issue if you want an address.'

What a first-class – scrub that – second-rate bitch, Paul thought to himself.

Paul weighed up the phone call. He supposed that overall it was good news that his tactics of stopping the maintenance payments had provoked a response from Phoenix. He was now assured that any money deducted from his account should be going towards Kara's upkeep. On the downside, he was still no closer to getting a contact address for Kara. He wondered if Phoenix had planned this as a New Year present for him and Jenna. He was in little doubt that Phoenix had been extremely manipulative over the last few years, but now her vindictive streak was truly coming to the fore. She seemed determined to break any hope of a relationship between him and Kara, whilst at the same time screwing him for every penny she could get. It was at times like these that he seriously wondered if it was all worth it and whether he and Jenna would be better off selling up and doing charity work overseas.

That evening he recorded the latest events and added a special note for Kara.

Kara, if you ever read this, I do apologise. I wanted to try and sort this mess out in a friendly manner, but your mother flatly refuses to co-operate. I don't mind admitting I am very confused and fed up over all this.

Paul visited his parents on the Sunday of that weekend and understandably Phoenix and Kara were high on the list of topics of conversation. His mum re-stated her opinion that Phoenix must still be a very bitter woman, driven by hatred to behave in this fashion. His dad offered an alternative explanation.

'She may still be in love with you and this is her way of dealing with it,' he suggested.

Paul and his mum were quick to dismiss this theory. It made Paul feel quite nauseous. Regardless, they all agreed that if Phoenix continued to harbour feelings of revenge and behave in this vindictive manner, it would ultimately be her own undoing. Paul's dad ultimately felt sorry for her and Kara. Paul and his mum felt sorry for Kara, but found it difficult to have any sympathy for Phoenix.

On the Tuesday morning whilst at work, Paul received a phone call from the head of year at Kara's school. They discussed his request about the forwarding on of Christmas and birthday cards.

'I apologise for the delay in response, but we have given the matter a lot of thought and I am pleased to inform you that the school is in support of your idea. We will however need to confirm that Kara and Phoenix have no objection. We will be in contact soon.'

Paul was delighted. This solution appeared a suitable compromise for all parties. Phoenix could continue to keep her address a secret from Paul (for whatever reason) and he would at last be able to let Kara know how he felt. This reignited his hopes of reconciliation, but he was realistic enough to recognise it was still some way off. At least this appeared a move in the right direction.

On the Thursday of that week, Paul arrived home from work to find a letter from Phoenix.

Paul,

Kara has asked me to write this letter to you on her behalf, since she does not want direct contact with you. Here are some specific quotes from her.

'I do not want contact with you by phone, letter or in person and I do not want you to know anything about me. How dare you contact my school! I do not want you contacting me at home or via any other means. I am fed up with you thinking you are part of my life.'

'Mum has a wonderful new man in her life now and we all want to enjoy our lives without you. I want him to adopt me.'

'I will contact you if ever I feel I am ready, not when you are.'

Kara has asked me to ring you next week, demanding an explanation as to why you contacted her school. Perhaps if you had listened in the first place, you would not have ended up in this situation.

Paul was filled with absolute rage, yet gutted at the same time. He could not believe what he was reading. Apart from the very rude and disrespectful tone of the letter, all the good work he had been trying to do was being completely undermined by Phoenix for her own selfish, vengeful desires. Was this really how Kara felt or had Phoenix written this letter without Kara's knowledge? If Kara really felt this way, why had Phoenix allowed this situation to develop? The sheer disrespectful tone alone was unforgiveable. Had Phoenix actively encouraged it? What was this nonsense about wanting to be adopted? How could Phoenix continue to be so blind to the damage she was causing? Not just to him, but ultimately to Kara? He had had suspicions all along that Phoenix might need psychiatric help, but now it appeared she was inflicting her troubles on their daughter. Kara would ultimately end up having psychological issues of her own if her mother carried on in this manner.

He showed the letter to Jenna and she was absolutely livid.

'Has she no conscience?' she angrily remarked. 'How can anybody encourage a child to be so nasty?'

Paul prepared himself for Phoenix's phone call. He was not looking forward to it, but if he prepared himself carefully he might be able to get some useful points across. He made the best of another sleepless night by jotting down some thoughts in preparation.

+ As a father, I have unconditional love for my daughter and I obviously care for her. I am not taking an active interest in her welfare to upset her, but to ensure her wellbeing. The same goes for my family, who also care about her.

+ I have a moral and legal obligation to check Kara is okay. My role is not just about making maintenance payments, but ensuring her whole overall safety and security.

+ Since Phoenix does not give me any information, I have no choice but to use alternative means. The school is an obvious option. Can Phoenix offer any preferable alternatives?

+ I don't trust Phoenix, especially since she has not even had the decency to give me a contact address or telephone number for Kara. She has not bothered to keep me informed of Kara's wellbeing and she continues to use Kara to get at me, which is so unfair on Kara.

+ I am concerned for Kara's welfare. Our divorce appears to have hit her significantly harder than other children who have been through equally trying circumstances. I am sensing Kara is harbouring a lot of bitterness and resentment that she really needs to let go. She doesn't seem to want to communicate with me, even if only by letter. We all have to do things we don't like every now and then; it's part of growing into a mature adult. Frankly, I am wary of what the future holds for her if she continues to behave in this way.

+ With respect to the new man in Phoenix's life, I am pleased this brings Kara some comfort. However, she needs to be aware this does not have to be an either/or decision. She can still have a stepfather and her natural dad in her life. She could have the best of both worlds!

+ I want an address for Kara so I can send her birthday and Christmas cards, nothing more. She can then throw them in the bin if she wishes.

At the end of January, Paul received a letter from the head of year at Kara's school stating that the school governors had spoken to Kara and her mother regarding his suggestion about forwarding on cards. The letter conveyed the school's apologies, but since Phoenix and Kara had objected so strongly to Paul's request, there was nothing further the school could do. On a more positive note, the letter informed him that an Open Evening was going to be held the third week in February. If he wished to attend, would he please let the school know so they could ensure the timing of his appointment did not overlap with that of Kara and her mother?

Paul was back down in the dumps again. Whatever he tried to do in Kara's interests was somehow thwarted. It appeared there was now no alternative to pursuing the court route. This was by no means what he wanted, but as far as he could make out, he had exhausted all other options. He booked an appointment to see a solicitor the Friday of that week, who happened to be a friend of a friend.

Paul spent the whole of that Friday afternoon discussing his dilemma with the solicitor and the best course of action to take. They spoke at length about the pros and cons of going down the court Contact Order route. Key snippets of information Paul gathered included:

✦ He would need to get Phoenix's address via a private detective or enquiry agent in order for her to be notified of court proceedings. If this were not possible, he would need to involve the school to deliver the notice, or have an initial court hearing to find her as part of court proceedings.

✦ There would then be a meeting with a CAFCASS (Children and Family Court Advisory and Support Service) representative followed by a five-minute court hearing with a judge present, to see if rapid agreement could be reached with respect to contact. If yes, then all well and good.

+ If agreement could not be reached, then the judge would most likely ask for a full CAFCASS report to be made out. This could take up to six months.

+ There would then be a third court hearing to see if agreement could be reached from the report. All this could take the best part of a year.

+ If agreement could still not be reached, then the court would most likely go with Kara's wishes, particularly since she would be twelve, going on thirteen by then. Even though the court would recognise that breaking contact with the father could be damaging and her mind had likely been poisoned, forcing unwanted contact at this stage could be even more distressing for Kara.

+ If a Contact Order were imposed by the court and Phoenix did not abide by it, she could theoretically go to jail, but in the real world this rarely happened, since it would not be considered in the best interests of the child. As a consequence Phoenix could easily get away with disobeying any Court Order if she were so-minded. Knowing Phoenix's past behaviour and how strongly she felt, Paul felt sure this was exactly what she would do.

+ With respect to maintenance payments, the solicitor agreed he should continue paying them via the CSA, for Phoenix had made it clear she was not going to enter into any friendly arrangements. However he did point out that Phoenix may have shot herself in the foot, since if the CSA were to use their standard calculation for maintenance payments, he could expect to see a drop compared to the amount he had been voluntarily paying of about 30 per cent.

The solicitor then showed him several articles of past case histories detailing scenarios similar to Paul's, where the father involved had taken his case through the Family Courts. They made gruesome reading. Most fathers went into court in the understandable expectation that their case would be dealt with in a rational, fair and effective manner. Instead they came away enraged and bitter, convinced the system was biased against them. In a lot of instances, the ex-wife had deviously made up awful allegations of child abuse against the father in order to discredit him and strengthen her case, usually so she could get custody or residency with the child. These allegations were invariably proven to be false, but in some cases the child had been brainwashed into believing the accusations to be true and thus the damage had already been done. Paul was absolutely horrified.

By the end of their conversation, going down the court Contact Order route had certainly lost any appeal it might initially have had.

'I'd be prepared to represent you if that's what you want,' said the solicitor, 'but I do urge you to think carefully. If we do go down this route, I cannot guarantee any sort of request for contact will be successful.'

Paul was seriously questioning whether it was all worth it. It would put everyone through unnecessary stress and likely aggravate the situation between him and Kara further. On top of all that, it would cost him upwards of £3000, possibly going into tens of thousands. The only positive Paul could see coming out of it was an address for Kara, but Kara (via Phoenix) had made it clear she did not want any correspondence from him.

'Mull it over for a few days and then get back to me if you want to pursue this route,' the solicitor suggested.

Although Paul felt totally dejected, he thanked the solicitor for his time and appreciated his candidness.

Back at home Paul was in despair. This was not only because of the situation which he firmly believed Phoenix had orchestrated, but also at the apparent futility of the family judicial system. Had this been Phoenix's intention all along? Would she really be so malicious, selfish and underhand to take advantage of the potential flaws in family legislation? Was it coincidence things had got to this stage just before Kara's twelfth birthday? Had it all been meticulously planned? All these thoughts revolved round and round in his head.

He spent another sleepless night mulling things over and making entries in his journal. One particular message for Kara read:

Kara, once again I am not sure what to do for the best. Whatever I do appears wrong. From the feedback I am getting from your school and the fact that you never return my letters, I think at this stage in your life, you would not appreciate me going down the court Contact Order route since this would cause you further upset. Please understand that it is not the money stopping me from going to court, it's just that I think the way things are, it would make matters worse. If in hindsight this proves to not be the case, please forgive me. In the meantime, I will not give up exploring alternative routes to make sure you know I will always be there for you. As your father, I will always love you and you can contact me at any time. I want to try and make sure you know this, in a way that will not cause you any distress.

On the Monday, Paul replied to the school via letter. He thanked the head of year for his efforts in trying to progress the forwarding on of cards to Kara and informed him of the spiteful letter he had recently received from Phoenix (allegedly on Kara's behalf). He recognised that his request for the school to forward on any correspondence from him to Kara was not a viable option at this time. He then went on to explain his continuing concern for Kara's welfare and although he took comfort in her good school reports, he requested that the school please contact him should they ever notice anything that could be cause for concern. He finished off by saying he would very much like to attend the next Open Evening and would arrange an appointment by phone in the next few days.

Paul considered he had one option left with respect to getting birthday and Christmas cards to Kara. He would mail them to Phoenix's parents in the hope that they would pass them on. Additionally, he could let them know of his concerns and find out if they were aware of the latest situation. He had made a note of their new French address when he had carried out his internet search a couple of years back. He was acutely aware that Phoenix had asked him not to involve them, but since she refused to communicate, this was his only option. Were they aware Phoenix had denied him a contact address and phone number for Kara? Perhaps they could talk some sense into her?

Just over a week after receiving her letter, Paul got the phone call from Phoenix: the one he had not been looking forward to. It started off awkwardly.

'Have you read the letter?' Phoenix asked.

'Yes,' he replied.

Phoenix did not give him time to say anything else. She immediately started to interrogate him in a very forceful manner.

'Why did you contact Kara's school? You have really upset her.'

'I would rather explain this to Kara herself,' he replied. 'She is approaching twelve years old and should be capable of speaking up for herself.'

To his surprise, Kara came onto the phone.

'How are you?' he asked. To his delight they shared a few snippets of information. She told him that she was enjoying her new school, even though it was hard work. 'I'm concerned about you, that's why I was talking to your school,' he added. 'I'm looking forward to going to the Open Evening. You do know I love you, don't you? I do miss you and I'd love to start our father–daughter relationship again. I'd like to continue sending birthday and Christmas cards, but I haven't got your address.'

'I don't want contact with you,' she informed him and handed the phone back to her mum.

'Why is Kara behaving like this? What's the real problem?' he asked.

'She just wants to be left alone.'

'But you are leaving me with no choice but to send birthday and Christmas cards to your parents if you continue to refuse me a contact address.'

Out of the blue Phoenix then came out with an extraordinary request.

'Would you agree to Kara's stepfather adopting her?'

'Sorry, what did you say?' he asked.

'It's a simple question: would you agree to Kara's stepfather adopting her?'

Paul was caught off guard. 'No. Why? There's no reason for that to be necessary. I don't think I'd be happy with that at all.' What planet is she from? he thought to himself.

'Well, at least we know where we stand,' she replied.

At this point the conversation dried up.

'I'd love to speak to Kara again sometime,' said Paul, trying to keep the discussion flowing in a civil manner.

Phoenix didn't respond, but hung up.

Paul came away from the phone and Jenna poured him a whisky. She had heard most of the exchange. Although annoyed by Phoenix, he felt good having spoken with Kara, even if the conversation had been stilted. It was the first time he had spoken directly to her in about two years!

Paul went to the school Open Evening the following week as planned. He enjoyed conversing with Kara's teachers and was pleased to hear she had settled into her new school. She was doing well in all subjects, in particular languages, sciences and performing arts. This was similar to himself when he was her age. There were some slight concerns over her spelling (which he found a little surprising, since he remembered Kara used to read a lot) and a particular history test, but the teacher said that was probably attributable to her absence, when Kara had not been feeling well (something Paul felt peeved he knew nothing about). Most teachers remarked that Kara was quiet in class and generally only put her hand up if she was confident she knew the answer. Again, this reminded him very much of himself when he was her age, and even now to a degree. He was glad they confirmed there was no hint of her being an unhappy child.

One evening that same week, Paul and Jenna sat down and reflected on what had transpired over the last couple of months. It was not all doom and gloom. He had confirmation from the school they would keep him up to date with Kara's progress via photos and end of term reports. They had agreed to contact him in case of extreme emergency. Furthermore, he now had a route to get cards and messages to Kara via Phoenix's parents. At least he could let Kara know how much he loved her and she was welcome to contact him anytime she wished. He was also assured via the CSA that his maintenance payments were getting through. If he could content himself with these comforts, then it would not be necessary to go down the court route and risk further upset. It was just a matter of waiting for Kara to come round.

'Maybe Kara has a friend whose father does not bother with them much? Perhaps this is having an influence on Kara?' Jenna suggested.

They went on to discuss a number of different scenarios, but ultimately they all ended with the same conclusion. They would need to wait for Kara to grow out of this phase before they could do much more.

The following morning, Paul woke up feeling a little more refreshed than normal. He had still woken up a few times in the night with it all buzzing round in his head, but he did feel a little more at ease having made some progress. He had finally made some decisions on the best course of action. It was now a matter of waiting.

Chapter 9

The waiting game

✧ Coping
✧ Kara's name change
✧ Getting on with life

Over the next year, Paul kept himself up to date with Kara's wellbeing and progress via the school. It was not ideal, but he reasoned that this option would cause her the least distress. In accordance with his parental rights, he continued to request end of term reports and photographs, which the school were happy to provide. Kara continued to do well and the school confirmed there was nothing for him to worry about unduly. He was especially thrilled that she was taking such an interest in music. Although he was saddened he could not say, 'Well done!' directly, he contented himself sending birthday and Christmas cards via Phoenix's parents, with little notes inside wishing her well and congratulating her on her achievements. He wanted to make sure she was aware of his on-going support and that he would dearly love to hear from her when she felt ready.

His job kept him very busy, particularly now he had transferred into a procurement role and had assumed full global responsibility for his department, necessitating an ever-increasing amount of international travel. He continued to play sax during the spare time he had and became friendly with a number of musicians. Together they would often while away their free hours playing music and generally socialising.

Occasionally he would talk to other fathers in a similar position to his own. A significant number mentioned having similar contact issues with their children, so he did not feel too isolated in this respect.

His life with Jenna went from strength to strength. They were very happy together and supported each other in their careers and activities. He would help out at her dance school and they enjoyed some wonderfully romantic dancing holidays. At weekends they were like most couples. They liked visiting friends and family, and entertaining at home. They particularly loved snuggling up for quiet nights in when they got the opportunity.

Another important milestone for Paul and Jenna during this period was the arrival of their triplet nieces. Between them they already had numerous nephews and nieces of all ages of whom they were very proud, but none to date from a multiple birth. They were invited to see the baby girls at the hospital the day they were born.

'Would you be godparents once again?' asked Jenna's younger sister, smiling proudly from her hospital bed, her husband at her side.

'We'd love to,' replied Paul and Jenna almost simultaneously, huge grins all over their faces. They were absolutely thrilled to take on the role. Inwardly Paul was more overjoyed and honoured than anyone could imagine. He had missed out on such a lot of Kara's childhood. Having been denied the opportunity to be there for his own daughter, the joy and importance of the role he was about to take on was really moving for him. He made a promise to himself there and then that all his nephews and nieces would get all the love and attention they could possibly want from him for the rest of their lives. He realised that regrettably this would not make Kara feel any better, but it helped assuage some of the guilt he felt for not being personally involved in her life. In a funny sort of way, he saw it as a chance of redemption. He was determined these children were not going to miss out in the same way as his own daughter.

Overall the year was turning out very well for Paul, apart from missing Kara. He felt he was coping admirably, but a day never went by when he did not think about her, hoping she was okay too. As each day passed, he saw it as a day closer to their reunion.

Father's Day in particular was a day of mixed emotions. He

was glad to contact his own father and see his friends and family with their children, but he also experienced sadness in that he and Kara never got to share this day. Even a short phone call would be such a marvellous step forward. Occasionally he would brood over it a little bit too long for his own good. Why was Kara so angry with him and why was she taking it out on his family as well? He had no explanation; he was stumped. He could only put it down to Phoenix bad-mouthing him and he looked forward immensely to the day when Kara would be independent of her mother's influence.

He kept abreast of newspaper articles, documentaries and high-profile court activities that detailed circumstances similar to his own, in the hope that one day fathers would get a better deal. The subject was quite often raised in the media and it would get a lot of lip service, but ultimately nothing changed. He would keep any interesting articles he came across and insert them in his journal. He would often reminisce about old times, some good and some bad, including anything he considered of relevance. Entries over this period included:

16 June

Today is Kara's twelfth birthday. I hope everything is going well for her. It upsets me that I cannot tell her in person. Hopefully this awful situation will not go on much longer.

3 July

Today I came across the original correspondence between myself and Phoenix's solicitor when we first separated nine years ago. From the content of the letters and with the benefit of hindsight, it appears she was trying to cut me out of Kara's life even then, but was obviously having difficulty because of Kara's age. Kara was only three at the time. Phoenix had been reluctant to give me a contact address and telephone number and I had to specifically request it from her solicitor. I needed the number so I could arrange contact visits and speak to Kara on the telephone. When I eventually did get a number and tried to call, Phoenix would either answer it in a belligerent manner, or not answer at all. Phone messages I left asking her to return my calls were rarely acknowledged.

It seems that Phoenix has now got what she wanted. I don't know how her conscience allows her to sleep at night. I just hope that all the damage can be repaired one day.

10 July

I have been on the internet viewing the websites of different organisations that may be able to help with the situation Kara and I find ourselves in. One in particular cited numerous examples where vindictive mothers had unfairly influenced their child(ren) to stop having contact with their father. This poisoning typically took place over a number of years. It went on to say how a number of these same mothers had at the same time tried to 'screw' the father for every penny they could get. The website made it clear that these particular types of women were not out to get a fair deal. Their main objective was to try and destroy the man in an act of revenge. Is this the game Phoenix has been playing?

Paul continued to have his eyes opened to this type of cruelty and wickedness. He had not realised how common a problem it was in the UK. He looked at a number of e-mail conversations that had been posted to this particular website. These people (both the vindictive mothers and the bitter fathers) were full of rage and hatred towards one another. The more the courts were involved, the worse the situation became and it appeared to him that everyone involved was a loser, particularly the children. This gave him greater affirmation that he had done the right thing at the beginning of the year by not taking it through the courts. Although he was angry with his ex-wife for having let these circumstances develop, he did not bear her the awful levels of animosity being exhibited here.

Later that summer, Paul and Jenna got another opportunity

to go and stay with their friends in Sri Lanka. Once again they experienced the jungle and simple village life and felt very honoured to be welcomed into the local villages and mix with the locals. They were fortunate enough to be invited to a traditional wedding, which they found mesmerising. They could not help but notice how happy the local people were, particularly the children, despite little material wealth. They made many new friends and were sad to leave, but were extremely thankful for such a wonderful opportunity to recharge their batteries.

They arrived back in England feeling very much rejuvenated. After forty hours of non-stop travelling, they were greeted by their friends who had stayed at their house whilst they were away. They talked excitedly for about an hour, catching up with all the news.

Paul started opening up the post and then got an unwelcome wake-up call. Phoenix had been her usual self and managed to put a 'damp squib' on their return. Somehow she always managed to do this either when they returned from holiday or over the Christmas period.

'Phoenix must have spies out so she can time her actions to upset us the most,' remarked Jenna half-jokingly, although she was now seriously wondering whether this had become an unsettling reality. Paul read the letter out loud.

'Phoenix has instructed a solicitor to request my permission for Kara to change her surname from Nelson to Tucker. It threatens me with court action and says if I fight it, I will most likely lose and have to pay everybody's costs.' As he read on, it became clear that Phoenix was going to remarry in the imminent future and wanted Kara to take her stepfather's surname of Tucker.

'I get the feeling she loves twisting a knife in your back,' said Jenna. 'You shouldn't trust her. She's up to something. You can call it woman's intuition if you like.'

Jenna had spoken with Paul on many occasions about bitter mothers and how they would purposely make their ex-partner's life painful, just for their own satisfaction. She came across it on a regular basis in her job when she came into contact with parents. She acknowledged that fathers could also behave badly, but in her experience, it was mainly mothers that exhibited this spiteful behaviour. Paul had a lot of respect for Jenna's viewpoint and she was rarely wrong on such matters.

Paul spent the next few days mulling over this change in surname request before giving a reply. His first instinct was to refuse to give his consent. How could he be sure that this request was Kara's wish? Perhaps it was another of Phoenix's efforts to further break ties between him and his daughter? He wrote back to the solicitor asking for confirmation that this change of surname request was actually what Kara wanted and it was not being forced upon her by her mother.

Five days later he received a response from the solicitor. Included in the response was a copy of a letter written by Kara. The letter was addressed to the solicitor and it described how the request for a change in surname was entirely her idea and not her mum's. She then went on to describe how Paul had been an immense let-down to her and how she had previously told him on a number of occasions that she wanted absolutely nothing to do with him. Despite this, he had gone behind her back and contacted her school. Her mum had met a wonderful new man and Paul had been made aware of this, so this change in surname should not have come as a surprise.

Paul noted that she had asked the solicitor not to pass her contact details onto him, emphasising that she wanted no contact with him. He showed the letter to Jenna, who read it open-mouthed.

'What parent would allow a child to send such a letter? No child should have that much spite in them,' she remarked.

Paul was once again feeling totally gutted, reminiscent of how he had felt after receiving Kara's first devastating letter three years earlier. It wasn't just the hurtful words; it was the whole tone of the letter. It made her sound like a very spoilt child. Instead of mellowing over the last three years, her anger and resentment appeared to have now reached fever pitch. She didn't even refer to him as 'dad', but called him 'Paul'! She appeared to have no appreciation that the reason he had been in contact with her school was to support her and ensure her wellbeing, nothing more. This horrible letter struck him as one more emotional outpouring of spite and venom. As well as being hurtful and disrespectful, he was convinced it was not healthy for a twelve-year-old girl to be harbouring such emotions.

Yet again he was left asking himself the same old questions. How had things sunk to such a low level? How had this situation developed? Why had Phoenix let things drift on? He was fearful that Kara's psychological health was at risk, but he did not see what he could do. His attempts to patch things up were futile, simply regarded as him not going along with Kara's wishes. Court action would be ineffective now she was over twelve years of age, since her wishes would take precedence. The fact she had most likely been brainwashed would be difficult to prove and probably not carry much weight.

With respect to the name change, he felt most dejected but concluded he had no choice other than to go along with Kara's request, for fear of making the situation even worse (if that was possible!). He spoke to his father that evening to get his opinion on the matter. His father pointed out that perhaps Kara would find it embarrassing having a different surname to her mum and stepfather when they married. Paul agreed this could possibly be the root cause of her request. A change in surname was probably the least of his worries in the grand scheme of things and if it made Kara happy, then so be it.

The following day Paul telephoned Phoenix's solicitor, verbally giving his consent to the name change on the understanding that it would not affect his parental rights and responsibilities. The solicitor confirmed this to be the case. Paul sadly sent a formal letter providing his written consent.

That evening he made the following entry in his journal:

This is all so sad. It really does appear that Kara is taking on her mother's anger and bitterness. I sincerely hope for Kara's sake she is going to grow out of this phase, otherwise I am afraid she is going to end up a very unhappy person. I really feel at a loss as to what I can do to help her. Whatever I do will be considered wrong. I will continue to go along with her wishes for the foreseeable future, but make sure I am there for her if she changes her mind.

Kara, if you ever read this, I am so sorry it has come to this, but I am sure you will appreciate the hopeless position I am in. I never abandoned you, but if I try and make contact with you at the present time, you will only throw it back in my face. I hope you feel you can come to me if ever you are ready. You must realise that as your father I have never stopped loving you, and you are constantly in my thoughts, but with your feelings the way they are, perhaps it is best we stay apart until you make contact.

Once again Paul was resigned to the fact he could only wait for Kara to come around. Unfortunately playing the waiting game had so far proved very ineffectual. If anything, the situation had deteriorated even further, but he was absolutely stumped as to what else he could do. He did take some comfort in recognising Kara was about to enter her teenage years and perhaps problems such as these might be expected to a degree. Regardless, he considered these circumstances to be extreme. Jenna cheered him up a bit, though, and brought a smile to his face. 'Kara will have some of your good-natured genes. They just need a jump start,' she remarked.

Paul continued to keep abreast of Kara's welfare as best he could via the school. Although he was not being denied his parental rights, he could sense things were becoming more awkward. Photos and reports he requested were not always being sent and he had to chase things up more frequently. He did however get written assurance from the school's student support manager that she would let him know of any issues that in her judgement required his attention. This went some way to placating him.

He continued to send Christmas and birthday cards to Phoenix's parents, never giving up hope that one day Kara would realise he had never abandoned her. He never got any response. He resorted to his journal for comfort.

Unfortunately I have not heard anything from Kara. Hopefully next year will see some sort of breakthrough. For now, I still think it best to keep my distance and hope Kara softens a little, but I am not holding my breath, particularly now she has entered her teenage years.

This remained pretty much the situation for the whole of the next year. He got on with his life, waiting and keeping faith that Kara would get in touch when she felt ready. He kept his journal up to date and purposely focused his energies on the many positive aspects in his life. Life was much more fun looking at it from this perspective.

Paul and Jenna kept in regular contact with all their friends and family. They enjoyed spending time with their nieces and nephews, and buying them little presents. He naturally missed doing these things for Kara, but as consolation, he felt he had been given a second chance not to miss out on such life experiences. He kept up his hobby playing the saxophone and they both continued with their dancing. Despite missing Kara, overall it was a very happy time. One particular journal entry read:

17 March

I still think of Kara every day and although it gets easier to be apart, it still does not feel right. Hopefully one day we will be able to put all this behind us and start again. In the meantime, I will concentrate on the many, many positive aspects I have in my life and try to be the best person I can.

During that year, Paul had no direct contact with Kara whatso-ever. He continued to send cards and the school sent him reports. No one had informed him of any issues, so he assumed everything was working out okay. Additionally he had received no nasty phone calls from Phoenix. Surely that had to be a good sign?

Christmas came and went. Paul enjoyed himself as usual, but that same tinge of sadness remained, for he missed Kara.

In the spring, partly due to the global recession, it was announced that major cutbacks were going to be made at Paul's firm and as a consequence the branch where he was based was going to be shut down. This did not come as a complete surprise, for he knew it had been on the cards for some time and he had been quietly preparing himself for such an event, emotionally and financially.

He was given the choice of applying for another position overseas or taking an early retirement package. He did not need to consider the offer for long. He was growing tired of working for a large corporation and there was no way he was going to uproot Jenna from her dance school. He had been working in the construction industry for nigh on thirty years. He acknowl-edged this as a wonderful opportunity to try something new. Additionally, his firm had offered to finance his retraining in a field of his choice. He decided to bite the bullet and fulfil a life-long ambition. He would retrain as a music teacher and go self-employed, teaching the sax.

During the next year, Paul spent time working with mentors and preparing his own teaching material. Quite by chance, he was also offered an audition for the lead saxophonist role in one of the county's finest jazz bands and he passed with flying colours.

Putting the Kara situation to one side, his life was running very happily. He could play the sax whenever he wanted and was able to spend more time with Jenna, helping out at the dance school. He found he had more time to see friends and family and get things done around the house. There was obviously a big drop in financial income to contend with, but fortunately his redundancy money would help tide them over for a while. Neither he nor Jenna were materialistic and they were more than happy to live within their new means, especially if it meant they had more quality time together.

Another Christmas came and went. Paul and Jenna enjoyed time with friends and family as usual. He once again sent a Christmas card with a small note inside for Kara, via Phoenix's parents. The note read:

Dearest Kara,

I hope you are well and enjoying life. Are you looking forward to Christmas? Are you still playing the cello?

I am currently retraining as a music teacher and hope to be teaching the saxophone in the near future for a living. I am really enjoying it, especially since it means I can spend more time at home. Of course I still love playing the sax and I have joined a new band.

Jenna and I continue to look after some wonderful pets for friends of ours (including a spider!).

I still think about you every day, hoping you are OK. I will always be there for you and my Christmas wish is that you will want to contact me one day soon and we can be friends again.

Have fun over Christmas and enjoy your New Year!
Lots of love,
Dad, xx

Predictably he heard nothing in return. Five years had now passed since direct contact with Kara. He had continued to pay maintenance via the CSA and keep abreast of her wellbeing via the school. He had tried to keep her up to date with his activities by including small notes in the Christmas and birthday cards he sent. What else could he do apart from wait for Kara to come around?

Following correspondence with the CSA, Paul updated them on his new employment status. He also took the opportunity to inform them that he was still being refused a contact address and telephone number for his daughter, meaning he was unable to send her birthday and Christmas cards directly.

The representative he spoke to was sympathetic and replied, 'Although we can't get involved directly, if you would like to send us a letter, we can forward it on.'

Paul thought this was great news, although he was disappointed he had not been informed of this option earlier. He drafted the following letter.

Dear Phoenix,

I hope everything is going well for you and Kara.

It is now over three years since I have heard anything from you about Kara and how she is doing, despite me sending Christmas and birthday cards for her to your parents' address. I have not seen Kara in person to talk to for over five years, against my wishes.

I recognise you say that it was Kara's decision at the time to break contact with myself and my family, but five years on, I wonder if there is something we can now collectively do to rectify the circumstances in which we find ourselves. I am sure this would be in all our interests, in particular Kara's.

I appreciate you will have become much closer to Kara than I over the last years and will be in a much better position to judge the situation. I would dearly love to see Kara again and try and make amends for what upset her, but if you don't think the time is right, then perhaps it would be possible for me to at least have her address so I can send Christmas and birthday cards directly, without bothering your mother and stepfather. I would like reassurance that she knows her father still loves her and will always be there for her whatever.

I hope to hear from you soon and ideally we can agree on the best way forward.

Best wishes,
Paul

Paul sat back and pored over the contents of his draft. He felt it accurately portrayed his feelings, but he would not want it to be misconstrued by Kara as unwelcome hassle. She had resolutely stated she would get in touch with him when she was ready, not the other way round. He knew she had his address and telephone number. Nevertheless, he felt he had to say something to Phoenix, so he mailed the letter to the CSA for forwarding on the following day.

Paul continued to play the waiting game. He never did get a response to his letter. Instead his life was turned upside down and he and his family were drawn into a very nasty, dark and unfamiliar world.

Chapter 10

Court matters (1)

✧ Kara's adoption request
✧ Meeting Kara's stepfather (Ross)
✧ Involvement of Social Services (the SS)
✧ False allegations
✧ First court hearing

Two days after mailing his letter, quite unexpectedly, Paul received a phone call from Phoenix. He was instantly on edge, for past history told him she was unlikely to be the bearer of good news.

'Kara has just mailed you a letter. She has requested your consent for her to be adopted by her stepfather,' she told him.

Paul was quite taken aback and required significant effort to stay calm.

'No way,' he replied, following his instinctive gut reaction. He was extremely upset that Phoenix had let things get to this stage without talking to him.

Kara then came on the phone and very forcefully (and somewhat selfishly, Paul had to reluctantly admit) put her case forward. He listened to her, feeling both sad and stunned.

'You have never loved me,' she told him. 'You have been a bad influence in my life and I want nothing to do with you or your family. My stepfather is the opposite. He's everything I ever wanted and is like a real dad. He makes up for all your failings and makes me feel truly wanted.'

Paul's head reeled as he listened. His heart was pumping fast and he could feel that all too recognisable feeling of simultaneous frustration and sadness bubbling up inside him. He knew what she was saying about him was untrue. These thoughts must have been seeded and nurtured in her head by someone else, but he dared not say this to Kara for fear of causing more upset. He was shaking, despite his efforts to remain calm. Why was Phoenix still allowing, or possibly even encouraging, their daughter to go down this self-destructive path? Couldn't she see that whatever perverse pleasure she might be getting in seeing him suffer, Kara was also going to lose out? He continued to try and remain composed as best he could and endeavoured to find the real reason behind her adoption request.

'But it's what I want,' Kara kept repeating, whatever question he asked her. It was as if she had been programmed.

'I don't think it's what I want,' he gently informed her. 'I also need to take the views of others into account. What about your gran and granddad? What about your uncle and aunt? What about your cousins?'

After about five minutes of talking, going round in circles and not really making any progress, Kara swore at him and handed the phone back to her mother.

'I'm not happy about this adoption request,' Paul re-stated. 'I'm not impressed with Kara's telephone manner either. Where has she got these bad manners from?'

'Kara is usually a polite girl, but her strong feelings about this adoption are causing her to be a little headstrong,' Phoenix replied.

Paul was still unimpressed. He did agree to give the adoption matter his full attention however and would try to see things from Kara's perspective. He agreed to respond soon, although in his mind he was not sure how, since he still had no official address or telephone number for Kara. He did a '1471' at the end of the call, but predictably got the response, 'The caller withheld their number'. It pained and saddened him, but his first impression of Kara after all these years was that she had become a spoilt and rather rude girl.

The letter to which Phoenix had referred arrived the following morning. It was the first direct communication he had received from Kara since her first letter over five years ago. He opened it with trepidation. His palms were sweating and he was trembling slightly. He started to read it, but then had to sit down. Once more he had trouble accepting what he was reading. It tugged at his heart strings, whilst fuelling intense frustration at the same time.

Paul,

As you are aware I now have a loving family around me. I really love my stepfather. He is good-natured and makes me feel loved, whereas you never had any time for me. He is a lovely man and your exact opposite. I am truly happy with him.

I have told you on many occasions that I don't want anything to do with you or your family due to past issues. My feelings are now even stronger. I want to be adopted by my stepfather and as such want your consent on the matter.

Kara

Paul read it through a number of times and concluded this was too big for him to handle on his own. He talked it through with Jenna and forwarded copies to his family before deciding on any action.

The whole letter had a spiteful and vindictive tone. What were the 'past issues' she was referring to? He noted that Kara had once again made a point of referring to him by his first name, which he found very disrespectful. He could not understand how or why Phoenix was allowing her to behave in this manner. At the very least, if this was what Kara truly wanted, then Phoenix should be encouraging Kara to write her letters in a much more pleasant tone. That way, he might be more amenable to her requests. He was not saying it would necessarily change his views on the subject, but it would help him take it more seriously.

Paul spent the next few days mulling over the letter, discussing it with friends and family. He also consulted numerous professionals including solicitors, the Citizens Advice Bureau, the CSA and Social Services.

Opinion from friends and family was unanimous. There was no way he should give in to this latest crazy demand for a number of reasons, all of which he recorded.

This surreal nightmare continues and Kara has written to me asking for my consent for her to be adopted by her stepfather. My instinctive reaction is to say 'No', but I have reluctantly agreed to give it my full consideration. I have been speaking to others and they agree with my first instincts. Amongst the reasons are:

- *My family does not want to lose the last bit of contact we have with Kara. This adoption request feels like a misguided attempt, likely fuelled by Phoenix's bitterness, to cut me and my side of her family from her life.*
- *I want to keep my parental rights and exercise my responsibilities so I can continue to assure myself of Kara's wellbeing. I have always kept up to date with her progress via the school and despite her hurtful letters, I am still proud of her. If I gave my consent to the adoption, I would lose all my parental rights.*
- *I and my family are totally flummoxed as to what Kara means by 'past issues'. We have no idea what she is talking about. Whenever she was with us, we always went out of our way to look after her and showed her nothing but love and affection.*
- *If Kara is as happy as she makes out with her new family, then why should adoption be necessary? Why upset the status quo? Surely a truly happy girl would not be interested in such matters.*
- *I do not know anything about her stepfather. He could be a convicted axe murderer for all I know.*

On another sinister note, Paul acknowledged it was not unheard of for mothers to blackmail fathers with false allegations of child abuse if they could not get their own way (as he had previously read in various media articles). He considered that anyone would have to be totally engulfed in bitterness and likely mentally disturbed to ever consider going down this route, but at the same time he did not rule it out as a possibility. His sister-in-law went one step further and hypothesised that maybe this had been Phoenix's crazy plan all along.

Perhaps her next goal would be to try and split him and Jenna up, get him incarcerated, or make him feel so low that he committed suicide! This actually brought a smile to Paul's face. He had occasionally suspected his ex-wife was 'not playing with a full deck', but surely she would not sink that low, would she? They both laughed and admitted that they were probably getting a bit paranoid, but would stay wary just the same.

The next day Paul visited the offices of the Citizens Advice Bureau. Two representatives dedicated the best part of two hours of their day to him, discussing his circumstances. He described the situation from the point of his marriage breakdown to the present date. He showed them Kara's original letter from six years back and her latest letter. They were most taken aback by the disrespectful way Kara had referred to him by his first name. Without prompting, they both commented on how the letters had an obvious spiteful and vicious tone. They were particularly suspicious of Kara's original letter and stated that in their view, this letter was not solely the work of a nine-year-old child and any court would likely agree. It was too deep and full of adult emotion. They strongly believed there had been some significant adult influence in its authorship. They were also surprised to hear Paul was still paying maintenance via the CSA.

'If mother and daughter genuinely want nothing to do with you, why are they still asking for your money?' questioned one of the representatives.

They agreed that Kara's mind could have been poisoned against him and this could have been on-going since his marriage breakdown. Out of spite, Phoenix could have continually tried to make his life as unpleasant as possible.

'Unfortunately this is not uncommon behaviour for women bitter about a break-up,' one of them added. 'Regrettably, it is the children that suffer.'

None of this came as any surprise to Paul. Citizens Advice recommended two courses of action.

'You could reply to Kara's letter, if you can find a way of getting it to her. Tell her that you are not in favour of the adoption and hope and pray that one day she will recognise the truth and get in touch with you. You could also get some legal advice and, if necessary, take legal action.' They handed him a list of useful solicitors in the area that dealt in Family Law.

'Ideally I want to sort this out amicably without using solicitors,' replied Paul. 'I was planning on working with Social Services and CAFCASS, without the need for going to court. It would be a very hollow victory for me if I won a court case but alienated Kara even further.'

They agreed. As he left, they wholeheartedly and sincerely wished him the very best of luck.

After returning home, Paul tried phoning Social Services, but they were very difficult to pin down. For the best part of two hours, he was passed from department to department, having to explain his dilemma a number of times. The only person able to provide any useful information was a woman from an independent body providing a contracted service to Social Services, called 'Kinship and Children'. She was interested to hear his story and very sympathetic to his plight. She knew from personal experience that fathers in his position got a rough deal and it was difficult to identify where to go to for help. She admitted she could not offer much help herself, but did provide a direct telephone number for his local Social Services branch. He rang the number and left a message on an answering machine.

Later that afternoon Social Services returned his call, but were not helpful at all. They were not prepared to pass on any letters to Kara and suggested he contact a solicitor. They advised he would not get legal aid, since he had some savings. Also, since Kara was nearly fifteen, the courts would give her views highest priority. They made it clear that they did not consider this a serious enough problem to warrant any more of their attention.

As a last resort, Paul rang the Child Support Agency and got through to a man who was much more helpful. Once again Paul explained his dilemma and how he needed to respond to Kara's adoption request.

'If you mail us an open letter for Kara, together with a covering letter stating that you want us to forward it on to her, we can do that for you.'

Paul was pleasantly surprised at the man's co-operative nature and expressed his thanks, adding that he would give his offer some serious consideration.

At the end of the week, Paul arranged to see a female solicitor. He had prepared a list of questions to which he was hoping he would get answers. He and Jenna went together and managed to obtain the following information.

✦ Kara could not be adopted without his consent. If he refused to give his consent, then Phoenix would have to take it to court to go further. If it did go to court, it was unlikely he would be able to stop the process completely, but he should be able to retain his parental rights and responsibilities. This would entitle him to continue receiving school reports and photos. Additionally Phoenix would need his agreement in order to leave the UK with Kara.

✦ Grandparents did not have any such rights.

✦ The court would listen to his side of the story before any decision was made regarding the adoption, but only he would be allowed in the courtroom itself. No other members of his family would be permitted to join him.

✦ The court could ask for a report to be prepared by CAFCASS, taking into account relevant persons' views, should there be any disputes.

✦ He could send a letter to Kara detailing why he felt it was not in her best interests to give his consent to the adoption, but all correspondence after that concerning the adoption, should be with Phoenix and the stepfather, not Kara.

✦ It might be a good idea to have a meeting, with or without Kara present, to ensure everybody's views were heard, including grandparents and other family members. One possible successful outcome would be the stepfather having some share in the parental responsibility or 'Legal Guardianship' until Kara was eighteen, but Paul should categorically not give up his parental responsibility.

+ If it did go to court, he did not necessarily have to have a solicitor present and could represent himself.

+ In the solicitor's experience, proving poisoning or brain-washing had taken place was always very difficult. However, Paul's journal and the detail it contained within would be very useful in demonstrating how he had tried to maintain contact with Kara over the years. Also Kara's original letter, which appeared to be from an angry woman rather than a nine-year-old child, would go in his favour.

+ If Kara or Phoenix tried to blackmail Paul with false allegations of child abuse, it would be seen as a last-minute act of desperation. He had not seen Kara for five to six years and for any allegations to be taken seriously, they should have been reported straight away at the time. Additionally there would be no evidence, unless they were to falsify it, which would be an extremely dangerous act on their part.

+ Paul would have to pay his court costs, whatever the outcome. They would be around £3000, unless he wanted to pursue a Contact Order, in which case they would be an awful lot more. If he did pursue a Contact Order, he should be aware that he would likely lose and risk alienating Kara further.

'It's a shame you didn't get solicitors involved a lot earlier and make an application to the court when Kara was nine years old,' remarked the solicitor. 'It will now likely go against you that you have not had direct contact with Kara over the past five to six years.'

'I did consider solicitor involvement at the time,' replied Paul, 'but seriously thought I could sort things out amicably with my ex-wife. I reconsidered getting solicitors involved a couple of years later when my ex-wife moved house without giving me a contact address, but I was then advised that since Kara was approaching twelve years of age, I would be wasting time and money. Apparently Kara's views would have taken precedence over mine and I would have risked alienating her further.'

'That may well have been the case,' agreed the solicitor. 'A strong positive on your side, however, is that you have tried to maintain contact over the years. You've sent cards and letters and stayed in touch with the school, despite difficulties put in your way.' She looked at Paul pensively. 'Have you considered whether there might be a large inheritance at stake? Could this be Phoenix's motivation for the adoption, i.e. to ensure Kara has a legal right to her stepfather's money?'

'It's something I have considered, but not dwelled upon. It could be a possibility,' he replied.

For the time being they agreed to put these thoughts on hold since this was purely speculation, but nevertheless a possibility worth mentioning in the absence of other information.

'I can see no legal reason why the adoption should go ahead with you losing your parental rights,' she added. 'Even if the adoption were to progress, the process would require a minimum of six months, maybe even up to three years before a decision is made, by which point Kara would be approaching eighteen years of age anyway.'

Paul and Jenna thanked her for her time and went away to mull things over.

Paul spent the weekend reflecting on everything that had transpired over the past week. The fact that the adoption could not easily go ahead without his consent gave him some comfort. If he opposed the Adoption Order, the court would likely appoint an officer from CAFCASS to investigate the consent issue and decide whether it should be over-ruled in the child's interest. A worker from Social Services would also make a recommendation to the court regarding the application, but the court would make the final decision. He felt that this was all good news. In fact he would welcome Social Services and CAFCASS getting involved. He recalled the times in the past when he had tried to involve Social Services, for example when Phoenix had moved house without telling him. They hadn't been interested then. Perhaps now he would get the opportunity to show just how badly he had been treated and this would be a fantastic opportunity to start building bridges with Kara.

Overall, he was starting to feel much more at ease with the situation. He could not see why anyone would consider it in Kara's best interests for the adoption to go ahead and there was absolutely no valid reason why the court should dispense with his consent. He carefully constructed a letter with help from his family and mailed it to Kara via the CSA with a covering letter as per their instructions. The gist of the letter was as below.

Dear Kara,

I am pleased to hear you are enjoying family life with your stepfather. At the same time however, I must confess to feeling sad that you want nothing to do with me and my side of your family. We all still love you and miss you very much.

At this time I find it too difficult to give my consent to your request for adoption. I am sorry this does not meet with your wishes, but I hope you will understand. I would dearly like to rebuild our relationship, whereas this adoption feels like a move in the opposite direction. As your father, I naturally care about you and love you very much. I continue to regard myself as at least partly responsible for your future happiness and wellbeing.

Over the last years I have always tried to go along with your wishes and I have purposely remained in the background as per your requests. However, I want you to know that I will always be there for you and I hope one day we can enjoy a father–daughter relationship again.

If you ever feel the need to contact me, you will always be ever so warmly welcomed.
Wishing you peace, joy and love,
Your Father

A few days later, Paul got a call from Phoenix. She opened the conversation.

'Have you considered Kara's request?'

'Yes,' he replied. 'I have put all my thoughts in a letter and mailed it to the CSA and they have agreed to forward it on to Kara.' Phoenix was noticeably irritated.

'Why have you got the CSA involved?' she demanded.

'It's the only way I could ensure Kara got the letter. Surely you remember refusing to give me a contact address?' He tried not to sound too sarcastic. Phoenix was obviously not pleased that the CSA were acting in his interests for a change.

'What decision have you come to?' she asked impatiently.

'I have not reached a final decision yet, since I don't have enough information.'

'What information?' asked Phoenix. He could tell by her voice that she was getting increasingly frustrated. Nevertheless, he tried to keep the conversation civil.

'I know nothing about Kara's stepfather. How can I be sure he is the right person to take on this role? Also, if the adoption goes ahead and I give up my parental rights, how am I going to assure myself of Kara's future welfare?'

Phoenix didn't reply. She handed the phone to Kara, who essentially asked the same questions as her mother. He felt uncomfortable talking to Kara in such an official manner and wanted be more friendly with her, but she was making it difficult and appeared to have a fixed agenda she wanted to follow.

'I want you to meet my stepfather,' said Kara in what came across to Paul as a rather demanding tone. 'I want you to meet him on your own. I don't want anyone else there. Just you and him.'

'It might be useful to have others present to make sure no one is being bulldozed into anything,' Paul suggested. 'Perhaps they could act as mediators. They could help ensure we have all the right information to make the best decision.'

'No,' Kara replied firmly. 'I'm the only one that gets bulldozed into anything. You've not taken any interest in me over the last few years, so why do you want to keep your parental rights anyway?'

'That's not true,' replied Paul, trying not to sound too adversarial. 'A day never goes by when I don't think about you and I have consistently checked you are okay via your school.'

'Well, you've not been around for the last five years.'

'Yes, I know,' replied Paul, 'but that was not my choice. It was forced upon me.'

'How dare you! It's my mum that has been the major influence in my life and I won't have you saying anything against her.'

'I agree your mum has been the major influence,' he replied, 'but it's a pity I couldn't have been there more. If I had been, perhaps you would have a more informed and balanced outlook on this whole adoption scenario and life in general.'

'I have told you on many occasions that I don't want you finding out things about me, but you have deliberately gone behind my back.'

'I've tried to respect your wishes as far as practical over the years, but for all our sakes, I needed reassurance that you were okay. I was simply behaving as any responsible parent.' Once again Paul felt he could not win. He was damned if he did; he was damned if he didn't. 'Your gran, granddad, uncle and aunt all have a significant part to play in this adoption request. You do realise this, don't you?'

'No, it should just be about me and you,' she replied. She did not appear to understand his views at all.

'Neither I nor my family have ever neglected you and we will always be there for you. We just want what's best for you.'

At this point Kara got abusive, using foul language.

'I never get what I want,' she ranted. 'Why are you being so fucking obstructive? Just fuck off!'

Paul was shocked and would have been deeply offended if it

had not been so laughably ridiculous. He focused on keeping his composure.

'It pains me to say this, but I think you are acting very selfishly. My family is offering to always be there for you, but you are throwing it back in our faces. I can understand you being angry with me, but there is no need to take it out on the rest of the family.'

Paul sensed Kara was seeing this as some kind of fight, despite him trying to reassure her that he was only trying to act in everyone's best interests. He certainly did not want to fight with her.

'Whatever,' replied Kara. 'I'll give you a week to give me an answer. I told you I wanted to be adopted over two years ago, so you have been given enough warning.'

'Well, my answer at that time was categorically "No", but now you are older, I am prepared to reconsider. The letter I have mailed to you explains my feelings in detail and perhaps we can discuss it further once you have had a chance to read it.'

Kara seemed to go along with this, albeit reluctantly.

'You must still meet my stepfather,' she replied, then handed the phone back to Phoenix.

'You can hear for yourself how strongly Kara feels. Don't upset her. We would appreciate you reaching your decision quickly. We'll be in touch.' She then hung up.

For the next few days, Paul's phone did not stop ringing. On top of all the issues with Kara, he received the bad news that his gran (Kara's great-gran) was very ill in hospital and the doctors were not sure if she was going to pull through. He had not mentioned anything to Kara about her illness on the phone the previous week, since from what he had experienced of Kara's attitude, he believed she could not have cared less.

Friends and family also rang to hear the latest update with respect to Kara. One particular friend, now living in Crete, was absolutely appalled when he heard the news. He had known Paul and Phoenix when they were once a happy couple and was of the firm opinion that Phoenix's latest behaviour was down to her ego and 'point scoring'.

One night in the middle of the week, Paul and Jenna were feeling particularly down. Jenna had been his source of comfort and solace throughout this whole ordeal and it was obviously having a draining effect on her too. She rang one of her teacher friends who had worked with Social Services in a professional capacity in the past. This friend had a lot of experience working with children from difficult backgrounds. Jenna explained their dilemma in detail and put the phone on loudspeaker so both she and Paul could hear what her friend had to say.

'Be warned that girls of Kara's age behaving in this spiteful fashion are capable of all sorts if they don't get their own way. Don't be surprised if she goes on to make up nasty allegations against Paul. This could be her misguided way of giving a gift to her stepfather. Kara is behaving in a very naive fashion and either isn't aware or doesn't care about the full far-reaching consequences of her actions. There could be an extreme amount of upheaval and unpleasantness with respect to court costs, slander, false allegations, and at the end Paul could still lose his parental rights and would have pushed Kara even further away. Is it worth going through all that?'

Jenna sighed heavily. 'I just don't know,' she replied. 'I'll support Paul whatever he thinks is best.'

'Another way of looking at it,' her friend suggested, 'is if Kara does change her mind when she's older and eventually does comes back, which ultimately I think she will, then great. If on the other hand she doesn't, then what have you lost? She can't be a very nice person in that case. Regardless of the outcome, that woman Phoenix has a lot of bad karma coming her way unless she changes her attitude.'

They continued chatting for a short while longer. Jenna thanked her for her wise words and frank advice before they said their goodbyes.

Paul was now really distraught, pacing up and down. Jenna tried reasoning with him and poured him a whisky, but he was inconsolable.

'What if Kara goes on to make up false allegations about me? What if people believe her? I've done nothing wrong.'

'I know,' replied Jenna, and she put her arms around him. 'I'll be here for you.'

He felt like his own daughter was tearing out his stomach, whilst his ex-wife was stabbing him in the back, cruelly enjoying twisting the knife. He decided to ring his father. His father could sense Paul was in a state and calmed him down.

'You have absolutely nothing to worry about,' he said. 'You have behaved impeccably throughout this whole sorry affair, from the divorce right up until now. You have a clear conscience. Wait for a response to your letter and we can take it from there. No allegations of any sort have been made and Kara and Phoenix would be unlikely to be so malicious as to make some up. The most likely outcome will be some sort of "hissy-fit" response and that will be the end of it.'

Paul hoped he was right.

Towards the end of the week, Phoenix telephoned. She was very keen for Paul to meet with Kara's stepfather, who she let slip into the conversation was called Ross. This was the first time he had heard his actual name mentioned. She was pushing Paul for a date, time and venue. They agreed the meeting would take place the third Sunday in May, at a café equidistant from them.

Paul wondered what Ross must think of all this. Why couldn't he see through Phoenix's facade? Perhaps he could, but was too controlled by Phoenix and Kara to say anything? Why had he not phoned Paul himself? Was he a weak man? Was he still in his honeymoon period?

Paul's father rang later that same evening to enquire how everything was going. His parents were obviously concerned and hated to see anyone going through emotional suffering, particularly their son. Paul relayed the latest news.

'It sounds like everything is working out okay,' replied his father. 'You might find the meeting with the stepfather doesn't even go ahead. They might be trying to call your bluff to get your consent. Regardless, if you get the chance to meet him, I think you should. It would be a step in the right direction. I wouldn't worry too much about Kara at the moment. She's just behaving like any other typical fourteen-year-old girl who unfortunately is too used to getting her own way.

'Changing the subject slightly, you might be interested to know that your mum and I received a short note from Phoenix's stepfather over the Christmas period. I didn't mention it before, for fear of bringing up bad memories, but we've exchanged the odd Christmas card with Phoenix's parents over the years. He appreciates you have tried to stay in contact with Kara by sending Christmas and birthday cards via their address. He wrote in the card that Kara is doing well at school and continues her interests in music and acting. He even suggested that perhaps we could meet up the next time they were visiting England.'

'I don't think Phoenix would like that,' said Paul with a wry smile.

'Probably not,' his father agreed, 'but regardless, he did come across as being sympathetic that we had not seen Kara. I got the impression he was more on our side than Phoenix's, but for obvious reasons couldn't come straight out and say it.'

All this sent Paul's head into another spin. It so happened that he and Jenna had a trip booked to visit Poland the following week. He was hopeful that this would be a good opportunity to take a break from the latest happenings and he would come back refreshed in preparation for his meeting with Ross. He continued to make entries in his journal, recording all the latest developments, using it as a repository to collect his thoughts.

30 April

Although my head is spinning, I have started to make some firm conclusions as to how to take this forward.

I will meet with Kara's stepfather and get some more information.

- *What are his views on the adoption?*
- *Why does he want to adopt Kara? Why is it so necessary?*
- *What evidence can he provide that he has a stable and enduring relationship with Phoenix? I was also married to her and that all went pear-shaped!*

- *Has he been married before? Any children from a previous relationship? Any other family?*
- *Is he in a position to provide financial stability? What are his work prospects?*
- *What state of health is he in? Anything I should be aware of that could affect his ability to look after Kara?*

I need to know the answers to these questions before I can take it further. If the answers to all these questions are satisfactory, then I will give serious consideration to sharing parental responsibility, or agree to him having legal guardianship up to the age of eighteen. Regardless of the answers, I will not agree to give my consent to total adoption since:

- *I do not want to give up my parental rights and responsibilities which are currently my only way of ensuring Kara is okay. Phoenix has proved herself totally untrustworthy with respect to passing on any information. She has purposefully obstructed me from getting any information about Kara over the last five or six years, including denying me a home address/phone number. She has:*
  - *denied me the right of sending Kara weekly letters by refusing to disclose her address*
  - *requested I do not visit or contact the school*
  - *requested I do not contact her parents, and*
  - *blocked any form of contact between my family and Kara.*
- *Even if Kara did not want contact with me herself, as a responsible parent, Phoenix should have kept me reasonably updated. Instead, I feel she has purposely contributed to the breakdown of my father–daughter relationship, resulting in me being effectively pushed out of Kara's life. I am not prepared to lose the last little bit I have. I will continue to respect Kara's wishes and not contact her or meddle in her new family life, but I will always make myself available, should she ever wish to contact me.*
- *Adoption is a very serious matter and once an Adoption Order is made, the law no longer recognises the other birth parent as having any parental links with the child. Other relations such as grand-*

parents and other birth relatives on that parent's side are also considered legally unrelated to the child. In Kara's case this would be grossly unfair. There are no logical, legal or ethical grounds as to why it should go ahead. A blood/DNA relationship cannot be denied! If anything, I find it 'twisted' that Kara and Phoenix are even considering this adoption approach.

• *If I gave my consent to adoption, it could lessen the chance of ever being united with any possible grandchildren of the future.*

If this adoption matter goes to court, then I will represent myself.

Rightly or wrongly, Paul, Jenna, friends and family all came to the conclusion that the real reason Phoenix and Kara were pursuing this course of action was to try and hurt him as much as possible. Interestingly, this view was very much supported by other women he spoke to. They believed that Kara was only acting in this manner because she had been brainwashed by her mother.

Paul was wary that even if he gave his consent to the adoption, he had no guarantee that he would not be persecuted further. They could additionally try to split him and Jenna up, get him sent to prison, or pressurise him to the point of a heart attack. Phoenix could claim that the fact he consented to Kara's adoption was proof he never cared for her. Although this all sounded far-fetched, it was something he had already discussed with Jenna and relatives, for they believed Phoenix might be 'unhinged'. The more this situation continued, the more convinced of this possibility they became.

Paul's brother telephoned the following morning to check he was okay and get an update.

'How are you bearing up?' he asked.

'Not too bad,' Paul replied. 'I'm meeting Kara's stepfather in the near future and I'll try and move things forward, but I don't want to give up my parental responsibilities.'

'I'm right behind you,' he replied. 'You have been far too accommodating to Phoenix over the years and it's about time you put your foot down. It's not right she gets her own way all the time. Do bear in mind though if this goes to court, Phoenix and Kara will most likely try and rubbish you in some way to get what they want. You will need to be very sure of your facts if you are going to represent yourself.'

They agreed that keeping his journal up to date had been a true blessing. Little had he known when he had first started it just how useful it would become.

The following week Paul and Jenna travelled to Poland on their short break. This was a belated Christmas present from Paul to Jenna, who had an avid interest in both world wars. They visited Oswiecim, where they had a haunting and unforgettable visit to the Auschwitz concentration camp. Although they were aware of what went on during the Holocaust from books and TV documentaries, it was still very much a stark eye-opener for them. Walking round Auschwitz was a timely reminder of just how evil man can be. The museum was resolute in being a reminder that humanity had a responsibility to not fall into the trap of such evil again. Paul acknowledged his problems were absolutely nothing in comparison, but he and Jenna both admitted to thinking of Phoenix when the evil deeds of mankind were discussed. He wondered whether Kara had visited this place, or if she was planning a visit with the school.

After Auschwitz, they visited the old town of Krakow, which was a much more charming experience.

Being away did give Paul the chance to clear his head of all the recent turmoil. Before they had left, it had felt like they were constantly being deluged with bad news. His gran had been taken seriously ill and a number of their close friends had been dealing with their own personal tragedies. To top it all, both Paul's and Jenna's cars had died and had been towed to the breakers. This short spell away came at a very welcome time and helped get things back in perspective. However, nothing really prepared them for what was coming their way over the months ahead.

Whilst he was away, Paul desperately tried to see things from Kara's viewpoint. From whichever perspective he looked at it, he still did not believe adoption was in her best interests. He documented his reasons.

8 May

- *I and my family do not want to break any more ties with Kara. For us, it's more a matter of waiting for the day when we can welcome her back into the family. We will always be there for her, no matter. We recognise her heart has been poisoned against us from a young age, through no fault of her own.*
- *Over the years Phoenix has made my life difficult, particularly with respect to seeing Kara and maintaining contact. Adoption would be the last straw. Examples of obstacles she has put in the way include:*
  - *changing arrangements for me to see Kara at the last minute*
  - *not answering my phone calls*
  - *allowing and likely encouraging Kara to disrespect me and my family*
  - *refusing to give me a contact address or telephone number*
  - *making it difficult for the school to allow me to exercise my parental responsibilities*
  - *encouraging Kara to distance herself from me, rather than forging a good relationship.*
- *What would happen if Kara changed her mind and wanted to start rebuilding bridges with her natural family in the future? If the adoption went ahead, all legal ties would have been irreversibly broken.*
- *I recognise Kara claims to be very happy with her new stepfamily, but it does not make sense for her to turn her back on her natural family for no good reason. We all still love her very much. She could have both families if we go down the 'shared parental responsibility' route. Who knows what events could happen in the future when access to both loving families would be extremely valuable?*
  - *Something could happen to Ross and/or Phoenix, rendering them incapable of looking after Kara.*
  - *The relationship between Phoenix and Ross could break down.*
  - *Kara may have children of her own and when they grow older, they may want to find out more about their roots and meet their natural grandfather.*

On the third Sunday in May, Paul went to meet with Kara's stepfather. Paul was at the arranged venue on time, but after twenty minutes there was no sign of Ross. He wondered if he had changed his mind about their rendezvous.

After a further ten minutes, Ross finally appeared, looking a little flustered. Although Paul had no idea what he looked like, he guessed it was him when he entered the café by his general demeanour. Ross looked around, acknowledged Paul and walked over. Paul thought he looked vaguely familiar, but he could not quite register where he might have seen him before. They shook hands and Ross apologised for being late.

'Phoenix directed me to the wrong place,' he said in a rather embarrassed fashion. 'I had to stop and ask for directions. I recognised you from a photograph Phoenix had shown me.'

Paul smiled and beckoned the waitress in order to buy them both a drink.

The conversation flowed easily from the start. They appeared to understand one another and there was a growing mutual respect. Paul showed Ross a copy of the letter he had recently written and mailed to Kara via the CSA.

'I've not seen this,' Ross said to Paul's surprise.

Neither of them was sure whether this was because the CSA had not forwarded it on, or Kara had neglected to tell Ross she had received it. It made Paul wonder if there was anything else Kara had not seen. What about the cards he had sent via Phoenix's parents? Were things being intentionally kept from her?

Ross started reading the letter whilst Paul took a sip from his coffee.

'I would have written something similar if I was in your shoes,' said Ross once he had finished reading. 'I'll take this letter back with me and show Kara, just in case she hasn't seen it.'

'Would you mind answering some questions about yourself?' asked Paul. 'I don't want our meeting to turn into an interrogation akin to the Spanish inquisition, but I feel very much at a disadvantage, since you obviously know a lot more about me than I know about you.'

'Please do, fire away,' replied Ross. 'I can understand how you must feel.'

Paul had come pre-armed with his list of questions and did not hold back.

'What are your views on the adoption?' he asked.

'It's what Kara wants. She first mentioned it about a year or two ago. I have no problem with it. I regard Kara as my own daughter, although I recognise you will always be her biological father.'

'Why do you want to adopt Kara? Why do you consider it necessary?'

'As I say, it's what Kara wants. I love her as my own daughter and I think it would be best for her physical and mental wellbeing, making her feel part of the family unit.' Paul found this last comment a little unsettling, but let it go. 'I recognise that adoption will not cause the family unit to change as such,' continued Ross, 'but Kara probably feels a bit sidelined bearing in mind I have two sons of my own from a previous relationship who live with us.'

Paul raised his eyebrows and wondered how Kara would feel about having two stepbrothers.

'How sure are you that your relationship with Phoenix will pass the test of time?' enquired Paul. 'After all, I was with her ten years and that went sour.'

'Well, I'm as sure as I can be,' replied Ross with a smile. 'It's six years we've been together now.'

Paul did some quick mental arithmetic. That meant he had come on the scene the same year Kara had started becoming distant from him, then wrote her devastating letter. He did not say anything at this point, but logged the information in his head.

'You mention two sons. Any other family?'

'No. My parents passed away a few years back. I have no brothers or sisters.'

'Are you in a position to provide some sort of financial stability for Kara?'

Ross smiled again and replied, 'I'm not loaded, but business is going reasonably well. I'm the proud owner of two hardware shops.'

'How's your general state of health?'

'Well, as you can see, I'm a little overweight, but other than that, fine.'

Paul smiled. 'Has Kara any new hobbies?' he enquired.

'She's thinking of working in theatre, but her main passion remains the cello. Her goal is to play in a world famous orchestra one day, perhaps the London Philharmonic, but she also enjoys writing scripts and would like to direct her own Broadway production. Phoenix and I support her in these activities and get involved where we can. I assume she gets her musical abilities from you.'

Overall Paul felt this meeting was turning out to be much more pleasant and productive than he was expecting. Ross bought some more drinks and they continued chatting as if old friends for another couple of hours. Paul was able to get all his points across and additionally gave Ross a brief synopsis of events since his marriage break-up with Phoenix. He explained how things had taken a turn for the worse about six years ago, when she had moved house and refused to give him a contact address and phone number for Kara. He described how embarrassing it had been going to Kara's new school to try and find out what was going on. Ross understandably looked a little uncomfortable at hearing some of this, for it was likely the first time he had heard Paul's version of events.

It was then Ross's turn to ask Paul some questions.

'What are your hobbies? Are you still playing sax?'

'Yes, very much so. It's a big part of my life.'

'Still playing in bands?'

'Yes, and I've retrained as a saxophone teacher.'

After further pleasant conversation, the subject moved on to how Paul considered Phoenix to have likely poisoned Kara's mind against him over the years, whether intentionally or not.

'What other rational explanation is there for Kara's behaviour?' he asked.

'I don't think Phoenix would be that manipulative,' replied

Ross, but try as he might, he could offer no alternative as to why Kara was behaving in this fashion. 'Kara has said at times she felt you did not listen to her. Perhaps that has had some influence? I must admit I find this whole adoption scenario most bizarre. It's a first for me.'

'I think "twisted" or "warped" might be a more accurate description,' said Paul, trying not to sound too antagonistic. 'What was it exactly that you were referring to earlier, when you mentioned Kara's physical and mental wellbeing?'

'Oh, I don't think there's anything to worry about at the moment,' replied Ross in what Paul regarded a suspiciously quick manner, 'but more something going forward.'

'Don't you think reconciling with her natural father is just as important?'

'Yes, I certainly do.' Ross then told the story of how Kara had been very scared the night Paul had gone to see her at the school Open Evening six years previously when all this business had started. 'She was terrified you were going to kidnap her! She came running to me for protection and didn't want to leave my side.'

Paul looked at him in utter disbelief and then it dawned on him why Ross looked familiar. 'That's exactly the type of mind poisoning I'm referring to,' exclaimed Paul. 'Where is Kara getting these ridiculous notions from if it's not from Phoenix?'

'I honestly don't know,' replied Ross. 'I can understand you only attended the Open Evening in Kara's best interests. Phoenix badly regretted not being there that evening to calm Kara down.'

The conversation continued to flow and Paul felt they were being remarkably open with one another considering the circumstances.

'I can see how you are in a very awkward position,' admitted Ross. 'It must be difficult to know what to do for the best. If you try and contact Kara it seems to upset her, but when you don't, you get accused of abandoning her.'

'For the foreseeable future, I think it best if I keep my distance as per Kara's original request,' replied Paul. 'I'll wait for her to approach me. I will continue to send Christmas and birthday cards, though. Does this sound reasonable to you?'

Ross nodded in response.

'Can I have a mailing address for Kara?'

'I'm afraid I am not prepared to give it, since this would be going against Kara's wishes,' replied Ross, appearing sympathetic.

'In that case, I have no choice but to continue mailing cards to Phoenix's parents' address.'

'I don't think Kara has actually received any birthday and Christmas cards from you,' Ross replied. He could see Paul was taken aback and back-tracked a little. 'For all Phoenix's parents' faults, I don't think they would intentionally do anything to hurt Kara, so I am sure she most probably has seen them. What's more likely is that she has received them, but she hasn't told me. I suppose another explanation could be that Phoenix's parents may be waiting for an opportune moment to give them to her.'

The conversation continued in a friendly manner. Neither Paul nor Ross mentioned the possibility that Phoenix could be intentionally hiding the cards from Kara. Ross granted that when he had heard Kara speaking on the phone, or had seen some of her written communications to Paul, her tone had appeared spiteful and hurtful.

'Kara is normally a polite girl,' he commented. 'From now on I will encourage her to be more respectful where you are concerned.' Paul was notably pleased at this response.

'I'm not expecting miracles overnight, but it would be nice to receive the odd Christmas or birthday card.' Ross agreed that this was a totally reasonable expectation.

'Do you think Kara will think less of you if you let her be adopted?' Ross asked pointedly.

'No, more the opposite. At this time she'll probably dislike me all the more for opposing the adoption, but maybe in time she will understand and might even come to respect me for it one day.'

Ross appeared to concur with these sentiments.

'I would really appreciate your help in trying to rebuild my relationship with my daughter,' Paul said.

They agreed this would be in Kara's interests, but recognised it would take some considerable time, bearing in mind her age and current attitude.

'What are your final views on the adoption?' asked Ross.

'From what I have seen, you come across as a very reasonable man. I would be prepared to consider sharing parental responsibility with you, or agreeing to you having legal guardianship. Total adoption, however, would mean legal ties being cut between Kara and myself, including my family. That's totally unnecessary. I can't comprehend how this would be in Kara's or anyone's best interests.'

'The remit I have been given for this meeting by Kara and Phoenix is to get your consent to total adoption,' replied Ross. 'However, I do appreciate where you're coming from and I think your requests are fair. I'll take them back to Kara, along with the other positives that have emanated from our conversation. Kara is aware of other options such as sharing parental responsibility, because she's been the main person researching the subject. It's not her choice, however, to pursue these middle ground options at this time.'

Before they parted company, they agreed it had been good to finally meet and jested that in another life they might have been the best of friends. They exchanged phone numbers so they could contact each other in the future, should they ever feel the need. They shook hands before Ross made one last comment.

'I'm sure you realise that Phoenix, Kara and I are holding all the trump cards with respect to this adoption process.'

This surprised and disappointed Paul. He wondered if he should be a little concerned, for it sounded like a threat. He decided it best to not respond, but thanked him for a useful conversation and wished him a safe journey.

When Paul returned home, he spoke with Jenna and the rest of his family, relaying the conversation as accurately as he could. They shared the opinion that it appeared to have gone very well considering the circumstances. They agreed this was probably the most constructive thing to have happened since his break-up with Phoenix. His sister-in-law did rightly urge him to be cautious, reminding him of the time they had been to see Phoenix about five years ago at her local café and how she had come across as all sweetness and innocence, just before absconding with Kara.

'My overall impression is that he was genuine,' replied Paul, 'although he did reveal he's into theatre and playing dastardly villains!'

They laughed, but agreed to stay cautious, particularly bearing in mind Ross's parting comment.

After the meeting, things appeared to calm down. Paul sent Kara her customary birthday card (she was now fifteen) with a gift voucher inside via Phoenix's parents. When his birthday arrived, predictably he heard nothing in return. He was quietly confident however that following his meeting with Ross, all suggestions of adoption would blow over and they could now get on with their lives. He continued to get end of term reports from Kara's school showing she was doing well in her studies. There appeared nothing to unduly alarm him.

During the second week of September, Paul received a phone call from the CSA.

'We've reviewed our files and asked Phoenix if it is okay for us to forward on your hand-written letters to Kara,' the representative informed him. 'She has said "Yes", so we are now forwarding them on.'

'But I sent those to you ages ago,' Paul protested, 'well over six months ago!'

'Yes, I know,' the anonymous voice replied. 'We get very busy.'

Paul was flabbergasted! How come they had only just got round to sending them, over six months later? When the CSA wanted something from him, they were on his case immediately. When he wanted them to do something for him, they obviously considered it a very low priority.

'Well, I'm not very impressed with your service,' he informed them. 'It's a good job I wasn't relying on you.'

He remembered that fortunately he had handed a copy of his second letter to Ross when they met back in April, so hopefully Kara should have already seen it. He did not want it opening up old wounds for her now. His faith in the efficiency of this organisation had taken a bashing. He could understand why the CSA had a poor reputation, particularly amongst fathers.

Even though things remained quiet, Kara was constantly in Paul's thoughts. He wondered if he should telephone Ross for an update, but he didn't want to get accused of meddling. He remained optimistic that Ross would have been able to talk rationally with Kara and perhaps even succeeded in laying some foundations for him to rebuild his relationship with his daughter. Any such hopes were soon dashed to the ground, however, when in November he received the following Recorded Delivery letter from Social Services.

Dear Mr Nelson,

I understand you are aware that Kara's stepfather has made a Court application to adopt Kara as his daughter. Since you have Parental Responsibility for Kara, this Adoption Order can only be granted if:-

a) You give your consent, or

b) There are grounds for the Court to dispense with your consent

It is important you understand that should an Adoption Order be granted, you would lose all rights regarding your daughter. Should you wish to contest the application, I would strongly advise you consult a solicitor.

For the purposes of preparing a report regarding this application, could you please contact me to arrange a suitable time to discuss the matter more fully so I can get your opinion.

Yours sincerely,

Ms Nerys Staines

Paul was gutted at receiving this letter. He had not been expecting it. He spent the next couple of days trying to crystallise his thoughts and talked it through with his family. They were all upset, but they could also see a positive in that perhaps now he would get a chance to bring everything out into the open. Perhaps now others would see how unjustly he had been treated. They shared the opinion that Kara could not be as happy as she made out if she still felt the need to go ahead with this adoption. Was she using it to try and fill an empty space in her life? One obvious void to consider was the absence of a good relationship with her natural father, directly as a consequence of Phoenix's conduct. Was Kara misguidedly using this adoption process as a way of filling this void? Surely the best way forward would be to rebuild the relationship, not break it down further? Although Phoenix appeared blind to this, surely a trained social worker would see it?

Paul remained reluctant to get solicitors involved. He was not sure how a solicitor could help. There was also the substantial financial burden to consider. He still had faith that everything would work itself out. He found it difficult to admit to himself how much his relationship with his own daughter had deteriorated and would struggle with the humiliation of having to explain it all to a solicitor. He felt very foolish for having believed Phoenix for so long, particularly when she had repeatedly said, 'Leave things to me' or 'Just give me a little more time to sort things out. Kara is coming round.' How could he have been so naive?

Members of his family were also of the view there was no point in involving solicitors. None of them had anything to hide or be ashamed about. If Kara still wanted to go ahead with the adoption and the court believed it to be in her best interests, then so be it. However, he would continue to make it clear that his door would always be open for her to come back at any time, should she change her mind.

That evening Paul made the following entry in his journal:

Kara and I should be rebuilding our relationship as father and daughter, not breaking any remaining fragile ties that currently exist. I and my family will always love and be there for her. At the same time, we would never do anything to jeopardise the loving relationship she has built with her stepfather and his family. Where has all her hatred come from?

The following day Paul telephoned Ms Staines and discussed his views on the proposed adoption. He explained how he felt Kara had been poisoned against him over the years. Ms Staines did not seem very receptive, but agreed they should have a two-hour meeting in a couple of weeks to discuss it further. She could then prepare her report.

'That's fine. I can bring evidence to support any claims or statements I make,' said Paul, trying to be helpful. 'Are you acting independently?' he asked her directly.

'Yes,' she replied brusquely.

She doesn't sound the 'happy family type', he mused to himself.

During the course of the next week, Paul prepared a number of short memos covering relevant topics, ready for the meeting. He also collated evidence to support specific statements within those memos. He recorded the details.

14 November

Tomorrow I meet with the Social Services. I am taking the following with me in preparation.
- *A summary of relevant events since my break-up with Phoenix to the present day.*
- *Examples of how I and my family have desperately tried to stay in contact with Kara.*
- *Reasons why I do not think adoption is in Kara's best interests.*
- *Examples of how I believe Kara has been poisoned against me and my family.*

- *A copy of the first devastating letter I received from Kara, when she was aged nine.*
- *A copy of my reply to the above letter.*
- *Copies of the weekly letters I sent to Kara, over the following eighteen months.*
- *Examples of my correspondence with Kara's schools.*
- *Correspondence with regards to Kara's change of surname.*
- *Kara's letter requesting my consent to the proposed adoption.*
- *A copy of my reply to Kara's adoption request letter.*
- *Copies of birthday and Christmas cards I have sent over the years.*
- *Various memorabilia including cards, photographs and school reports.*

Paul went to meet with Ms Staines on the day as planned. He arrived at the council's Adoption Services building ten minutes early and had to wait in the reception area for an extra half an hour. When Ms Staines finally arrived, she was pretty much as he had visualised from their telephone conversation. He considered her a rather sour-faced lady, in her mid to late fifties. She looked as if she had not smiled for at least ten years and had no idea what an enjoyable relationship was all about. He forced a smile in her direction, but it did not appear to register with her at all. She led him to a small, sparse meeting room where they sat down on uncomfortable plastic chairs placed around a small table.

'I'm going to ask you some questions,' she informed him.

Paul immediately got the impression she considered herself his superior, unjustifiably judging and treating him as some sort of criminal low-life. Regardless, he gave her the benefit of the doubt and remained polite.

'First I want to confirm some details concerning your physical appearance.' She started asking personal questions about the colour of his eyes, the colour of his hair and his height.

'Why do you want these details?' enquired Paul.

'To fill out my report,' she replied.

She continued to ask all sorts of seemingly irrelevant personal questions concerning his childhood, including which infant school he attended. Paul was getting impatient, but tried not to show it. As she moved on to asking questions about his marital relationship with Phoenix and the circumstances that led to their divorce, the meeting felt more like an interrogation than a discussion. Despite feeling it inappropriate, he couldn't help thinking of the initials 'SS' and their connotations. Eventually she got round to asking questions about his relationship with Kara.

Paul answered all her questions as honestly as he could and then showed her the material he had brought with him. She spent the next ten minutes going through it and seemed genuinely interested. She paid particular attention to the summary cataloguing significant events since his marriage break-up and how he and his family had cared and provided for Kara over the years.

'You can keep copies of all this information,' Paul offered.

Once Ms Staines had finished reading, she took off her glasses and looked uncomfortably at him.

'I have to inform you that a Court Order has been mailed to your home address. Included in that package is a Statement of Facts, authored and signed by Phoenix, Kara and her stepfather.' She handed him a copy to read.

The Statement was a request for the court to dispense with Paul's consent regarding the adoption of Kara by her stepfather. The reason given was that he had never exercised his parental rights responsibly and had never bothered to stay in contact with Kara, whether in person, by letter or by phone. It went on to say that the few times he and Kara had spent together were very unsettling for her, leaving her feeling angry, confused and let down. His behaviour had led to her feeling very low. Conversely, with support from her new loving family she was now starting to enjoy life and had put all the unpleasant history with Paul behind her. The hearing with regard to Kara's adoption had been set for the 14th of December.

Paul was speechless. He felt hurt, angry and humiliated. Why were they saying these things about him? It was all so unfair. How could he possibly be accused of not trying to stay in contact? What about all the weekly letters he had sent prior to being denied an address? What about his correspondence with the schools? He looked at Ms Staines, making sure to make eye contact.

'I've just shown you undeniable evidence that clearly demonstrates this Statement of Facts to be complete nonsense. Surely you can see that?'

Ms Staines didn't answer. Instead she went on to inform him that allegations of child abuse had also been made against him. Paul felt sick as he listened to what she had to say.

'Kara alleges that when she was with you, there were times when you beat her as a form of punishment, locked her in a room, took her to see inappropriate and explicit shows and prohibited her from contacting her mum.'

Paul was absolutely horrified. Not only were these allegations totally preposterous and untrue, they tore right through his insides, hurting him so very deeply. How could this be happening? Why was Kara acting in this way? Where was she getting these ridiculous notions from?

Once he had gathered himself together, he looked Ms Staines firmly in the eyes once more.

'This Statement is based on outright lies and the associated allegations are ridiculous,' he said firmly, trying not to sound too emotional. 'Furthermore I have just presented you with concrete evidence to prove it.' He was desperately trying to hide his frustration at having to justify himself to this woman. 'I have never beaten my daughter, or anyone for that matter. Like any normal human being, I find the whole subject of abusing children totally abhorrent.'

Ms Staines sat there emotionless, urging him to continue.

'I have never, ever forced Kara to do anything she did not want to do and there is no way I would ever permit her to watch, let alone take her to, shows of the nature you appear to be implying. I am certainly not in the habit of visiting "strip-joints". Are you suggesting I took my daughter to a "strip joint"? Even if I tried, do you really think a child would be permitted to enter such an establishment? The most explicit show I took her to was "Peter Pan"! This whole thing is rubbish.'

Paul was conscious he was doing all the talking and went quiet. There was an uneasy pause in the conversation for about ten seconds. Ms Staines once again gestured for him to continue.

'With regards to locking Kara in a room, again, this is all lies. There are no locks fitted to any of the doors in the house and there never have been. It's utter nonsense. I admit I might have threatened to send Kara to her room if she was misbehaving, since I consider this an appropriate form of discipline, but this never actually happened in reality. Kara was very rarely naughty.'

'What about denying Kara phone contact with her mother?'

'This is a gross distortion of the truth. There was one Saturday afternoon when Kara came to visit with a mobile phone and she kept ringing and texting her mum every ten minutes. After about the fifth time, I did try and gently discourage her from doing this, since I wanted some quality time with her without distractions. That's all.'

Paul could not tell if Ms Staines believed him or not, or whether she was even interested in his version of events. He was too shocked to totally absorb the Statement of Facts, but he had taken in enough to know it was a fabrication. He was relieved he had brought along evidence to prove these outrageous slurs on his character were all rubbish. In particular he had copies of his communications with Kara's schools over the years. These showed beyond any doubt that he had tried his utmost to act in Kara's best interests and how he had exercised his parental rights responsibly, despite Phoenix making it difficult for him.

'Why don't you ring my parents?' he suggested. 'They'll be able to support my version of events and also vouch that these allegations are totally unfounded. Also, I know many, many people that would be prepared to act as character referees for me. They know how much I tried to ensure Kara's welfare. They know I would not carry out these deplorable acts.'

Ms Staines looked at him and nodded.

'I think this has now escalated into more than an adoption issue,' Paul continued, regaining his composure. 'Kara might need professional counselling. Why is she making these things up? If she really believes they happened, then she needs psychiatric help.'

'She has been receiving counselling,' Ms Staines informed him.

Paul was taken aback. 'Well, it doesn't seem to have been very effective,' he replied angrily. 'Why was I not involved, or at least informed about this?'

Ms Staines did not respond.

He was understandably annoyed that he had not been consulted about his own daughter's welfare. Where was the justice and common sense in this system? Why hadn't Phoenix had the decency to mention anything to him?

'I think the best course of action I can take now is to make sure that the supposed "experts" involved in making a decision about Kara's adoption, i.e. Social Services, CAFCASS and the courts, have access to all the facts, to make sure the right decisions are taken. If that means Kara is adopted by her stepfather, then so be it, as long as it is for the right reasons and not based on a catalogue of lies and false allegations.'

'If you want CAFCASS to be involved and carry out an investigation, you will need to contest the application for adoption,' replied Ms Staines.

'I'm more concerned about challenging the wisdom behind the proposed adoption than the adoption itself,' he explained. 'I think more emphasis needs to be placed on Kara's psychological wellbeing.'

Ms Staines made no comment. She looked at the clock and announced that their two-hour slot was over.

Before he left, Paul enquired as to her current opinion on the matter. She gave a rather long-winded reply, basically saying that she could not comment at this point, but all would be made available in her report.

'CAFCASS investigations invariably support the initial investigation carried out by Social Services,' she added. 'Any judge will be extremely reluctant to go against the joint recommendation of Social Services and CAFCASS, this being virtually unheard of.'

Paul considered she was very confident in her own power and ability, to the point of arrogance.

Although he was deeply hurt and confused by the allegations made against him, he wasn't overly concerned at this point with respect to the adoption. He was naively confident that Social Services and CAFCASS (assuming CAFCASS were even required) would easily be able to see how Kara had been poisoned against him in support of Phoenix's perverse intention to eliminate him from their lives. Without his consent, the adoption could not go ahead. Anyone could see these ridiculous allegations of child abuse had been deviously concocted in an attempt to do away with the need for his consent. All the evidence was on his side, whereas Phoenix had none, simply hearsay. Of more concern to him at this stage was Kara's state of mind.

Paul drove straight from his meeting with Ms Staines to his parents' house, still with that horrible sick feeling in his stomach. He informed them of what had happened and they too were shocked. They were obviously distressed and fully supported his proposed course of action. It was essential that the supposed 'experts' had access to the truth before making any decision.

'Kara has probably backed herself into a corner with all these stories,' his mum added. 'She may be frightened of the consequences if the truth comes out. Being a fifteen-year-old girl, there's also the added embarrassment of losing face.'

Whatever the reason, they all ultimately felt sorry for Kara. They believed she had been, and was continuing to be, used by Phoenix for her own selfish desires. Unfortunately Kara was not mature enough or sufficiently experienced in life to recognise this yet.

That evening Paul spoke with Jenna, his brother and his sister-in-law and they were also fully supportive of his proposed actions. They shared the opinion that trained counsellors and social workers should easily be able to see through the tissue of lies and get to the heart of the real matter. They agreed the issue of adoption was not so relevant now. What was of more concern was Kara's psychological welfare.

Paul made an entry in his journal that evening. Part of it read:

15 November

It appears that all the hatred is now emanating from Kara and not Phoenix. My guess is that the seeds of poison were wickedly planted when Kara was younger and now she is wilfully removing me and my family from her life, while the perpetrator watches on. The vengeful baton has been successfully handed over. I find it despicable that Phoenix can stand by and let Kara do this to herself. It should be seen as a criminal offence. Has she no moral compass?

The following evening, Jenna rang Paul's mum to let her know that she could understand what she must be going through. Jenna had witnessed her own mother in tears over the breakdown of family relationships. Jenna assured Paul's mum that she would be fully supporting Paul every step of the way. His mum, although still upset over the whole situation, was very grateful to Jenna. Paul's father then came to the phone and told Jenna that the social worker (Ms Staines) had telephoned him that afternoon. At this point Jenna called Paul to the phone and suggested he talk with his dad.

'How are you doing?' asked his father.

'My head's still spinning with all this, but I guess I'm coping okay,' he replied.

Paul's father relayed the gist of his phone call with Ms Staines.

'The conversation opened with Ms Staines checking that I was aware of all the implications of adoption and how if it went ahead, the family would irreversibly lose all legal ties with Kara. She asked for my views on the matter.'

'Go on,' said Paul.

'I let her know how much the family still loved Kara and, despite current circumstances, would never want to lose contact with her. I explained how upset you and the whole family have been over these latest developments and how utterly ridiculous we consider these allegations. I let her know that ever since I had known Phoenix, I had always been a little concerned with regard to her mental state, and I gave her some examples of how she used to mistreat your mother and me. I told her about the time you and Kara came to visit and Kara unexpectedly asked if she could come on holiday with us. Do you remember? She must have been about six at the time.'

'How could I forget?' Paul replied.

Together they recalled how his father had responded to Kara's request. 'Of course, if that's what you want, we'd love you to join us. Ask your mum to contact me and we can arrange it.' Once Kara had returned home, Phoenix had immediately telephoned Paul's father, viciously ranting and raving, 'How dare you agree to such requests. How dare you influence Kara in this way.' Despite the volume of Phoenix's rant, Paul's father could clearly hear Kara crying in the background.

Bringing back that recollection disturbed them both. Paul wondered how many other times Kara may have been harshly interrogated after returning from a visit to see him and his family. Could it be that Kara had become reluctant to stay with him for fear of the interrogation she would get when back home with her mother?

'I asked the social worker if she was acting independently,' continued Paul's father. 'She gave me the impression she was and then she went into more detail about these wretched allegations. Apparently eighteen months ago, Phoenix and Kara went to Social Services and the police to report these alleged offences.'

'How come I knew nothing of this?' interjected Paul. 'Why didn't the social worker tell me about this?'

'I don't know. Apparently neither the police nor Social Services took the allegations seriously. Unsurprisingly there was no supporting evidence, and secondly they were purported to have happened such a long time ago.'

152

'Even if they were true, why didn't Phoenix report them to the police when they were alleged to have happened, all those years ago?' asked Paul.

'I challenged the social worker with that same question, but she never gave me a response to that one,' his father replied. 'However, she did suggest it would be a good idea for you to prepare your own Statement of Facts to defend yourself. That was essentially the end of the call. I got the impression that the social worker believes your version of events, but couldn't come straight out and say it. I don't think you have anything to worry about, but it's probably worth preparing a statement as suggested, in case it's required.'

Paul agreed and thanked his father for the update.

Paul and his family were astonished that things had sunk to these new depths, fuelling their concerns over Phoenix's and Kara's psychological wellbeing. All Paul's family continually told him not to worry, assuring him that the truth would quickly come out in the court hearing, but he was back to having sleepless nights again. He used this time to question how things had turned out so terribly and how he could best address the situation. He wondered how Kara was coping. Was she having sleepless nights too? Was she experiencing levels of anguish like him? Why couldn't they make up for both their sakes? Was Phoenix purposely standing in the way?

Once again his journal proved invaluable, not only to look up previous entries, but to record all the thoughts going through his mind, helping him plan what to do next. What was it that was really troubling Kara? She was obviously distressed about something and she appeared to be taking it out on him and his family. Again he asked himself that same question: why had Phoenix allowed this to happen? He knew from previous conversations with her that she seriously believed she had never done anything wrong. She was convinced she had played no part in their marriage break-up. Had she convinced herself he was some sort of monster to help her cope with the loss of his love? Could she not accept that he simply did not love her any more? Was this her way of coping with rejection? Could this explain some of the outlandish allegations she had made against her previous boyfriends when those relationships had gone sour? Were those allegations false as well? Was he simply a target or scapegoat for her frustrations with all men?

The day before the hearing, Ms Staines telephoned Paul to let him know she was going to recommend the adoption go ahead. He could not believe what he was hearing.

'Why?' he asked in exasperation.

'I am convinced Kara is fully aware of the implications of adoption and she is adamant it is what she wants. I have questioned her on more than one occasion about the allegations she has made against you and she repeatedly says they happened. As a consequence, I am going to recommend adoption, basing my recommendation on allegations of child abuse.'

Paul felt helpless. Why was a child's word being taken over his, with no supporting evidence whatsoever? To him it was painfully obvious that the allegations had been concocted so the court could simply dispense with his consent. All the evidence was on his side. Why couldn't this social worker see it?

'But surely you can see these allegations are not true? Why aren't you putting more effort into getting to the bottom of what is really troubling Kara?'

'We could try, but we may never get to the bottom of it,' she replied.

Paul felt drained. How could a social worker get away with this? His confidence in her ability had taken a major blow.

'Can I see a copy of your report?' he asked.

'There's not enough time now and I don't think you are allowed access anyway,' she replied. She then explained how busy she was and that was essentially the end of the call.

Paul was shocked and felt extremely let down. Why had she left this call so late, just one day before the hearing? For something as important as this, why couldn't she have written something in a letter or even e-mailed him? What if he had been out? He decided it was imperative he have his own Statement of Facts ready for the following day in court, meaning another sleepless night. Although the social worker had afforded him precious little time to prepare, he recognised if he did nothing the court would get a very one-sided version of events. He started working on his material immediately after the call.

Later that afternoon, Paul and Jenna drove to his brother's house where they stayed the night. It was more convenient to stay there, since he and his family lived closer to the courthouse and they did not want to be late for the hearing as a result of getting caught up in traffic. As evening approached, they went out for a meal together. They tried to keep the mood as buoyant as possible, but the injustice of what was happening hung over them like a black cloud, dominating their conversation. Regardless, they remained confident that the court would see through the weaknesses of the social worker's investigation and ultimately common sense would prevail.

On the 14th of December, Paul and Jenna set off on their journey to the court building to attend the directional hearing for Kara's proposed adoption. They were joined there by his parents, who had come along to give moral support. They were all predictably early, about 45 minutes. None of them had been in a courthouse before, so this was a new experience for them all. They went in through the front doors and were immediately subjected to a routine search procedure, similar to that of an airport security point. Once they had the all-clear, they were free to move around the building. There was not much in the way of facilities, just a small basic cafeteria area, some toilets and a vending machine. That was about it. Whilst they were drinking substandard-quality cups of coffee from the machine, Paul realised he had left some paperwork in the car which he required. As he was walking back to the courthouse from the car park, his eye caught the image of someone waving at him from their car. It was Phoenix, with a big smile on her face. He could not believe her audacity and it made him feel sick. She appeared to have no idea of what he and his family were going through. He slightly raised his hand to acknowledge her as a reflex action, but that was all he could muster before hurriedly making his way back into the courthouse.

They all had to wait outside the allocated courtroom for an additional uncomfortable 30 minutes, since the judge was late. During this time, Ms Staines greeted Paul and briefly acknowledged his father when Paul introduced them to each other. She then went to stand with Phoenix and Ross, spending the rest of her time chatting with them. Although Paul and his family were not familiar with court proceedings, they considered her conduct most unprofessional if she was truly independent. When he and his father had spoken to her separately a few weeks previously, she had led them to believe she was independent and impartial.

When the judge finally arrived, those allowed were ushered into the courtroom. Six people were present: Phoenix, Ross, Ms Staines, Paul, the judge and a scribe. Paul felt very much alone. There was no one allowed in the room to support him. The judge opened the proceedings and then addressed Paul.

'Mr Nelson, it is my understanding that you wish to contest this application for adoption. That being the case, I must point out that if you continue along this route, you are facing an uphill battle that you are most likely to lose. I would urge you to reconsider, particularly bearing in mind Kara is a fifteen-year-old girl. If you let things take their natural course, it is most likely you will be the best of friends again in a few years' time. It will be in everyone's interests to get this sorted as soon as possible. The courts are very busy places and we would not want a case like this to drag on.'

Paul was taken aback by the judge's comments and started to feel everything was against him right from the start.

'I feel I have no choice but to contest the adoption,' Paul replied. 'A number of serious allegations have been made against me that are all groundless and I am worried that whatever is truly troubling Kara is being overlooked. I am concerned my daughter might need psychiatric help.'

The judge looked at Paul with disdain. 'I am certainly not going to recommend Kara sees a psychiatrist and I am surprised you even mention it.'

At this point, however, things took a major turn.

Ms Staines addressed the judge. 'Your Honour, Kara is already seeing a psychiatrist.'

The judge looked markedly surprised and irritated that he had not been made aware of this information. This news also came as a surprise to Paul. He was aware that Kara had been seeing a counsellor, but not a psychiatrist! If she was suffering from some mental illness, could that explain why she was making up these allegations?

Paul then addressed the judge, taking Ms Staines's example, referring to him as 'Your Honour'.

'Your Honour, I've only been made aware verbally of allegations made against me. I've not seen anything actually written down. I'm not sure exactly what I am being accused of, but I do consider something is seriously troubling Kara that we need to get to the bottom of.'

The judge now showed more empathy with Paul's position and turned to Ms Staines.

'Has Mr Nelson seen a copy of your report?' he asked in a rather berating manner.

Ms Staines looked uneasy. 'I telephoned Mr Nelson yesterday to inform him that since Kara has made allegations of child abuse against him, I was going to recommend adoption. I considered this sufficient information for Mr Nelson. I did not consider he would need a copy of the report or a full breakdown of the allegations made.'

The judge turned to Paul, urging him for a response.

'Yes, I can confirm we had a five-minute call. Ms Staines informed me she would be supporting the proposed adoption, based on allegations of abuse. When I asked her if I could have a copy of the report, she gave me some vague response about not being allowed access. That was the end of the call.'

The judge then noted that he himself did not have a copy of the correct report in front of him and consequently appeared even more put out. He asked for a copy immediately, then turned to face Paul.

'Would you be prepared to read the report over the next two

hours, then give your consent to the adoption?' He said it in such a manner as to imply he was doing Paul a favour.

Paul was dumbstruck and did not say anything. The judge could tell from his body language that Paul was extremely uncomfortable with this request.

'It would be preferable to resolve this case as quickly as possible,' the judge continued. 'I would encourage you to take a break from the hearing and read the report. Then you can give your consent to the adoption before lunchtime.' Once again he was acting as if he was doing Paul a good turn.

Paul's mind was racing. How did the judge expect him to make such an important decision in two hours? What about the views of his family? This could affect their whole lives. He concentrated hard on regaining his power of speech.

'No, I'm not happy to do this. I would like time to properly digest the contents of the report.'

The judge tried one last time to dissuade Paul from this line of action. He repeated how overworked the courts were and how it would be in everyone's interests if they could come to a conclusion that day, otherwise another hearing would be required.

Paul felt the judge had already made his mind up that the adoption was going ahead regardless. He stood his ground, however.

'I'm not happy to give my consent today, without consulting my family. I'd also been given the impression that today was simply a directional hearing and a full and independent investigation was going to be carried out by CAFCASS before any decisions were made.'

This time the judge accepted Paul's point of view. He briefly made reference to Paul's human rights and then arranged for a further hearing to be held in four months' time. This would follow a full CAFCASS investigation.

'CAFCASS will leave no stone unturned,' remarked the judge, looking pointedly at Paul.

Paul was delighted and expressed his gratitude. He now had some assurance that a suitably rigorous investigation would be conducted and CAFCASS would get to the root of what was actually troubling Kara.

The judge ordered that the CAFCASS report be made available to the court, with a copy sent to Paul by March 15th, thus allowing him at least three weeks to provide his responses prior to the second hearing, arranged for the beginning of April. Before ending the proceedings, the judge turned to Ms Staines.

'Make sure Mr Nelson gets to see a copy of your report immediately after this hearing.'

Ms Staines initially provided some resistance.

'Your Honour, I believe some of the information in the report is personal and it would be better if not shared.'

The judge was clearly not sympathetic to her view at all. He turned to face Ross and Phoenix.

'Have you any objection to Mr Nelson having a copy of this report?' he asked pointedly, clearly pressing for the response, 'No objection'. Ross and Phoenix had not said a word throughout the whole hearing up to this point.

'I've no objection,' replied Ross. Phoenix on the other hand looked very rattled. The judge pushed her for a response.

'No, I suppose not,' she replied reluctantly.

As the judge brought the hearing to a close, Paul mentioned he had prepared his own Statement of Facts, together with supporting evidence. The judge gladly received these items and requested he also make them available to Ms Staines immediately afterwards, who in turn would disseminate to all relevant parties.

That was essentially the end of the hearing.

On leaving the courtroom, Paul was relieved to see Jenna and his parents outside and he smiled wearily in their direction. The hearing had been a very solitary experience. It had felt like him against all the rest. It had all been so very matter-of-fact and devoid of feeling. Outside the courtroom, it was entirely different. Here he had support, whilst Phoenix and Ross noticeably had no one present from their respective families. Was this because their families did not agree with what they were doing?

Perhaps their families wanted to play no part in this debacle. His mum and Jenna both noticed that Ross and Phoenix came out of the courtroom separately and Phoenix had a face like thunder. From her body language, it was obvious the court proceedings had not gone as she had anticipated.

Before Paul left the courthouse, a copy of the 'Staines' report was tracked down and handed to him.

Paul, Jenna and his parents drove to a restaurant for lunch. During the journey he gave an account of the morning's events. They agreed it sounded as if things had gone reasonably well once the judge had heard what he had to say.

Whilst waiting for their food, Paul opened the copy of the report that had been provided to him. After reading a couple of paragraphs to himself, he once again was horror-struck and the awful sick feeling in the pit of his stomach returned. It was full of gross inaccuracies and the full extent of the allegations was unveiled. He fretfully read out some extracts to Jenna and his parents. They were equally horrified.

'It's reported here that I beat Kara with a stick when she was on holiday with us as a means of disciplining her. When she visited, it alleges I took her to inappropriate establishments and made her watch "explicit shows". How can they say such things? It also says that during her visits I locked her in her bedroom and denied her any phone contact with her mother.' As he read on, things got even worse. He flicked the pages to the concluding parts of the report. 'It's not even reporting these despicable acts as allegations now, but is reporting them as if they actually happened! How can they get away with this? It's all rubbish. Surely this is libel!'

All of them felt quite sickened and had lost their appetites. He turned to another section of the report that presented Phoenix's views. He was getting really angry now. He showed this section of the report to Jenna and his parents. Nauseating statements had been provided by Phoenix and Ross, projecting themselves as angels. They described each other as dazzling, beautiful, delightful, playful, warm, family-focused people. A vision of 'the Waltons on Ecstasy' came to mind. Phoenix had also made some ridiculously boastful claims about her previous employment history, grossly exaggerating her qualifications and positions of responsibility.

In contrast, all sorts of fabricated and deprecating nonsense had been reported about Paul and his family, with facts intentionally twisted to make him look as bad as possible. He had been portrayed by Phoenix as some work-shy, deadbeat father who never loved or cared for his own daughter and never had any time for children. The whole thing was very biased against him and portrayed him as some sort of child-hating ogre. Phoenix had denied he had sent regular letters to Kara, claiming she had only ever received a couple of cards and these had upset Kara. Even Phoenix's mother had taken the opportunity of putting the boot in, fully supporting the adoption proposal. Very little of what had been discussed during his interview in support of his good character had been included.

When he turned to the concluding sections, he read aloud how Ms Staines was recommending there be no future contact between him and Kara whatsoever, not even birthday or Christmas cards, for fear of causing her further distress.

'What distress?' he exclaimed in exasperation. 'It's all lies. This is outrageous!'

The report went on to say that if Kara should change her mind in the future and decide she wanted contact, it would have to be be under the supervision of a third party to guarantee Kara's safety.

'How utterly ludicrous! They've made me out to be some sort of dangerous criminal. How can they get away with this dreadful tripe? They've made it even harder now for me to try and repair my relationship with Kara. They've compounded the damage. There must be something I can do about this. There must be somewhere I can protest or complain.'

Understandably Paul and his family were deeply hurt, angry and felt totally 'stitched up'. Why were Social Services allowing the 'Tuckers' to get away with this garbage? If anything, they were supporting it. How could someone in Ms Staines's position not see she was being lied to? Why had she ignored his evidence? He had shown her copies of over fifty letters he had sent Kara. Surely someone of Ms Staines's apparent status should be a better judge of character? He knew social workers were not well paid and he was also aware of the expression, 'Pay peanuts, get monkeys'. Had he now had- first-hand experience?

'Look at this,' he pointed out. 'She has the outright impudence to write, "Although Paul now knows Kara's address, to his credit he has not used it to cause trouble". What planet is she from? I have never been involved in trouble of that sort in my life and she could have easily confirmed this, had she bothered to check. She's basing her opinions of me on a two-hour interview, where she wasted a large amount of that time asking irrelevant questions about the colour of my eyes and what infant school I attended! She didn't even bother to interview any of you in person, but simply relied on a short phone conversation with you,' he remarked, looking at his father. 'Is she so incapable of distinguishing fact from fiction? It looks like she has been totally fooled by the Tuckers, or I wonder if there is something more sinister and underhand going on? Perhaps she's received a back-hander of some sort, possibly monetary? Is she a friend of the Tucker family? Perhaps Ross or Phoenix have done her a few favours and this is her way of compensating them.'

When Paul returned home, he e-mailed his Statement of Facts plus the supporting evidence to Ms Staines as had been agreed with the judge. It included a history of how he and his family had been effectively forced out of Kara's life against their wishes by Phoenix. It described how he and his family still loved and cared for her and wanted to start building bridges, not destroy them further. It described his concerns that Kara must be deeply troubled in some way and this was manifesting itself as unfounded resentment against him and his family. In conclusion, he requested the court get to the root cause of Kara's unhappiness before considering the adoption request. Adoption at this stage would just be wallpapering over the cracks and likely storing up more problems for the future. It was simply substituting one emotional problem with another.

He also expressed his acute dissatisfaction at the content of Ms Staines's report, highlighting that it contained a significant number of serious factual inaccuracies and he considered it extremely biased against him. He was particularly concerned that the allegations Kara had made against him were repeatedly reported as if they had actually happened.

Was Ms Staines intentionally trying to mislead the reader?

Paul got a reply from Ms Staines the following day, thanking him for his Statement of Facts and apologising that he found her report one-sided. Since it had been issued, however, it would not be amended. She recommended that he wait until he had seen the impending CAFCASS report before taking it further.

Paul groaned inwardly. Just what he needed. Another woman telling him what to do! Considering the gravity of the situation, he did not consider this response good enough and replied to Ms Staines telling her so. He informed her that he would be taking legal advice and would be writing to the court in due course. He would copy her in on his correspondence.

In the meantime, Paul re-read the report over and over again. He tried looking at it from different angles, but whichever angle he came from, it was an appalling piece of work as far as he was concerned, full of lies and inaccuracies, totally misleading the reader. Phoenix had been portrayed as some sort of angelic superwoman, Ross as a child-loving hero and Kara as a child saved from the edge of madness, caused by her biological father's neglect and abuse. In contrast, Paul had been portrayed as an out-of-work layabout who had never wanted children and had no time for his own daughter. He could not really comment on the description of Ross, for he had only met him once, but the description of Phoenix was truly farcical.

Paul was becoming increasingly of the opinion that Kara's adoption had been Phoenix's plan all along. The contents of the report had been fabricated in order to support the adoption recommendation. Ross came across as a simple pawn in Phoenix's game. On the plus side (if there was one), the template design of the report meant Ms Staines had included some noteworthy and relevant information to which he had not previously had access. Amongst other useful snippets, it included histories of employment, personal relationships and medical details. At least he now had some information to help him work out what was really going on. No wonder Phoenix had not wanted him to see a copy of this report.

Since the court hearing, Paul had hardly slept. He knew the same went for Jenna and his parents. His brother and sister-in-law were also keeping up to date with the latest news and they all remained in a state of semi-shock and dismay. Thoughts constantly went round and round in his head as to how this situation continually managed to degenerate.

He felt the psychiatrist's account within the Staines report needed further investigation. It described how following a referral from Kara's GP, the psychiatrist had diagnosed Kara with a serious depressive disorder. Kara had required medication ever since. It went on to say that correspondence received from her biological father a couple of years back was thought to have catalysed the condition. The condition had been aggravated by the fact that her father had never bothered to see her from a young age and in the last six years had cut her off completely. The very few times she had seen him when she was younger were very frightening for her.

Paul knew this was complete and utter rubbish, but was at a loss as to what he could do about it. He had been given no opportunity whatsoever to challenge any of the psychiatrist's statements or provide his version of events.

The psychiatrist concluded her account by stating, 'In light of these circumstances, I consider the proposed adoption would be a very positive step for Kara.'

Paul went back through his journal and reviewed the correspondence he had mailed to Kara over the last three years. This was not a long task. He had only sent birthday and Christmas cards and these had been via Phoenix's parents, since he had been refused a direct contact address for a number of years. One particular item he had sent around this time was a card with a photograph of Kara when she was younger, sitting at a table with all his family, blowing out the candles on her birthday cake. She had a beaming smile over her face and the family were looking on lovingly. Could this be the correspondence they were referring to? Was it possible that Kara's depressive disorder was emanating from feelings of guilt? Perhaps she felt she had unfairly disowned her natural family. What was this serious depressive disorder exactly? He had mixed feelings about the diagnosis. Was it genuine, or something faked to help build the case for adoption? He did not wish his daughter to have mental health issues, but on the other hand, perhaps it could explain some of her irrational behaviour and if diagnosed early enough, could hopefully be successfully treated. Could she be suffering from some sort of delusion-causing illness? Could such delusion-causing disorders be the cause of her making up these allegations? Did she think this alleged abuse had really happened? Originally he had thought Kara's behaviour was out of spite, fuelled by early-age poisoning from her mother, but perhaps it was more accurate that she was suffering from delusions of persecution caused by some sort of mental disorder. Perhaps it was both. Had the poisoning of Kara's mind sparked the mental illness? It was already common knowledge that children suffered when in the middle of a parental battle. He remembered the wise words of Kara's school head of year a few years back when he had remarked, 'I am concerned problems are being stored up for the future.'

Closer scrutiny of the Staines report led to other significant revelations. It suggested a mental health issue running through Phoenix's family. Could this confirm his long-term suspicions that Phoenix was not the 'full ticket'? Should he ask for an independent psychiatric investigation to be carried out on Phoenix?

Paul concluded Ms Staines and the psychiatrist, who were both recommending adoption, had clearly had the wool pulled over their eyes and this had influenced their judgement. From the correspondence he had seen, it appeared he had been unfairly stereotyped and neither of them had taken the time to diligently find out the truth and get to the root of what was really troubling Kara. He considered it unfortunately too common in a number of professions these days. People were too busy to give the job their full attention, with priority being given to covering their own arse, rather than doing a thorough job in the interests of all. Another explanation could be that they were acquaintances of Phoenix and this was all one big scam. He considered this latter explanation a little far-fetched and surreal, but then again, so was this whole adoption scenario.

After days and days of considerable thought, Paul continued to believe the proposed adoption was not in Kara's best interests. He would however be prepared to compromise and back off until there was an improvement in her condition, assuming this concurred with expert medical opinion. Would CAFCASS go along with these sentiments? Bearing in mind Kara's reported mental illness, he was now of the opinion that the adoption should now not be so much about 'what Kara wants', but more about 'what Kara needs'. He was becoming increasingly concerned for her welfare and mental health. He wondered if a follow-up psychiatric investigation should be carried out, where he could make it clear that no actual abuse of Kara had taken place. Surely a psychiatrist needs to be aware that these are just unfounded allegations being made by Kara, he pondered. If the psychiatrist had been aware of his version of events at the time of assessment, would she have reached the same diagnosis? Would other avenues of explanation have been explored? Would she still be recommending the proposed adoption? Unfortunately the psychiatrist only had Kara's and Phoenix's version of events to go on.

Paul thought about all the evidence he could provide to CAFCASS to ensure the best decisions were made for Kara and her welfare. There were many witnesses who could corroborate his version of events. He was becoming increasingly confident that the truth would come out and common sense would ultimately prevail. He needed to make it clear that any distress caused to Kara was categorically not due to the alleged abuse by him. In fact, her mental condition had deteriorated since having less contact with him. He now needed to make sure all her needs were properly met and as always, he was committed to giving his full support.

He continued to make entries in his journal, recording his feelings and his thoughts.

16 December

I have spent many sleepless nights trying to fathom what is spurring Kara to continue on this path of adoption. I am sure something must be seriously troubling her or she has been brainwashed. The following possibilities continue to go round in my head:

- *She is jealous of her stepbrothers and resents the fact that she is not the centre of attention any more.*
- *She is worried about her inheritance rights, in that she may lose out to her stepbrothers.*
- *She misguidedly sees this as a gift to her stepfather.*
- *She feels a lack of security in her current family set-up. She may feel her stepfather will not look after her if Phoenix dies, or perhaps his family would disown her should something happen to him and Phoenix.*
- *She has been denied a good relationship with me by Phoenix and this has created a void in her life. Unfortunately she is too young to recognise this yet and as a consequence cannot start to address it constructively.*
- *She has a genuine delusion-causing mental illness.*

With respect to the allegations, I wonder if she made them when she was younger and dreamt them from a wild imagination. It could be she feels she cannot now undo them for fear of losing face.

Perhaps she has been so poisoned against me that she actually believes all the lies of child abuse. Could the abuse have been perpetrated by a previous boyfriend of her mother's and she (or they) is now taking it out on me?

Would she/they make them up solely for the purpose of getting 'what she/they want', i.e. adoption, effectively eliminating me from their lives?

I think the situation is now far too big for me to handle and I need the help of a solicitor.

That afternoon Paul made some initial enquiries, researching various solicitors' firms on the internet to help take matters forward. He conceded he needed expert legal advice to avoid getting truly 'stitched up'. He found the list of local solicitors given to him by the Citizens Advice Bureau back in March that year.

This whole state of affairs obviously continued to take its emotional toll. Paul, Jenna and his family were now living this nightmare 24/7. Paul was heartbroken, frustrated and angry at the same time. He was heartbroken that his daughter had mental health issues and refused to acknowledge him. He was frustrated at the lack of help he was getting from authorities such as Social Services and he was extremely angry with Phoenix for having let things get this far without consulting him.

Fortunately there were also positives to help divert attention from all the nastiness. He and Jenna had fantastically supportive families around them and they shared a wonderful network of friends. This was perfectly exemplified on the Saturday before Christmas when they invited their younger godchildren (including the triplets who were now three) over to see Santa. Paul and Jenna had decorated their house to look like Santa's grotto with lots of fairy lights and decorations. They also invited friends and family over, who dressed up as Santa's elves, fairies and general helpers. The children were mesmerised and loved every bit of it. Then in walked Father Christmas (it was in fact Paul's brother) and they were totally blown away. It was a lovely, magical afternoon that all would treasure. It didn't totally take Paul's mind off all the horrible things he and Jenna were having to endure, but it did provide some very welcome relief.

Little did they know that things were about to get a lot, lot worse.

Chapter 11

Court matters (2)

- ✧ Paul responds to the Staines Social Services (SS) report
- ✧ Paul gets a solicitor
- ✧ The deposition
- ✧ Gathering further evidence
- ✧ Dealings with Children and Family Court Advisory and Support Service (CAFCASS)
- ✧ Introduction to False Allegations Support Organisation (FASO)
- ✧ Involving a barrister
- ✧ The second hearing

On the Monday of the week running up to Christmas, Paul sent a letter (Recorded Delivery) to the court, candidly expressing his acute dissatisfaction with Ms Staines's report. He stated his frustration with regard to the large number of factual inaccuracies and how he considered it extremely biased against him. There appeared no impartiality and he was not being treated fairly. He detailed his concern for the psychological welfare of his daughter and whether the delay in the issue of the report could have put her mental health at risk. He made it clear that he would provide his support wherever required to help expedite any treatment she might need.

He also e-mailed a copy of this letter to Ms Staines and let her know he had no objection to her forwarding it on to the relevant parties. Why should he object? He had nothing to hide.

Whilst out in town that same day Christmas shopping, Paul bumped into one of his long-term friends, one he had stayed with for some months following his separation from Phoenix. They had not seen each other for some time, so they had plenty of news to share. Paul gave him an update on the situation with

Kara. His friend listened in utter disbelief. Paul could see the look of shock and horror on his face.

'No, no, no. This is appalling,' his friend kept repeating. This was a reaction with which Paul was unfortunately getting very familiar when broaching this subject. 'Why didn't you phone me?' asked his friend, once he had taken it all in.

'I didn't want to bother you with my troubles,' replied Paul. 'I thought this was something I could handle on my own.'

'With all due respect, you can't deal with this on your own. I knew things were not good between you and Phoenix, but I never thought things would sink to this level. There appears to be something far more sinister going on here. It's just not normal. No father should ever have to go through this.'

'I'm thinking of getting a solicitor involved.'

'I really think you should, as a matter of urgency,' his friend replied. 'I think all your troubles could easily stem from Kara having been poisoned against you.' Interestingly, his friend had an eight-year-old daughter of his own. 'I know how easy it would be for me to convince my own daughter to hate her mother in less than a year if I were so wickedly inclined,' he continued. 'Children can be so impressionable during their formative years.'

Paul appreciated his friend's advice. This particular friend had provided him with so much valuable support in the past concerning his problems with access to Kara. He had known Phoenix ever since she and Paul had first met, but he never really took to her much. Phoenix had made it clear she did not like him, but then again she didn't like any of Paul's friends (or family for that matter). After they were married, Paul felt she didn't like him that much either.

The following morning, Paul got up at 6am. He got dressed and walked into town with the list of local solicitors the Citizens Advice Bureau had given him. It was a typical December morning, cold, dark and wet, which pretty much reflected his mood. The early morning street cleaners and shopkeepers were going about their daily business, getting set up for the day. He had skipped breakfast. He had not been able to stomach food recently. This had gone on for the last few days. He had been relying on coffee as his main sustenance and this morning was no different.

Once in the centre of town, he happened to look up and noticed a solicitor's office window on the top floor of an old three-storey Victorian building. The amber glow of the street light was reflected in the window, allowing him to read the text written on it. It advertised that the solicitor dealt in 'Family Law'. This particular solicitor was not on his list, but he noticed the solid wooden front door to the building was open, so he went in anyway. He walked up a long, narrow wooden staircase to the first floor. He noted the empty store room with a few discarded cardboard boxes lying around on the floor. It was still early morning and not yet fully light, so it all felt a bit spooky. He followed the signs up the next flight of stairs to the solicitor's office. Once at the top he crossed the small landing and went through a doorway. He could see three or four rooms leading off a narrow passageway. It was eerily quiet.

'Who are you?' enquired a tall gentleman suddenly in a loud booming voice. The man came out from one of the rooms, walking towards him.

Paul was startled and turned to face him.

'I'm looking for a solicitor well versed in family law to represent me for a court case,' he explained rapidly.

'What, this afternoon?' asked the gentleman.

This made Paul smile. He wondered what sort of clients this man was used to dealing with.

'No, not this afternoon, but in about three months' time,' he replied.

The gentleman introduced himself as Ashley and led Paul into a meeting room.

Paul spent the next fifteen minutes relaying his dreadful tale. He felt embarrassed at having to relate his story to a stranger, but was hopeful it would be worth his while. He knew he could not let his desperate situation go on any longer. During this time, Ashley mainly listened, with very few interjections. He then asked some very direct and outright questions.

'Did you do any of these things you are being accused of?'

'Absolutely not,' replied Paul, shaking his head.

'Is there a possibility that these allegations could be elevated to something more serious, for example sexual abuse?'

'I sincerely hope not.' Paul was a little shocked that he had even asked the question.

The meeting went on for another fifteen minutes and Paul felt absolutely drained by the end. He felt like he had been through some sort of war-type interrogation, even though it had been only short-lived.

Ashley sat back and smiled. 'I genuinely believe you are innocent,' he remarked. 'I have been trained in the art of interrogation techniques and I am a recognised expert in interpreting body language. I'd be happy to represent you. I believe you have a very strong case for retaining your parental rights. My fees would be between £3000 and £5000, but you should get quotes from other solicitors before making a decision.'

Paul thanked him for his time and agreed he would do as Ashley had suggested.

'Cheers, mate,' Ashley said as Paul walked out the door.

As Paul walked back down the narrow staircase, he reflected on what had happened. Despite having been given the third degree by Ashley, he couldn't help liking him and felt he had a lot to offer. He had certainly shown a good understanding of his situation in the limited time they had spent together. He was perhaps a little unconventional for a solicitor, but that appealed to Paul. He was certainly not the 'stuffy' type he had been dreading. Paul considered him someone who would be prepared to think outside the box and go the extra mile should it be required. There was something that told him he had already found the solicitor he wanted, but he felt obliged to investigate others all the same.

Paul spent the rest of the morning visiting various other solicitors. He was confronted with a variety of responses. Some were very stuffy, which turned him off straight away. Others wanted to see full written documentation before they were prepared to even consider him. The remainder remarked that they were far too busy to see him now and requested he come back later. One did agree to represent him and suggested he book a preliminary appointment for sometime in mid-January.

Paul took offence at their apparent lack of urgency, particularly bearing in mind how grave he considered his circumstances. Those he did speak to did not appear to show a good understanding of his predicament and just upset him further. He got the impression that some were not taking him seriously, maybe even believing he had actually perpetrated the horrible acts of which he was being accused. He felt that none of these individuals were really interested in representing his case, nor had they met the standards he expected.

It had been an emotionally exhausting morning having to explain his painful predicament a number of times, over and over again. At least he had made one decision. He went back to see Ashley around lunchtime and they agreed there and then that Ashley would represent him. They arranged to meet again on the 23rd of December at 4pm, when they would discuss it in more detail and finalise terms and conditions.

When Paul returned home he discussed his morning's events with Jenna. She was interested to hear about Ashley and was keen to meet him. She offered to accompany Paul to their arranged meeting. Paul was really happy about this, for he considered Jenna an invariably good judge of character and he valued her opinion highly. She could help confirm that Ashley was the right man for the job.

The 23rd of December was a turning point for Paul. Up until that point he had given in to all Phoenix's requests, but now he was going to employ the services of a solicitor and take a much firmer stance.

There had been a heavy snowfall the previous evening making driving conditions treacherous. He telephoned Ashley.

'Should we still meet?' asked Paul.

'I'm not in the office currently, but I am still hoping to get there by 4pm. I'm happy to brave it if you are,' replied Ashley.

'OK, see you soon.' Once again Paul was impressed that Ashley was prepared to put himself out.

Paul and Jenna wrapped up in their warmest coats and

walked into town carrying his laptop. Although it was snowing, they were not full of Christmas spirit, which was unusual for them. They arrived at Ashley's offices at 4pm, but the building was locked up. They pondered over what they should do next. The snow was easing off a little and although it was no longer daylight, it was not dark. The street lamps and the festive Christmas lights were reflecting off the snow, lightening their mood a little. They waited for five more minutes and then Ashley arrived, apologetic with a beaming smile. He opened the wooden front door to the old building and they all made their way up the cold narrow staircase to the second floor. Ashley turned on all the portable electric heaters.

'Coffee?' he offered.

'Yes, please,' replied Jenna and Paul appreciatively.

'I'll make it,' said Jenna, trying to be helpful. She went into the small kitchenette area. There were seven different types of coffee, but no milk. She walked back in to the office. 'I don't think you have any milk,' she said in her soft voice. 'I'll go to the shops and get some for you.'

By the time she returned, the office area had warmed up and Paul had started to convey his sorry tale of woe in great detail. He continued for the next four hours, helped by Jenna who would interject every now and then, filling in details he had inadvertently left out. He stressed how much he felt he had been kept in the dark over the years with respect to Kara's welfare and how he considered his current predicament could have been purposely manufactured by others with wicked intent. Ashley appeared genuinely appalled at the way Paul had been treated, but not overly shocked.

'I have experienced this type of behaviour from bitter, vengeful women before,' he remarked. He put it to Paul that perhaps he had been far too soft with Phoenix over the years.

Paul gave Ashley all the evidence he had collected supporting his account, including an electronic copy of his journal. They agreed to build a case to exonerate Paul's name and ultimately contest the adoption application. Paul made it clear that he was not out to destroy Phoenix, but he did need to be vindicated of the allegations made against him and was adamant that people should know the truth. They shared the view that once the truth was out, there was absolutely no reason why he should have his parental rights and responsibilities revoked.

'It's pretty clear to me that Phoenix has been totally ineffectual in ensuring Kara maintained a good relationship with you. If anything, it should be her that is accused of child abuse, not you,' said Ashley.

Paul went on to explain how he still felt responsible for Kara's welfare and how he considered it even more important that he now had a role to play, particularly since he was not sure of the poison Kara continued to be fed, or by whom.

'My priority is repairing and building a good relationship with my daughter,' he added.

Ashley appeared to understand his predicament completely. He outlined his terms and conditions and agreed to e-mail them to Paul for signature. He urged Paul to spend the next two weeks scrutinising every detail in the Staines report and gather witness statements and character references. The first and foremost goal was to remove the blemish on his character. If not adequately managed, this could have a spiralling effect on his, and possibly Jenna's, dealings with teaching children. After that they would focus on the retention of his parental rights and responsibilities, proving that over the years Phoenix had systematically brainwashed Kara, poisoning her heart against him. They would then question her motives.

They eventually wrapped up their meeting around 8:30 that evening.

The following morning (Christmas Eve), Paul's father telephoned and gave him the sad news that his gran (Paul's dad's mum, Kara's great-gran) had passed away during the night. She had died in hospital in her sleep. Although Paul was very sad and would miss her, he was relieved that her suffering was over. She had lived a full and healthy life up until the age of 99, but her health had seriously deteriorated in the last six months and her quality of life was minimal. During her whole life she had been an exceptionally kind and remarkable lady, who never had a bad word to say about anyone. She kept photographs of all her children, grandchildren and great-grandchildren (including Kara) in her front room. Kara met her on a number of occasions when she was a lot younger. Under normal circumstances, Paul would have passed on to Kara the sad news that her great-gran had passed away. He would also have been sending her a Christmas card and choosing presents. However, the circumstances were not normal and he considered it best for all concerned to not attempt making contact for fear of inflaming the ugly situation further, if that was possible! Instead he put photographs of his gran in his journal, annotated with entries in the hope that Kara would read it one day and discover for herself this wonderful gracious lady.

He was glad his gran had known nothing of this adoption scenario before she died. He was not sure if there was an afterlife or not, but if there was, he knew his gran would be reunited with his granddad and that they would look down kindly and guide him through the awful experience he and his family were currently having to endure.

Paul and Jenna understandably struggled to whip up some Christmas spirit. They put on a brave face visiting friends and family, but they felt very heavy-hearted. They kept themselves busy, trying to take their minds off what was happening, but it was proving impossible.

Whilst looking through photographs of his gran, Paul came across some of Kara that had been taken when she used to stay with him and Jenna at weekends. She looked so cute and always had a cheery smile on her face. Interestingly, some of these photos had been taken over the Easter period, approximately six months before he had received Kara's first devastating letter in the October of that year. He and Kara looked so happy together, laughing and playing. How could things have gone wrong so quickly? What could have happened in that six-month period for Kara to write such a letter? On going through the Staines report, he was reminded that Ross and Phoenix had embarked on their relationship that same October. This was also the same year (around Easter time) that Phoenix had broken up with her previous boyfriend, Garth. According to Kara, this had not been an amicable break-up.

Paul mulled this over for a while. Could this indicate that his troubles started when Ross first came on the scene? Perhaps something had been brewing since Phoenix's break-up with Garth. He was not blaming Ross or Garth for his current predicament, but wondered whether these events might have had an influence on Kara. Could they have spurred her to write such a letter? Was Kara transferring her feelings of dislike or frustration with Garth, Ross or any of her mother's previous boyfriends on to him? Could it be that whilst Phoenix had primed Kara for Ross to enter their lives, simultaneously she had influenced Kara to have nothing more to do with Paul and his family? Was it possible Phoenix could have done it without even realising what she was doing? Kara would have been at a very impressionable age. Were these credible explanations?

Between Christmas and mid-January, Paul and Jenna were swamped with the adoption scenario. They had spent many, many hours working closely with Ashley and the deeper they dug, the more foul play they uncovered. Ashley had collated a deposition on Paul's behalf and had submitted copies to the court. The deposition included:

✦ **Character references and witness statements for Paul.** These were from friends, family and acquaintances all testifying to Paul's good character, describing him as easy-going, likeable, mild-mannered and a respected member of the community. They stated how good he was around children and bore witness to how his nephews, nieces and godchildren loved having him around and looked forward to seeing him. Particular mention was made of the loving relationship he had shared with Kara, from when she was born, up until she reached the age of nine. They described how following his separation from Phoenix, he had done his utmost to ensure Kara's wellbeing. He had shown her nothing but love and devotion. They confirmed that she used to stay at his house on alternate weekends and would embark on fun family-type activities. Those who knew Phoenix described how she had intentionally made life awkward for him, including how she had moved house and refused to give him a forwarding address or telephone number. A couple also mentioned her occasional 'odd' and sometimes 'erratic' behaviour. They all clearly stated how they considered the allegations made against Paul to be totally outlandish and utterly preposterous.

+ **Paul's own witness statement.** Paul gave his version of events commencing from his marriage breakdown. He described how he believed Phoenix had never forgiven him for his indiscretion and how she resented the fact he had moved on before she did. She was now getting back at him by cutting him and his family out of Kara's life and over the years had gradually poisoned Kara against him. He had desperately tried to stay in contact via letters, cards and the school, but Phoenix had purposely and systematically severed these avenues of communication. He was now being falsely accused of child abuse so as to discredit him, meaning they would not need his consent to go ahead with their adoption request and he would have his parental rights and responsibilities taken away from him against his will. He was concerned about the environment in which Kara was living and wanted to know the real cause of her unhappiness and depressive illness. Ultimately he wanted to start repairing his relationship with his daughter, not break it down further, and was looking to professional organisations for help.

+ **A statement written on Paul's behalf by Ashley.** This put Paul's position into context within the wider scheme of things, outlining significant events since his separation from Phoenix and his laudable standing in society. It gave a legal view on the adoption application, detailing failures in how the whole matter had been dealt with so far and made recommendations to the court as to how it should be taken forward.

+ A list of further supporting evidence that could be provided to the court if required. Paul had gathered photos and mementos demonstrating the loving relationship he had shared with Kara up until she reached age of nine.

+ A list citing examples of 'foul play' by Phoenix. This list gave many examples of Phoenix deliberately undermining and demeaning Paul, before and after Kara's initial devastating letter. It revealed a slow, yet determined and progressive poisoning of Kara's mind.

+ Examples of correspondence with Kara's school. Paul had copies of school reports, photographs, letters and e-mails clearly demonstrating how he had taken a very keen interest in Kara's wellbeing, despite obstacles being put in his way by Phoenix and ultimately Kara.

During this time, Paul wrote to the doctors involved in diagnosing Kara's major depressive illness and requested further details. He conveyed his dismay that he had not been informed about her illness until nearly two years after it was initially diagnosed. He expressed his utter astonishment that this illness had been attributed to his apparent abusive behaviour. Why had they not made any attempt to contact him and ascertain if there was any credibility in the allegations that had been made? How could they make an accurate diagnosis without knowing all the facts?

The doctors responded to Paul's letters stating they appreciated his concern, but their hands were tied due to patient confidentiality. Phoenix and Kara had explicitly told them, 'Do not forward any details to Paul.'

Ashley conducted further investigation and found a

conversation thread on the internet where a child had asked the question, 'How can I get adopted by my stepfather when my biological father refuses to give his consent?'

Someone had replied, 'You need to discredit him in some way, perhaps make up some allegations that he abused you, then you will not need his consent.'

Paul was normally a fan of the internet for obtaining useful information, but here was a classic example of how the internet could be misused. A bit like, 'Instructions on how to make a bomb'.

During the third week of January, Kara's school report arrived. Paul was pleased to note that there was nothing in it to give him serious cause for concern. He telephoned the school and personally thanked the headmaster for the report and the continued updates the school had been providing regarding Kara's wellbeing. Sadly he felt obliged to also let him know about the continued deterioration in his relationship with Kara and the false allegations of child abuse that had been made against him, necessitating instruction of a solicitor to act on his behalf.

The headmaster thanked Paul for his candidness and agreed to update his key staff so they were aware of the situation.

During February, life became even more frenzied for Paul and Jenna. Their whole life continued to be driven by the adoption business and it had become their sole topic of conversation. It was the first thing on their minds when they woke up, they thought about it all day, went to sleep thinking about it and then dreamt about it, assuming they got any sleep. There were days when Paul would get up at 4am and work round the clock until 1am the following morning, gathering and assembling evidence to support the initial deposition. A few cups of coffee would be his only respite. At the same time, they were trying to keep their respective businesses going, whilst keeping friends and family up to date with the latest turn of events. Usually they derived great joy from their work, but they both had to admit their hearts weren't in it at the moment. It was in fact a living nightmare.

As well as being concerned for Paul, Jenna was worried about the impact the allegations might have on her own business. She had conscientiously built it up over the previous twenty years and was not prepared to see it collapse due to a pack of lies, supported by incompetent professionals. She'd been wary and suspicious of Phoenix all along and there was no way she was going to let bitterness emanating from a vengeful woman destroy her livelihood. She was currently preparing for her school summer show, which was to be held at the local town theatre. She was desperately trying to choreograph new dance routines, but due to the current upset, her natural gift of creativity was eluding her and she was having difficulty finding anything from which to draw inspiration. She even contemplated cancelling the show, which was something unheard of in her book. In previous years she had always joked with the performers, 'The show must go on,' and although she said it playfully, they all knew she meant it.

To add to her woes, she was also becoming paranoid that social workers were visiting her classes, spying on her under different guises. There had been a couple of suspicious enquiries from supposed parents of late, wanting to watch classes before making a decision about their child joining her school. After class, these people had been very complimentary of the lessons, but then she had heard nothing more. Although she did not want to stereotype, her suspicions were further aroused by their rather unkempt appearance, looking as though they needed a 'good scrub'.

Jenna did not have a high opinion of social workers. She had worked with them in the past when they had requested her help concerning the domestic arrangements of some of her pupils. She also had a number of friends in well-respected professions who shared her concerns with respect to their working practices. Although she recognised that there were a number of excellent professionals in this field carrying out invaluable work under very trying circumstances, she felt there was still too high a proportion that were a clockwatching bunch, more concerned about going on courses and getting free lunches than focusing on the job in hand. All too often they appeared to take the easy option rather than getting to the real heart of issues.

Paul continued to play with his band, but he did not have time to learn new material. It was just a matter of churning out the same old songs for the time being. He became very wary of teaching children even though it had always been his policy to have a second adult present in all of his lessons.

Friends and family did try to keep their spirits up, inviting them out to various places, but general fun-time activities were currently way down on their list of priorities. The whole situation was having a detrimental impact on their health and they were showing signs of exhaustion. Paul's father made no secret of the fact that he was concerned about his son's state of mind. It was taking its toll on Paul's mum too. She was suffering from sleepless nights and panic attacks. The doctor had prescribed sleeping pills and anti-depressants to help her cope with the trauma.

Paul and Jenna continued to spend many, many hours with Ashley discussing the case, trying to determine Phoenix's motives. They meticulously studied the evidence they had collected and assembled the paperwork ready for presentation to the court. Paul had never known Jenna had such good secretarial skills! He was worried about the potentially huge costs building up and the likelihood that charges would go beyond the initial upper limit quote of £5000. He knew Ashley's hourly rates were well over £200, and that being the case, he must have already gone over his £5000 limit. Ashley did not appear to be charging him anywhere near his normal amount. When Paul mentioned it, Ashley smiled reassuringly, claiming he had a personal interest in the case and Paul had no need to worry.

Ashley was in his late forties and had built up his own solicitor's firm from scratch. He had trained to be a lawyer in his home county of Yorkshire prior to taking a year out travelling the USA. It was during his travels that he met his future wife. After returning to the UK he focused his energies on building up his law firm and settling down to start a family.

He and his wife had two children, a son aged four and a daughter aged nine. Ashley had already intimated that having a nine-year-old daughter of his own was one of the reasons he had a great deal of empathy with Paul's case. The more research he carried out, the more convinced he became that Paul's story should be made available to others. At the very least, it would be a helpful reference for fathers who found themselves in similar circumstances, but more importantly it could be a useful tool in helping to get draconian laws changed. This certainly gave Paul something more positive to think about.

Paul and Jenna had come to regard Ashley as a good friend as well as their solicitor. They frequently mentioned to each other how fortunate they were to have stumbled upon him. They found him a very charismatic and inspiring character. No matter how down they felt at times, he was able to lift their spirits. As well as being sharp-witted and a logical thinker, he had a comforting spiritual quality that appealed to them. They felt he would have made a good judge and told him so.

He smiled and remarked, 'I have considered it, but I'm not sure I'm ready for that level of responsibility, having such a dramatic impact on people's lives.'

The package of evidence Paul had built to date was quite formidable. It contained correspondence with Kara's school, Kara herself, Phoenix and solicitors, and all types of memorabilia including photos, birthday cards, drawings and much more. He had catalogued the evidence in an attempt to make it as reader-friendly as possible. He sat back and surveyed the overall package. If I can't convince a court of my innocence, then no father stands a chance in the UK Family Courts, he thought to himself. I have had more time than most to prepare, I have finances from my redundancy package, I have a fantastic solicitor and I have all the support from friends and family anyone could ask for. What more can any man do?

Once it was complete, Paul and Jenna took the package to Ashley's offices to get his views and get final confirmation it was ready for court. As Ashley surveyed the package, he was visibly taken aback at the level of spite and venom Phoenix and Kara had directed at Paul in their later correspondence.

'We could be dealing with nasty, vindictive and dangerous people,' he warned. 'Let me show you something.'

Ashley logged on to the internet and did a Google search on 'Parental Alienation Syndrome'. What came back disturbed Paul deeply. There were a number of articles from recognised professionals in the field. Key points included:

✦ Parental Alienation Syndrome (PAS) is the methodical vilification of one parent by the other, with the intent of alienating the child(ren) against the other parent. The ultimate goal is to eliminate that parent from the child's life and commonly extends to that parent's family and friends as well. In extreme cases, the 'alienating parent' will influence the child to work with them to successfully eliminate the previously treasured parent from the child's life. It is much more common for mothers to be the perpetrators of PAS, alienating the child against the father, but fathers can also act in this alienating role.

✦ Many 'child victims' of PAS are proud to state that the decision to reject their father is entirely their own, strongly denying any involvement or persuasion from their mother. Their mothers usually support this fanatically. Some mothers may even state that they have tried to encourage contact between the child and father, stating they fully recognise the importance of the father's involvement. All their actions, however, indicate otherwise. The child victim learns to appreciate that by stating the decision to not see their father is their own, they allay their mother's guilt, protecting her from criticism. The mother then praises the child for having their own mind and not being afraid to express their own opinion. Frequently, such mothers will pressure their children to tell 'the truth' regarding whether or not they

184

really want to see their fathers. The child comes to understand that in order to please the mother, 'the truth' is to claim that they hate their father and do not want to see him ever again. After a period of such programming, the child may not know what the truth is any more and is likely to have false memories. The child eventually comes to actually believe the father deserves the hatred being directed against him.

+ Mothers who indulge in PAS commonly have a history of emotional and psychological illness. Only a small percentage of mothers who indulge in PAS are normal, stable, and independent. These would more typically be professional women who have another partner and exploit loopholes in the law to unashamedly get rid of the father. It can be argued that these women display sociopathic tendencies. In most cases the mother needs help.

+ There are no advantages in a child not having free access to both parents. The disadvantages include suffering the loss of half a family and all the support and experiences that represents. The child may suffer from mental issues, including confusion and depression. The child will go on to have a higher than average chance of suffering from many social problems, which may include repeating the PAS cycle over again.

These extracts were accompanied with short film clips showing the distressed and confused expressions on the faces of children separated from a previously cherished parent.

Paul could feel that familiar uncontrollable sadness and rage bubbling up inside him and his eyes started to well up. He could not hold it in any longer and the tears rolled down his face. He had not cried in many, many years, but here he was sobbing. He felt so tragically sad for Kara, yet angered by Phoenix at the same time.

'This whole scenario could have so easily been avoided,' he

said whilst gasping for air. 'How can she possibly think that she is acting in Kara's best interests? How can she be so malicious? She must be quite mad!'

Paul felt very embarrassed and rather needlessly apologised for losing self-control in front of Ashley. Jenna comforted him as best she could, whilst Ashley looked on sympathetically, at the same time showing genuine concern.

After a couple of minutes, Paul regained his composure. They agreed it best that they should wrap up the meeting and continue another day.

That evening Ashley rang Paul.

'Are you okay?'

'Yes,' Paul replied. He apologised once more to Ashley for breaking down in his office.

'Absolutely no need for apologies,' remarked Ashley. 'I'm surprised you haven't cracked before. We are all feeling the strain of this case.'

Paul went on to tell him that since their meeting that afternoon, he had further researched Parental Alienation Syndrome and found it appeared to fit his situation exactly. Furthermore, he and Jenna were concerned and indeed a little frightened that there might be a serious personality disorder running through Phoenix's family, maybe of a sociopathic or narcissistic nature. Apparently, this was very common in parents who engaged in the act of alienating a child against the other parent. As a consequence, they were worried that this adoption and the associated allegations might not be the end of their torment. Paul had looked up narcissistic behavioural traits on the internet and collated the following snippets of information:

✦ Narcissists are hypersensitive to insults, defeat, criticism, and often tend to react aggressively when faced with these.

✦ They are introverts, hence they don't make it obvious even if they are hurt.

186

+ They are preoccupied with fantasies related to power, wealth, success and love.

+ They feel that they are special and hence desire to be treated in a special way.

+ They lack the ability to understand human emotions. They don't try to understand other people's needs, feelings or viewpoints.

+ They are self-centred and consider themselves to be superior to others.

+ They are extremely reluctant to admit anything is their fault.

+ They are boastful and often indulge in exaggerating themselves and their achievements.

+ They set unrealistic goals for themselves and don't hesitate in taking extreme measures to attain these goals.

+ They like being constantly admired and always crave to be the centre of attraction.

+ They appear very arrogant in nature and sport an unnecessary attitude or ego most of the time.

+ They are always envious of others, but simultaneously think that other people are envious of them.

Could this description fit Phoenix's behaviour? Worryingly, Paul and Jenna felt there were some striking resemblances. Some of these patterns of behaviour had even been exemplified and described in the Staines report.

Ashley was not surprised by Paul and Jenna's concern, claiming he had reached a similar conclusion.

By the second week in March, approximately eight weeks after Ashley had submitted the initial deposition to the court, they still had not received a response from the Tuckers or their representatives. Paul and Jenna were also waiting to hear from CAFCASS for their interview. At the first hearing, the judge had ordered that CAFCASS circulate their findings and report their recommendations for everyone to review by March 15th at the latest. They were leaving things a bit late!

Paul discussed this with Ashley and they concluded the lateness could be due to one of two reasons. It could be that Phoenix and Ross were now being forced to backtrack and carry out damage limitation for fear of being exposed as liars, which would result in them having to pay Paul's legal costs. Alternatively they could be trying to strengthen their position by coming up with more fictitious allegations.

The letter from CAFCASS finally arrived on the third Tuesday in March. It informed Paul that his interview would be held on the Friday of that week, at 3pm at their offices. This meant he and Jenna would have to cancel their classes and do a 70-mile round trip, which neither was thrilled about. Apart from being an obvious emotional nightmare, this whole scenario was incredibly inconvenient. It was always Paul who was expected to drop everything, do all the travelling, incur all the expenses, whilst at the same time being treated as some sort of criminal low-life. He noted his allocated interview slot had been left late in the day and he was horribly suspicious that the CAFCASS report might have already been written, without having even met him. The deadline for the final report to be with the court was on the Monday, which meant it needed to be completed over the weekend. He wanted to make sure his appointment did not become a typical 'Friday afternoon job'. It was imperative that he get all his points across clearly and concisely.

He telephoned the CAFCASS officer involved to find out what he should bring with him. There was no answer, so he left a message on her voicemail. The CAFCASS officer never did return his call.

Paul met with Ashley on the Thursday, the day before the CAFCASS interview.

'This organisation does not have a good reputation within the legal profession,' Ashley advised him. 'A number of my professional colleagues regard them and Social Services as potentially highly dangerous. Although these organisations are trained to look for abuse, too frequently they are dismissive of the possibility of parental alienation perpetrated by a resident parent, and are slow to recognise it as an abuse in its own right. I can give you countless examples where they have shown an unfounded bias against absent fathers and drawn incorrect conclusions, unfairly influencing Family Courts. I do not want to alarm you unduly, since in your case there is an overwhelming wealth of evidence that should easily enable CAFCASS to see through the lies that have been made up to discredit you. Nevertheless, I recommend you go "wired up".'

Paul looked puzzled and Ashley smiled. He reminded Paul how unfairly treated and misled he had been during his Social Services interview with Nerys Staines. He went over to his desk and pulled out a small recording device.

'It's very simple to operate; simply turn on and off.' He showed Paul the button. 'In the unlikely event that the recording is used as evidence in court, you will first need to make sure that the CAFCASS officer is aware that such a record is being made. Okay?'

Paul initially felt a little uncomfortable at this prospect, but soon came round to the idea when he recalled how badly Ms Staines had distorted his version of events in her report.

Ashley re-checked the material that Paul intended to take with him.

'It's a strong package,' he commented. 'It demonstrates your innocence of the allegations made against you and your monumental efforts to be a good father, despite all the obstacles put in your way. I wish you well. Please update me as soon as you get an opportunity.'

That evening Paul and Jenna once again stayed at his brother's house. It was more convenient than staying at their own house, since his brother lived closer to the CAFCASS offices. His brother and sister-in-law read the package of material he intended to present to the CAFCASS officer. They were impressed, declaring it a very accurate and readable version of facts.

Over dinner, they commented on how tired and withdrawn he and Jenna were looking. Paul and Jenna were a little dismissive of this observation, for they did not wish to unduly upset anyone, but their well-intended actions were not helped when Paul suddenly suffered a major nosebleed. They all showed natural concern.

'This has been happening a lot lately,' he conceded and agreed to have a medical check-up at the earliest opportunity.

The following day, Paul and Jenna drove to the CAFCASS offices. They parked up and made their way inside the building. They were ten minutes early. The CAFCASS officer was running about 30 minutes late. They were offered a cup of coffee whilst they were waiting in the small reception area. Paul used this opportunity to look around and check he was correctly 'wired'. He regarded it as farcical that he was having to go to these lengths to prove himself, but what choice did he have?

There were lots of brochures in the lobby area detailing CAFCASS services and how they could provide a mediation service in difficult family circumstances. One leaflet in particular grabbed his attention with the heading, 'How damaging it can be for a child to be turned against a parent'. It went on say, 'Such poisoning can damage a child's self-esteem, since the child ultimately realises that 50 per cent of their genetic makeup comes from that parent'. He considered it a huge pity that this mediation service had not been available six years ago when he had first had issues with Phoenix and Kara. Nevertheless, it did appear that organisations such as CAFCASS were now recognising his type of family issue and it raised his hopes that he might finally be taken seriously.

When the CAFCASS officer did appear, she made it clear she wanted to interview Paul on his own, without Jenna present.

She was a corpulent woman of middle age, with a demeanour that reminded Paul of an over-officious prison wardress. He knew it was unwise to go on first impressions alone, but his heart did sink a little.

'I'm not happy about Jenna not being present,' he informed her.

'Jenna will be allowed to join us towards the end of the interview, but I want to speak with you on your own.' She directed him to a small meeting room. 'I have put 90 minutes aside for this interview, after which our offices close.'

They exchanged typical introductory pleasantries (which Paul found very false) and it was at this point that he asked if he could make his own recording, to which the CAFCASS officer agreed.

'How is Kara coping with this unpleasant business?' he enquired.

The CAFCASS officer looked at him with a little disdain, as if to say, 'I ask the questions, not you'.

'Kara is okay in herself, but very, very annoyed with you,' she replied in a haughty, officious manner. 'She has written a letter to the judge, requesting to be present in court alongside Phoenix for the second hearing. She is preparing her own Statement of Facts in anticipation.'

Paul felt very downhearted. Kara was obviously still intent on going ahead with this adoption, regardless of his feelings on the matter.

'I have seen your Statement of Facts and the letter you sent to the court conveying your concern over Ms Staines's report,' she continued in a condescending fashion. Paul sensed that she was very put out that he had had the audacity to question the validity of judgements made by someone in a profession related to her own.

'Have you seen the deposition provided to the court by my solicitor?' he asked.

'No,' she replied, 'but I will make contact after this meeting to obtain a copy. For now, I want you to expand on your version of events.'

Paul spent the next hour giving a history of events right up to the present day. He spoke of his marital relationship with Phoenix, his regrettable one-off lapse and how he believed Phoenix had never been able to forgive him. He now had strong reason to believe that as a consequence, she had damaged the loving relationship he had once shared with his daughter. She had deliberately made it difficult for him to maintain contact and had systematically brainwashed Kara into believing he was some kind of monster, whether intentionally or not. He suspected Phoenix and now Kara, after having been unfairly influenced by her mother, were trying to re-write history in an attempt to unjustifiably eliminate him from their lives. He presented a summary of events he had drafted in preparation for their meeting.

Pre-separation
✦ Marriage shows signs of difficulties.
✦ Paul's one-off extra-marital encounter.
✦ Phoenix immediately files for divorce.

Separation
✦ Paul leaves family residence.
✦ Kara starts to spend alternate Sundays with Paul.
✦ Divorce finalised.
✦ Paul moves into his new house, suitable for Kara to come and stay.

Contact with Kara
✦ Kara typically stays alternate weekends.
✦ Paul meets Jenna.
✦ Phoenix shows increasing antagonistic behaviour towards Paul.
✦ Jenna moves in with Paul.
✦ Everything works reasonably smoothly for next four to five years, then there is a noticeable change in Kara's attitude.
✦ Kara becomes reluctant to visit, but there is still essen-

tially a loving father–daughter relationship. (This period coincides with Phoenix breaking up with Garth and her new boyfriend, Ross, coming on the scene.)

Breakdown of contact
+ Paul receives bewildering and devastating letter from Kara.
+ All direct contact arrangements with Paul are broken, supposedly at Kara's request.
+ Paul's attempts to set up family counselling sessions thwarted by Phoenix.
+ Paul tries to maintain contact with Kara via weekly letters, phone calls, postcards, Christmas cards and birthday cards.
+ Phoenix moves house without warning and refuses to give Paul a contact address or telephone number for Kara.

Trying to maintain contact/carry out parental responsibilities
+ Paul tries to keep abreast of Kara's welfare via the school.
+ Phoenix appears content to let Paul's relationship with Kara suffer.
+ Paul tries to maintain contact with Kara via Phoenix's parents.

More recent matters
+ Paul receives first request from Phoenix, allegedly expressing Kara's sentiments, for his consent for Kara to be adopted by her stepfather. Paul states he is not prepared to give his consent.
+ Eight months later, Paul receives a rather threatening request from Phoenix's solicitor for his consent for Kara to change her surname to that of her stepfather. Paul reluctantly agrees.
+ Four months on, Kara is diagnosed with a serious depressive disorder, supposedly triggered by receiving correspondence from Paul the previous year. Phoenix/Kara specifically request Paul is not informed about this.

- Another year on, Paul receives a written request from Kara to be adopted. Paul responds saying that he is not prepared to give his consent at this time, since he does not have enough information.
- A couple of months later, at Kara/Phoenix's request, Paul has convivial meeting with Kara's stepfather. Stepfather is sympathetic to Paul's position and agrees to relay Paul's feelings back to Kara, with a view to changing her mind.
- Six months later Paul unexpectedly receives letter from Social Services stating that Kara's stepfather has applied to the court to adopt her.
- Paul meets with social worker (Ms Staines). He is made aware of hurtful and damaging allegations of child abuse that have been made against him, supposed to have happened many years ago.
- First court hearing takes place and judge makes an order for CAFCASS involvement.
- Post-hearing Paul is handed a copy of Social Services report written by Ms Staines that recommends it would be in Kara's best interests to be adopted. The recommendation is based on fictitious allegations of child abuse that are erroneously reported as if they actually happened. Report also makes reference to Kara's major depressive illness. This is the first time Paul is made aware of her mental condition.
- Paul officially employs the services of a solicitor.

The CAFCASS officer read the summary with interest. Once she had finished reading, Paul explained how he considered the proposed adoption to be potentially very damaging for Kara, particularly in the long term. It would perpetuate the lies that had already been told and store up more problems for the future. He was worried it was simply substituting one emotional problem for another and told the officer so.

'I think the best way forward would be for me, Phoenix, Ross and the other professional bodies involved to start working together, helping to rebuild the relationship between Kara and myself. If anyone should be investigated for child abuse, it should be Phoenix for allowing, maybe even facilitating, the breakdown of Kara's relationship with her natural father. As I have already told you, my top priority is to get the truth out before any decision is made regarding the adoption. I consider it of paramount importance to Kara's future welfare. Adoption is currently being recommended based on lies and false allegations, with little attempt or interest being shown in getting to the truth. I find it particularly disturbing that my daughter has been on prescribed medication for a mental health issue, the real causes of which are being swept under the carpet. To quote Ms Staines, "We may never get to the truth". I consider her response totally unacceptable, particularly bearing in mind all the evidence I have collected.'

Paul showed the officer the package of evidence he had prepared. The files included witness statements and records of all happenings since his marriage breakdown, supplemented with photos, documents and memorabilia, clearly supporting his version of events. He pointed out Kara's good school reports, which indicated she was performing well above average and showed no hint of unhappiness.

The officer read each of his witness statements and spent an additional fifteen minutes reviewing the evidence files. She complimented him on his organisational skills. She challenged him on a few aspects, but ultimately agreed it was an impressive package. Unfortunately she then destroyed any credibility she might have initially had in his eyes.

'You do realise that a good school report is the sign of an abused child, possibly sexually? The judge could also see it this way.'

Paul was most taken aback and displayed his obvious distaste for her comments. He wondered if she was trying to bait him, to see how he would react when challenged.

'I may not be an expert in child psychology,' he responded, 'but in Kara's case, I can tell you quite categorically, she has not been abused in any way by me and I find your comments quite sickening.'

He was getting angry at having to justify himself to this stupid woman. How dare she come up with such nonsense. What would she have made of it if Kara had been given a bad school report? No doubt she would have regarded that as a sign of an abused child too.

As the interview continued, it appeared that whatever he said, she was going to unfairly incriminate him. He got the distinct impression she had already made up her mind and she was not prepared to listen to anything he had to say. Nevertheless, he continued as best he could in his uphill battle.

'You do realise, don't you, that I have never, ever been in any trouble with the police or Social Services, nor have I ever been contacted by them?'

'You would not necessarily have been made aware of any police or Social Services investigations into your affairs, since you and your partner do not have any children residing with you. If you did, then it would have been a different matter and the children would have likely been taken into care.'

Paul found this utterly ludicrous and any confidence he might have initially had in this woman had regrettably now diminished to absolute zero. Did she not understand that both he and Jenna taught young children? They both had clean enhanced CRB certificates. Were they worth nothing?

To his absolute dismay, she then added, 'It is the remit of CAFCASS to always believe the child, regardless of what you have to say or your supporting evidence. The court, especially the judge, will likely not read any of your evidence due to time constraints.'

Paul was totally astounded and wondered what the judge would make of her comments. Why would their remit be to believe the child without question? Was she not aware of how devious teenage girls can be when they want to get their own way?

'Where's the cut-off point?' he asked demonstratively. 'What if she accused me of beating her mother up, stabbing her with a pitchfork and pouring bleach in her eyes? Would you still believe her then?'

The officer did not respond.

He paused for a moment to try and calm down and then asked her exasperatedly, 'What would you do in my position?'

'I do have sympathy with your case,' she replied. 'I advise you send your evidence to the court at the earliest opportunity to give it the best chance of being reviewed.'

Paul mentioned the website Ashley had found where a child had been advised to make up false allegations in order to discredit their biological father, so they could be adopted.

'That's a bit devious,' the officer replied. 'Regardless, I see no reason why we should suspect this has any relevance to your case.'

Once more Paul felt he was wasting his time. She apparently did not want to entertain anything he had to say.

The officer then stood up, opened the office door and beckoned Jenna to join them for the last 30 minutes. During this time Jenna added other useful snippets of information, corroborating Paul's version of events. They impressed upon the officer how the notable decline in Kara's happiness over the last few years had coincided with Phoenix denying her a loving relationship with Paul, despite his efforts to maintain contact. They had strong reasons to believe that Kara's mind had been systematically poisoned against him and the case bore all the classic hallmarks of Parental Alienation Syndrome, a recently recognised and professionally acclaimed phenomenon they had been researching on the internet.

'I made a specific point of interviewing Kara without her mother present, so I can assure you parental alienation is not an issue,' she replied indignantly.

Paul groaned inwardly. This statement alone signalled to him that she clearly did not have an understanding of this phenomenon. Had she not been trained in the concept or was she purposely not considering this as a possibility?

'I consider the alienation started when Kara was about three years of age,' he explained. 'I believe it has been an on-going process over the last twelve years and it is now manifesting itself in Kara's extreme attitude and behaviour.'

The officer looked as if she had been caught on the back foot somewhat. She dismissed his comment and brought the meeting to an abrupt close.

Paul enquired about the availability of the CAFCASS report.

'It's not a problem,' she replied. 'I will complete it over the weekend and then circulate to all parties.'

Paul and Jenna politely thanked her for her time and left. As they walked back to the car, they shared their views on how the meeting had gone. Neither was impressed. Jenna mentioned that although she had been made to wait outside the meeting room for the first hour, she and all others in the reception area could hear absolutely everything that was being said. They agreed the officer appeared ill-prepared, had a poor under-standing of the case and had not allocated enough time. They had the impression she had made up her mind about the case before the meeting had even started. The interview had come across as an unnecessary hassle for her. Furthermore they had both been made to feel inferior and criminal-like, even though they had done nothing wrong. They wondered whether she had to behave in a stand-offish manner as part of her job. To be fair to CAFCASS, they agreed to reserve final judgement until they had seen the contents of her report.

The following day Paul e-mailed Ashley with his thoughts on how the meeting with CAFCASS had gone.

Hi Ashley,

We met with the CAFCASS officer at 3:30pm yesterday and I was suitably 'wired' as planned. The officer informed me that we only had 90 minutes for the interview. Jenna was not allowed to join me for the first hour.

I asked the officer how Kara was bearing up. She looked at me with some degree of contempt and replied, 'Kara is fine in herself, but very angry with you' (meaning me) 'and is preparing her own Statement of Facts for the next hearing'. She was not prepared to give me any indication as to what Kara's Statement of Facts would contain.

I tried to convey to her my main concern was that professionals were basing their recommendations on a one-sided story and in my opinion, they needed to be fully aware of the truth in order to make the best decisions regarding Kara's welfare. She stated 'CAFCASS always believe the child' and that she had no reason not to believe Kara. I took her through the evidence I have prepared to date. I'm not sure how much of this she took on board, but she did agree to contact Kara's consultant psychiatrist to see if anything was being overlooked.

I got the impression that the officer was very suspicious of me throughout the interview, particularly at the beginning, but possibly relaxed a little as time went on and I took her through the material I had prepared.

I tried to explain my thoughts about Parental Alienation Syndrome, but she did not seem to understand and was not receptive at all.

The officer had not seen a copy of the deposition. Fortunately I had copies of your statement, my witness statement and the key witness statements with me, which I was able to provide. She said she would contact you for a copy of the full deposition during the week.

She remarked that I came across as emotional, not aggressive. She added that if I intended sending all the evidence I had prepared to the court, I should do it as soon as possible, otherwise it would not get read by the Judge or the court.

I remarked that she did not have long to write her report, since we are all supposed to have a copy by Monday. She was adamant that this would not be a problem.

As a general point, it continues to be very much an uphill struggle to make people listen to me, let alone believe me. However, I won't get too down about it. I know we have right on our side. If all we can achieve is clearing my name of the awful and ridiculous allegations, that will be some comfort.

I will drop off the record of the interview to you on Monday and hopefully we can meet later in the week.

Regards,

Paul

That evening Paul described the latest events in his journal and added:

This whole adoption nightmare is continuing. Although I don't blame Kara for any of this, I really think this is one of the worst things a child can do to their parent.

On the Wednesday of the last week in March, Ashley telephoned Paul to say that he had read the review of his meeting with CAFCASS and had listened to the recording a number of times. He was absolutely astonished at how badly Paul had been treated.

'You were effectively bullied by that officer,' he remarked. 'There was no sense of fair play whatsoever. The person being most abused in all of this is you.'

Paul wearily agreed. Ashley continued with a very serious tone in his voice.

'I'm getting concerned that further allegations could be concocted to support the Tuckers' case. I suggest you contact the police and Social Services as soon as possible to try and find out what exactly, if anything, was reported against you eighteen months ago, when this adoption scenario gathered momentum.'

Paul went to his local police station straight away and reported the possibility that false allegations might have been made against him by his ex-wife and daughter. They listened to his account with interest and were very understanding and helpful. They confirmed they would let him know the details of any allegations made against him within the next five working days.

He then went to his local branch of Social Services. The person to whom he spoke initially tried to be helpful, but, after consultation with some of their backroom colleagues, became obstructive and informed him they could not do anything until he had received something back from the police.

Once again he was made to feel like a criminal. The irony of it was that he had never been in trouble with the police in his whole life. He hadn't been arrested or convicted of anything; he hadn't even been issued a speeding ticket. Furthermore he had no history of drug or alcohol abuse and would purposely steer clear of violent behaviour. Not really the stamp of a hell-raising musician, he thought, jadedly smiling to himself.

That weekend Paul and Jenna assembled three additional copies of the evidence package. The original was for them; the three other copies were for the court.

On the Monday, they spent the whole day with Ashley in his office, carrying out last painstaking checks, getting the evidence ready to be delivered. They agreed it best if Paul deliver the copies personally and obtain a receipt as proof of delivery.

Ashley remained concerned he had heard nothing from the CAFCASS officer. She had still not requested a copy of the deposition as she had said she would in her interview with Paul. Furthermore, her report had not arrived, meaning it was now over a week late. As a consequence, he would have less time to respond and help Paul with a defence strategy if further unfounded allegations had been made. He had tried contacting the CAFCASS officer during the past week, but had constantly been put through to voicemail. He was becoming increasingly suspicious of further foul play and believed the impartiality of the court was being compromised. The officer herself had clearly stated on record, 'CAFCASS always believe the child', and there did not appear to be any sense of balance between the parties. No one seemed interested in hearing Paul's side of the story. Why was this?

Ashley suggested hiring a private investigator to see if they could get proof of foul play. Paul was not comfortable with this suggestion, not just because of the cost, but because he did not want to risk stirring things up any further with the Tuckers. Furthermore, there was no guarantee of any results. After discussion, they agreed to wait a little longer for the CAFCASS report before going down this route.

Throughout the course of the day, Paul continued to have heavy nosebleeds. It was not conducive to the working environment, but they wanted to take advantage of all the time they could, so they soldiered on regardless. By six o'clock that evening, after hours of toiling over the paperwork, the copies of the evidence package were ready to go.

They considered it grossly unfair that they had not received a copy of the CAFCASS report before making this submission. Paul was having to defend himself without even knowing if further allegations had been made against him. Regrettably, they could not leave the submission any longer. They needed to make sure the evidence they had prepared to date got the maximum chance of being read.

The following day, Paul and Jenna drove to the courthouse with the evidence package as planned. Paul delivered it personally, making sure he got a signed Receipt of Delivery note. He noticed the court offices were very disorganised, but the receptionist he spoke to assured him all relevant parties would get to see the package. Paul emphasised that this latest submission was a continuation of the initial deposition that had already been submitted in January.

Quietly he was pleased they had managed to get all the evidence prepared and delivered ahead of the time scheduled by the judge. It was quite an impressive achievement. It had been extremely hard work, but essential to support his case.

'Has the CAFCASS report been delivered yet?' he asked the receptionist.

'No, not yet,' she replied.

Paul could not understand how CAFCASS were allowed to get away with their conduct. It was now over a week late! It all seemed so unjust.

After leaving the courthouse, Paul and Jenna went to visit his parents, who continued to be very upset and traumatised by the whole affair. They could have done without this type of upset at this time in their lives. They were well into their 'autumn' years and struggled to fully grasp how human beings could be so wicked to each other. They were firm believers in 'Everything will work itself out in the end', but this was severely testing their faith. As far as they were concerned, they had already gone through the painful experience of losing their granddaughter many years ago through no fault of their own. They had reluctantly come to terms with it, but, like Paul, kept hope that as Kara matured, there would be a happy reunion at some stage. They had never considered things would sink to these depths. In their eyes, old wounds were being unnecessarily re-opened, whilst at the same time they watched their son suffer.

Paul's mum in particular had not slept properly for weeks. She hated seeing the way her son was being mistreated. She was in danger of hoarding a very intense, bitter hatred for Phoenix, which she knew would not be good for her own wellbeing. It was totally out of character for this usually very mild-mannered woman.

'It's like living through a horrific "Eastenders" soap plot,' she remarked.

Paul nodded. 'Yes, "Eastenders" on acid,' he replied.

That evening Ashley telephoned Paul at home to check the delivery to the courthouse had gone as planned and urged him to get a medical check-up. He was clearly concerned by how the circumstances were taking their toll on his health.

'I'm okay, just tired,' Paul replied, but he agreed to get checked out soon.

On the Thursday of that week, Ashley telephoned Paul and Jenna to let them know that the CAFCASS officer had left a message saying that she had delivered her report to the court. They immediately dropped what they were doing and went straight to his office. Whilst there, Ashley rang the court offices and asked for a copy of the report.

'The CAFCASS officer has left a note indicating she has already sent the report on to you,' the court spokesperson replied.

Ashley thought this strange. He rang the CAFCASS officer to confirm the court's response, since he had not yet received a copy. To their surprise, she answered her phone.

'I have not sent you a copy and the court is not obliged to do so,' she informed him.

Paul and Jenna could sense Ashley was getting extremely frustrated. He was not used to being messed around in such an unprofessional manner. The whole thing smacked of incompetence. Paul had been living on his nerves waiting for this report and he simply could not understand how others were allowed to get away with this shoddy practice, seemingly not bothered about doing their jobs properly.

Ashley telephoned the court offices once more and this time the court officer gave the same story as the CAFCASS officer, adding, 'I will make sure a note is left for the judge asking if the report can be forwarded on to you. However please note that if there is anything controversial in it, the judge is likely to refuse this request.'

Ashley was noticeably becoming increasingly annoyed at the way he, Paul and Jenna were being treated and apologised to them on behalf of his profession. He had many contacts in the legal profession, including top judges who had presided over very high-profile cases prior to retiring. He rang one of these legal friends and asked for their perspective on the matter.

'I see absolutely no reason why you should not be entitled to a copy of the CAFCASS report,' his friend replied.

Ashley telephoned the CAFCASS officer once more, insisting he get to see a copy of the report.

'I very much need to see a copy of your report in order to ensure a fair hearing for my client,' he informed her, 'but in the meantime can you please give me some indication as to its contents and what you are recommending?'

The officer was very offhand in her manner and begrudgingly replied, 'I am not overturning anything in the original Social Services report written by Ms Staines. The Tuckers have not withdrawn the allegations of child abuse and as a consequence I am recommending the adoption goes ahead. Additionally Kara has personally written to the judge requesting to take the stand in court.'

They were all bitterly disappointed, but not overly surprised. The officer had already made it clear that CAFCASS believed the child, no matter what the adult had to say. Whether CAFCASS could see through the lies or not, they had decided to support the adoption.

It made no sense to Paul. How could the unverified allegations of a child be allowed to cause so much turmoil to two families? It wasn't just his family that had to deal with the fallout, but it was having a knock-on effect on Jenna's family as well. He had already informed Social Services and CAFCASS that he was prepared to share parental responsibility with Ross, but this clearly wasn't good enough for those mad Tuckers. They were obviously not content with just the change in Kara's surname, having sole custody and blocking any contact between him and his daughter. They also wanted to destroy his good name and didn't care who else they brought down with him. Kara was nearly sixteen. If she was so happy with her life and new family, why did she feel the need to be adopted? Why was it such a big thing in her life? As a sixteen-year-old girl one would have thought she would be more interested in boys, music, make-up and fashion.

Ashley then significantly added to Paul's woes.

'In the absence of the report, I have been listening to the recording of your interview with CAFCASS in fine detail and there is something that worries me,' he remarked. 'When you were presenting Kara's school reports as evidence that you maintained an interest in her welfare, you mentioned to the CAFCASS officer that these reports portrayed Kara as a happy child, not giving the slightest indication of a child suffering from depression. The officer then interjected and said, "This could be a sign of sexual abuse and the child regarding the school as a safe haven. The judge could also see it this way."'

Paul did recall the officer saying something like that, but at the time he had just dismissed it as ridiculous and offensive nonsense.

Ashley continued, 'I am worried because this accusation appears to come out of nowhere. Since our evidence is so strong in support of your good character, I am wondering if the Tuckers might be sinking to new sub-gutter-level depths in their smear campaign to get their own way. After all, they have already accused you of beating Kara with a stick and have tried to bring your morality into question by suggesting you took

Kara to "inappropriate establishments". It's not a great leap of the imagination for them to now make up allegations of sexual abuse.'

Paul felt physically sick. How could they even think along these lines? How could they sleep at night?

Jenna was shaking with rage and forcefully pointed out, 'In this world there are genuine cases of child abuse that do require the resources from organisations such as Social Services and CAFCASS, but these Tuckers are selfishly depriving these deserving cases. If we had children residing with us, they would probably have been taken into care by now because of these ridiculous allegations. What happened to common sense and British justice?'

Jenna had now developed an understandable intense loathing for Phoenix. Paul's nose started to pour with blood again. Just when he thought this nightmare could not get any worse, it did.

Before they left, Ashley reminded them, 'No allegations of this nature have been made yet, but we need to be prepared for all possibilities, particularly since we have been denied access to the CAFCASS report. We need to be prepared in case there are some nasty surprises coming our way. It's plausible that the original allegations were deviously conjured up in this manner to purposely frighten you into thinking worse was still to come, simply trying to blackmail you into submission.'

They all cursed those nasty, miserable Tuckers.

That evening Paul surfed the web, trying to glean some information with respect to fathers in his position. He looked for any useful advice regarding the subject of false allegations. He needed to make sure that if the proposed adoption was granted, it was not given on the grounds of such allegations. He needed to clear his name for both his and Jenna's sakes. Both their businesses involved teaching children. As he was searching, he came across a website that took him into a very dark and disturbing world of which he had not previously been aware.

The website promoted FASO (False Allegation Support

Organisation). FASO described itself as a voluntary service dedicated to supporting anyone affected by false allegations of abuse. It quoted a speech by Earl Howe in the House of Lords:

Many innocent people are being wrongly accused of child abuse and whose lives in consequence are being turned upside down without due justification ... The climate is like that of a witch-hunt in which the voice of reason and all sense of proportion is lost.

It went on to say,

In the UK today, ordinary people with nothing to hide, can be accused of abuse on almost no evidence and without any proper witnesses to support the story.

- *The strain of child protection intruding into your family can make you depressed or ill for a long time, or push you into debt.*
- *Your children can be taken away from you, and then quickly and irreversibly adopted into another family.*
- *You can be arrested in your own home in front of your family and in full view of your friends and neighbours, held in a police cell, interviewed under caution, charged and called to appear in court.*
- *You can be convicted without proof, evidence, witnesses or corroboration and live for years in prison.*
- *You live forever after under suspicion by the authorities.*
- *Any other child you have now or later will be at risk of the same treatment and may be removed from you.*

You have done nothing wrong. But that does not protect you.

This was yet another new low that Paul was experiencing. Was it possible he could go to jail? Would he be the victim of a witch-hunt? Could he expect to face ill-informed lynch mobs? Had this been Phoenix's plan all along? Was it her vengeful way of getting back at him? Perhaps she was hoping the stress would kill him. She would clearly need to be psychologically unbalanced to pursue such action, but he had already considered this a possibility. Perhaps she was some sort of sociopath? If he hadn't before, he definitely now considered her a mad Tucker.

Paul rang the FASO helpline straightaway and spoke to a very understanding woman. She immediately recognised what he was going through. Their conversation covered topics such as:

+ CAFCASS and Social Services often appear biased.

+ CAFCASS may not be independent and do not always appear to support the family.

+ The system has no checks or balances that are controlled. What is in place is not monitored, therefore the system does not work adequately. Professionals providing information to the judiciary are listened to closely, whereas the respondents often appear to have no voice.

+ In Paul's case a fully enhanced CRB would be preferable to a police check, since a simple check may not disclose everything that might have been alleged against him. (A fully enhanced CRB is required where either children or vulnerable adults are gathered and individuals wish to work with them.)

+ He would need a very good solicitor (preferably registered with the Children's Panel).

+ He would need a very strong Statement of Facts, accompanied by supporting evidence.

+ He would need to thoroughly research Parental Alienation Syndrome.

'Stay calm and be positive,' she advised. 'You can ring again whenever you want should you feel in need of moral support.' She wished him the very best of luck in his endeavours.

Paul thanked her very much for her time and remarked he did feel better for talking to someone who understood what he was going through. He would let her know of any significant developments.

As he replaced the telephone receiver, he promised himself that once this ordeal was over, he would publicise the good work of this organisation.

Paul relayed his conversation with the FASO representative to Jenna. They were not overly surprised by the majority of the content of the discussion since they had witnessed a lot of the subject matter first-hand. What did surprise them, however, was the magnitude of the false allegations problem within the UK and how organisations such as CAFCASS and Social Services seemed to get away with their conduct. It appeared these organisations were making far too many serious errors of judgement. They either missed cases of genuine child abuse, or accused innocent people of abusing children in a desperate attempt to cover their incompetent arses. In his experience these organisations were causing more damage and emotional trauma than they were relieving and the UK would be a better place without them.

Paul hardly slept that night. When he did eventually drop off, he had awful nightmares about lynch mobs, media frenzy and prison. He woke in a cold sweat.

On Friday morning, Paul and Jenna met with Ashley. Paul relayed the previous night's conversation with FASO. Ashley could see they were feeling very low and tried to lift their spirits. He reminded them that they were not going to the Criminal Court, just the Family Court. The Family Court would not jail him. None of the allegations made against him had been taken seriously by the police. If they had been, he would have been investigated and arrested at the time, eighteen months ago, when the allegations were first made. The alleged offences were supposed to have happened eight years ago. If they were true, why didn't Phoenix raise it with the school, police or relevant authorities at the time? Any caring mother would have noticed nasty bruises or a change in their child's behaviour straight away. Had she reported something then, he would immediately have been taken in for questioning. As it was, she had done nothing. There was no credibility or evidence to support an investigation in the Criminal Court. Additionally, Paul had received a report back from the police stating that there was no mention of any allegations whatsoever on his police record, supporting his enhanced CRB certificate (which was a couple of years old now). He was 100 per cent clean.

They agreed this was great news, but Ashley did point out that the false allegations reported in the Staines report (and any future ones should they be forthcoming) needed to be managed appropriately. If ignored, there was always the possibility they could escalate into something that could tarnish his reputation in the future.

'It is imperative that the adoption is not granted on the grounds of these allegations,' Ashley explained, 'otherwise the Tuckers could try and come back at a later date and then threaten you with the Criminal Courts.'

Ashley suggested they employ the services of a barrister. He regularly used the services of one particular woman barrister for his more complex cases. He had not mentioned using her services before since barristers were notoriously expensive (typically up to £1000 per hour), but he was convinced someone of her calibre would be able to tear the Tuckers' statements to pieces, exposing them for the liars they were, ensuring all allegations were dropped once and for all.

There was silence for a moment before Jenna piped up and said, 'Paul, you have got to do it. We can't carry on like this. We need it all brought to an end for the sake of our health and sanity.'

Paul thought about it for a few seconds. It wasn't just the expense, he didn't want to put Kara through the unpleasant experience of being cross-examined by a barrister, but what choice did he have? He looked at Jenna and knew she was right.

Whilst they were in Ashley's offices, Ashley arranged for the three of them to meet with the barrister the following week. In the meantime, Paul agreed to prepare an additional copy of the evidence package and deliver it to her chambers so she could bring herself up to speed with the case.

As always, Paul and Jenna were feeling a bit better after having spoken with Ashley. Paul remembered the FASO representative's advice.

'Are you registered with the Children's Panel?' he asked.

'No, I am not. In order to qualify it is necessary to have served on 100 child cases first. I'm not quite there yet,' Ashley said with a smile.

This did not bother Paul too much. Ashley had been worth his weight in gold in so many other ways and he did not want to find a new solicitor at this stage.

That evening Paul went to his journal and for the first time he took out some of his anger on Kara.

This whole state of affairs is very worrying and draining for me, Jenna and all my family. I hate seeing my family put through this and there are times when I just can't bear to tell them the true horrors of the situation. We want it all over now and if that means Kara is adopted by her stepfather, then so be it. It really pains me to say it, but at this moment in time, I really do not want anything more to do with her until she makes a public apology. She is old enough now to know her own mind and must realise the stress and anguish she is putting me and my family through. I have done every-thing I can for her and this is how she has treated me. I am very sad to say it, but at the moment she is a big disappointment to me. I hope one day she realises her mistakes and we can rebuild our relationship, but until she is prepared to say 'Sorry' for what she has put me and my family through, I want no further contact with her. She is obviously harbouring a lot of resentment and bitterness, most likely fuelled by Phoenix, which needs to be off-loaded before she will be happy in her life. Unfortunately, there is nothing that I or my family can do for her now. She is making it quite clear she wants to cut us out of her life.

I find it particularly infuriating that professional bodies such as Social Services and CAFCASS have supported this behaviour in Kara. They have effectively fuelled conflict, rather than encourage relevant parties to get together and talk the circumstances through in an adult fashion. What kind of example have they set for Kara? These people have added to the damage that Phoenix has already inflicted on her. They have badly, arguably criminally, let Kara down. I hope one day she realises this and 'sues the arses off them!' They could be accused of 'identity theft'. These bodies are worse than a waste of space. They are dangerous and in this case permanently damaging. They should not be allowed to get away with it.

On the Tuesday of the following week, Paul went to the doctor's and had a routine check-up. Fortunately, the only concern was his slightly high blood pressure, but nothing too serious, particularly bearing in mind the stress he was under. He had been anxious about going since he was dreading further bad news, but this seeming change in fortune went some way to cheering him up. Perhaps this was a sign things were about to go in his favour.

During Wednesday morning, Paul, Jenna and Ashley prepared to meet with the barrister as planned. They all had high expectations and were incredibly interested to hear her views on the matter.

She arrived on time and sat down in Ashley's office, making herself comfortable. After some quick introductions, she turned to face Paul and started speaking in a slow, serious voice.

'I have read your evidence and sympathise very much with your situation. I believe you when you say these allegations are false. However, if we put the allegations to one side, the judge may still grant the adoption based on the fact that you have not had direct contact with Kara for many years. I know this was not of your choice, but it happened all the same. The court will additionally place high credence on Kara's views, particularly since she is prepared to take the stand. I am afraid Parental Alienation Syndrome is not taken that seriously in UK Family Courts and regardless, it would be extremely difficult to prove.'

There was an obvious drop in the mood. Ashley, Paul and Jenna were extremely disappointed with her response. They had genuinely felt they were in a more positive position.

The barrister could see their clear disappointment and reinforced her original points.

'I recognise the lack of contact has not been of your choice and Kara's mind has likely been poisoned against you, but to prove this in court will be very much an uphill struggle. It's as if this whole adoption has been meticulously planned from the start, many years back. Despite all your efforts, you have not been allowed to be a good father to Kara.'

Paul was back down in the doldrums. It appeared there was absolutely nothing he could do.

'The situation is so bad now,' he replied, 'that contesting the adoption is not so high on my list of priorities. I am more concerned with exonerating my name of any false allegations and protecting mine and Jenna's reputations. I feel I am being blackmailed into giving my consent. If I don't give it, who knows what other sorts of nonsense I or my family will be accused of? On the other hand, if I do give it, it's like admitting I actually carried out these acts. I feel in a no-win situation.'

The barrister understood his predicament and made no bones about the fact that he had been put in a very difficult position. She outlined three options.

1. Write a letter to the court explaining that you now give your consent to the adoption, but deny all the allegations made against you. The hearing would then not need to go ahead and would spare Kara having to speak in court. The adoption would then be granted. This would be the most cost-effective option and would require the least effort.

2. Turn up at the hearing and read an open letter in court stating your views and that you now give your consent to the adoption, but again deny all the allegations. You could also take the opportunity to speak directly to Kara.

3. Continue to contest the adoption and ask for a fact-finding mission to prove who is telling the truth. This would involve another four to five hearings and necessitate the presence of all relevant parties in court, including those who provided witness statements and character references. Each would need to be prepared to take the stand and be cross-examined. This option would be much more expensive, likely running into tens of thousands of pounds, and would probably mean the case continuing for another year or so.

'If you were a rich man,' she continued, 'I could do more for you. We could go for the fact-finding mission, have independent psychological and lie detector tests done on all parties, get the court to meticulously review your evidence and I would put the Tuckers on the stand for cross-examination in order to expose all their wrongdoings. However, if we were to go down this route, would it help you build your relationship with Kara? I suggest it could make things even worse.' Paul nodded in sad agreement. 'Please be aware that I would be very happy to represent you, but ultimately you have to work out what you are trying to achieve.'

That was essentially the end of the meeting. Paul, Jenna and Ashley thanked her for her time and agreed they would be in touch once they had reached a decision.

Over the next few days, Paul and Jenna spent many hours with Ashley trying to fathom the Tuckers' next move and imagined all sorts of terrible scenarios, the worst being that more false allegations would be forthcoming with Kara declaring them in court. They needed to make sure they were prepared for any such surprises. They were coming to the conclusion that the second option presented to them by the barrister would probably be the best way forward. Paul could get his point of view across and hopefully talk directly to Kara. This option would also negate the potentially confrontational experience of Kara taking the stand.

On the Sunday, Ashley went for dinner at Paul and Jenna's

house. He only just made it. He had driven there straight from the hospital. The previous night he had been admitted with a suspected gall bladder problem and had been kept in overnight for observation. He had been complaining recently of feeling very tired, but had put it down to all the work he had been doing. As well as Paul's case, he had other cases to deal with and was doing some very long days, sometimes seven days a week, as Paul had personally witnessed. Fortunately he felt better now, but conceded that he would take things a little easier and watch his diet.

Paul's brother and his wife also joined them for dinner and together they discussed the options put forward by the barrister. They rapidly confirmed their original conclusion. The second option would be the best path to follow. Paul would prepare an open letter, with the intention of reading it out in court. The letter would express his views on the matter and declare his consent to the adoption, but only on the assumption that the court truly believed this was the best course of action for Kara.

Ashley suggested the barrister's presence was probably not necessary now, to which they all agreed. He would thank her for the advice she had given and let her know of their decision.

That evening Paul expressed his feelings about Ashley in his journal.

Ashley has been so much more than a solicitor throughout this ordeal. He has become a counsellor and a good personal friend.

Three days later the CAFCASS report finally arrived at Ashley's offices. It was over three weeks late! Even worse, the front page stated that a copy had been sent to Ashley the first week in March, which was clearly not true.

Paul, Jenna and Ashley read the report with fervent interest and reached similar conclusions. Although the report contained a number of factual errors, remained biased against Paul and supported adoption, it was nowhere near as bad as they had feared it could have been. It did correctly state that the allegations were just allegations and, importantly, no more had been added. If anything, the allegations had been played down. In addition, the CAFCASS officer had stated in her conclusion, 'I empathise with Paul's difficult position'.

The report included a response from Kara to some of the evidence he had provided to the court. Kara had strongly defended Phoenix, stating that the adoption was solely her own idea with no involvement from her mother. In addition, she had accused Paul of 'never being there for her'. They knew this accusation was untrue and most likely planted in her mind by Phoenix, but Kara was unable to recognise this yet; a classic symptom of PAS. The truth of the matter was that he wasn't allowed to be there for her.

Ashley drew their attention to a statement that had been included from an independent psychological consultant: 'Any depression suffered by Kara cannot be attributed solely to Paul's alleged behaviour. Kara had previously required significant psychological support when Ross first entered Phoenix's life. Kara had tremendous difficulty sharing her mother due to previous experiences that cannot be isolated to Mr Nelson and as a consequence needed significant emotional and psychological support to help her through this difficult time.'

It took Paul and Jenna a little while to digest the full significance of this statement. How come Ms Staines had neglected to mention any of this in her report? They considered it absolutely scandalous.

'I think we may be getting a little closer to finding the real reason Kara initially suffered from depression,' said Ashley. 'It supports our claims that there is no truth in the allegations made against you.' Paul felt a weight starting to be lifted from his shoulders.

'It confirms here that Ross came into Kara's life when she was about nine, around the time I received her first devastating letter,' Paul pointed out. 'Could her letter have been precipitated as a result of this psychological support over-compensating, effectively forcing her to accept Ross into her life? Could it be that all the energy focused on helping Kara accept Ross was at the detriment of my own relationship with her? How come this is the first we have heard of this?'

As they scrutinised the CAFCASS report further, it was becoming more and more obvious how terribly misleading the original Staines report had been. Was this due to Ms Staines's incompetence, her lack of due diligence or something more sinister? Perhaps their suspicion that she was a family friend of the Tuckers was true.

Although they now had some substantial facts to help discredit the Staines report, there was nothing powerful enough to deter them from their planned course of action at the second hearing, which was to be held in two days' time.

Over the next couple of days, Paul and Jenna's phone was constantly ringing with friends and family wishing them well. Apart from their closest friends and immediate family, they had not made others fully aware of just how desperate the situation had become. Paul and Jenna did not want the ridiculous, but nonetheless potentially damaging, allegations to become public knowledge. They did take great comfort, however, in knowing so many people were on their side. Many wanted to be present at the hearing, offering their moral support. These supporters, both young and old, recognised that they would not be allowed in the courtroom, but they were so incensed at the perceived injustice taking place that they wanted to be there for them.

On the day of the hearing, Paul and Jenna drove to the courthouse with Ashley. He picked them up from their house at 7:30am. During the journey they spoke about the possible outcomes. They strongly believed they were still doing the right thing. It was important that the validity of an Adoption Order versus a Residence Order was challenged. If the adoption was granted, it was imperative it went ahead with Paul's agreement, rather than the court dispensing with his consent as a consequence of the nature of the allegations made against him. It was of paramount importance that the false allegations of child abuse were discounted, for fear of them coming back to haunt him at a later date.

They arrived at the courthouse at 8:45am and were shortly

joined by Paul's parents and his brother and sister-in-law. They all went to the small cafeteria for coffee. As they sat down, Ross unexpectedly walked in with Ms Staines and bought coffees to take away. Paul reluctantly acknowledged him with a nod of his head and Ross nodded back. Deep down Paul was disgusted that Ross was going along with this charade. Surely he could sense these allegations were nonsense? Paul's first reaction was that it would serve Ross right if Phoenix did something similar to him one day, but he recognised this would not be fair on him either. Paul returned to the table with the drinks.

Paul and his family were shortly joined by friends who had come along to provide moral support. Considering the gravity of the situation, they all remained light-hearted and there was a lot of good humour. Paul knew that one of their younger friends was very nervous in case she was called in to the courtroom to take the stand. She had never been in a courthouse before, hated public speaking and was worried she would let him down.

'All you need to do is tell the truth and everything will be okay,' he gently reassured her. Bless her, he thought.

At 10am, they left the cafeteria and went to wait outside the courtroom. Ashley went to the court offices to ensure the judge had a copy of the letter Paul intended to read.

The Tuckers and Ms Staines had been given their own private room just outside the courtroom and were studying some paperwork. Paul noted the Tuckers had no support from their own family or friends. The officer from CAFCASS arrived a couple of minutes later and waited in the public area outside the courtroom with Paul and his entourage. They did exchange pleasantries, but at this point Paul was not sure who he could and could not trust. It looked as if the Tuckers were very much prepared for a fight.

At 10:30am, Paul, Ashley, the Tuckers, Ms Staines and the CAFCASS officer were all called into the courtroom as scheduled. As they made their way to the entrance, Paul caught his first glimpse of Kara for over five years. He barely recognised her. If she had been walking down the street on a normal day, he would not have known it was his own daughter. This made him so sad. She was so much taller now, nearly as tall as him. He had to admit that she did not look very well, being a little thin and pale. She evidently didn't want to catch his eye. He exchanged a glance with his father as she walked past and it was obvious his father shared his opinion. As Phoenix walked past, he noticed she and Kara had the same small tattoo on their upper arm. He wondered if this had any significance. All the Tuckers noticeably avoided looking Paul, or any of his family, in the eye.

Paul and Ashley were the last to walk into the courtroom and were shown to their seats.

'You can see she's your daughter,' commented Ashley. 'She looks very much like you.'

Paul was sure Phoenix wouldn't like that, but it gave him a comforting feeling.

The judge then appeared from the front and they all rose. Once re-seated, proceedings commenced.

'I have read a letter from Kara and a letter from Mr Paul Nelson,' said the judge. 'I am pleased to say that it looks as though we have reached satisfactory resolution to this case and I am of the opinion that neither letter needs to be read aloud.'

Ashley spoke out at this point.

'Your Honour, considering the emotional turmoil my client has been through, I would like to respectfully request that my client, Mr Paul Nelson, be allowed to read his letter to his daughter, Kara, before the court.'

The judge looked at Paul, prompting a response.

'I do believe it would help bring a sense of closure to the whole proceedings,' Paul added.

The judge was suitably persuaded and agreed to the request.

Paul stood up and faced the court. The Tuckers still refused to look him in the eye. He took a sip of water, cleared his throat and started to read his letter.

Dearest Kara,

I have always loved you and always will. I hope one day in your heart this is something you will recognise. My love as your father is unconditional.

After receiving your upsetting letter over five years ago, I tried so hard to get things back on track by offering to arrange family counselling and mediation sessions. I desperately tried to get to the bottom of what was troubling you. I sent regular letters in an attempt to maintain contact and reassure you that I would always be there for you, despite not receiving any sort of reply. Once you moved house with your mum and I was refused an address or telephone number, I had no means of contacting you. Contacting your school was the only option left to me to ensure you were okay. I never meant to appear controlling in any way.

With respect to the allegations made against me, I don't understand where they are coming from. They are simply not true.

Paul turned specifically to face the judge before continuing.

I am not in favour of the adoption, but if the court genuinely believes that adoption is in her best interests, then out of love for Kara, I will once again give my own feelings lowest precedence and give my consent.

Paul then turned to face Kara.

I truly am at a loss as to how our relationship went so sour and I am hurt by how you currently feel about me and my family. I do take consolation however in knowing that you have successfully settled into another family and I wish you well. If you really want to be adopted so badly, then although it saddens me, you have my consent. Nevertheless, if you ever wish to contact me in the future, or you need my help in any way, I will always be there for you.

Ashley noted the facial expressions of those present whilst Paul read the letter. The CAFCASS officer looked touched, whereas

Kara, Phoenix, Ross and Ms Staines appeared emotionless. Ashley walked over to Kara and handed her a copy of the letter.

Once Paul had finished reading and he and Ashley were re-seated, Ashley quietly commended him on his reading skills.

'Kara, Phoenix and Ross will always remember what you said,' he whispered.

There was a brief pause before the judge turned to face Paul.

'Your letter will be kept by the court and remain on file indefinitely,' he said clearly for all to hear. He then turned to Kara and remarked in a rather berating tone, 'I hope you realise the anguish, stress and emotional suffering your father has gone through.'

Paul was pleased the judge made this point. He wondered what the judge would have made of it had he known the full extent of the torment and misery Paul and his family had endured and the total magnitude of the injustice that was transpiring. If only the judge had knowledge of all the facts, rather than the biased rubbish he had been fed by Social Services and CAFCASS, perhaps things would have worked out very differently.

After that, the hearing went very much downhill from Paul's point of view. Fortunately it only lasted another five or so minutes. The judge repeatedly got everyone's name wrong and then granted the adoption without question. Ashley just shook his head.

The judge turned to Kara.

'Would you like a celebration hearing?' he asked.

'Yes please,' Kara replied without hesitation. Paul turned to Ashley, looking bewildered.

'A celebration hearing is all part of the adoption process,' Ashley informed him. 'It is a hearing to which Kara's new family will be invited for a fifteen-minute celebration at the courthouse.'

Paul wondered how they could be so insensitive. He had just lost a child and here they were organising some sort of 'cele-bration party' in front of him.

The judge then thanked Ms Staines and the CAFCASS officer for all their hard work. This really hacked Paul off. He considered they had just been doing their jobs, and badly at that. It was he who had put in all the hard work, but no one was prepared to listen. No mention at all was made of all the evidence he had put together to try and get the truth out. He wondered if the judge even knew of its existence.

At approximately 10:50am, Paul and Ashley walked out of the courtroom. They had only been in there twenty minutes, but it had felt a lot longer. Paul was so glad to be met by friends and family. They didn't have to say anything. The reassuring hugs were enough. They were understandably keen to know how things had gone, but didn't want to press him too hard at this stage.

He invited them all out to lunch as a thank-you for their support. It was also an opportunity for them to share in the relief of the nightmare coming to an end. Unfortunately Ashley could not join them since he had further work appointments, but he promised to catch up later that afternoon.

Over lunch, Paul explained how bitterly disappointed he was that the adoption had been granted without question and how his evidence appeared to have been completely ignored. However, there were some positives. He was happy that:

+ he had had the opportunity to read out his letter in court and speak directly to Kara.

+ Ashley had personally handed a copy of the letter to Kara.

+ the judge had ordered the letter be held on file indefinitely by the court.

+ the judge had pointed out to Kara that she had put her father through a lot of emotional pain.

+ there had been no mention of the false allegations previously made against him and the mad Tuckers never got the opportunity to tarnish his good name further.

+ CAFCASS and Social Services had been taken by surprise and never got the opportunity to put a biased spin on the proceedings.

✦ most importantly, Kara had not had to take the stand. If she had, she would no doubt have been venomous towards him and made any chance of future reconciliation between them more difficult. The way things had been left, he still had a glimmer of hope that one day she would get in touch with him with a view to rebuilding their father–daughter relationship.

'At least all the nastiness of the court case is over,' said Paul, whilst raising a glass. 'Perhaps now we can try and get back to some sort of normality.'

They all drank to that.

Later that afternoon, Paul and Jenna met with Ashley. What he had to say took Paul by surprise.

'In court this morning, I witnessed malpractice and injustice of incredible magnitude, not dissimilar from the slave trade of old. The Tuckers might have thought they won today, but in reality, it was you that came across as by far the bigger person and this will come out in time.'

This cheered Paul up. 'I need to settle up with you,' he said with an apprehensive look on his face.

Ashley laughed. 'Don't look so frightened; it will be under £5000 as we agreed.'

Paul was mightily relieved and thankful. He knew Ashley had really gone out of his way on this case. They might not have got the result they were initially looking for, but considering the external forces working against them, it was probably the best they could ever have hoped to achieve.

Chapter 12

Conclusions

✧ Post-court matters
✧ Influencing change in the law
✧ Complaints through official channels
✧ Moving on

Over the next few days, Paul and Jenna were overwhelmed with visits and phone calls from friends and family, gladly sharing their relief that the nightmare of dealing with the courts was over. One of their friends who had come to the courthouse for the second hearing commented on how she had noticed that day she happened to be wearing the same coat as the CAFCASS officer. She went on to say how much she had loved that coat and that it was a special birthday present from her husband. Unfortunately she could no longer bear to look at it, since it brought back memories of the dreadful way Paul and Jenna had been treated. She sold it at a boot fair two weeks later.

Paul felt most touched by all the warm, heartfelt wishes he and Jenna received. Although the ordeal of the allegations and the court proceedings was indeed over, he recognised that the issue as a whole would never be completely over for him. He had never wanted Kara to be adopted and despite his valiant efforts to retain at least some, if not all, of his rights, it had all been to no avail. He had been hoping to start building a good relationship with his daughter, but the way things had conspired against him, he now felt there was zero chance of that happening.

Paul's father rang to let him know that his gran had left some money for the family in her will. It just so happened to be the same amount as Ashley's bill, give or take a couple of hundred.

'You're most welcome to it,' he said. 'If your gran had known what was going on she would have wanted to help in some way.'

Paul was not sure if he believed in guardian angels or not, but he took this as a firm signal that his gran was definitely looking after him and he still keeps a picture of her in his front room today.

Meantime, the CSA rang Paul and demanded to know why he had cancelled the standing order from his bank account for child maintenance. He could not believe how amazingly efficient they were when they wanted something from him. He had only just cancelled it, following the hearing. When he had wanted the CSA to deliver a letter to Kara on his behalf, it had taken them six months to respond! Useless, insensitive money-grabbing gits! No wonder they have such a poor reputation, he thought to himself. Talk about kicking you in the guts when you're down. He informed them about the adoption and the fact that his legal responsibilities had been effectively taken away. The CSA considered this highly irregular.

'We should have been informed,' they replied in an arrogant manner, as if they did not believe him.

'I suggest you contact my ex-wife Phoenix if you want further details,' he replied. 'She can provide proof if you need it.'

'Yes, we will, and we'll get back to you shortly.'

They never did get back to him.

Paul and Jenna felt quite humbled when they thought about all the people who had helped them and given so much support throughout their ordeal. As a way of thanks they spent the following week delivering flowers and bottles of wine.

As well as those who provided the more obvious support of providing witness statements and being present at the courthouse, there were others who had very willingly helped with the less visible tasks such as deputising for Jenna when she was absent from class, looking after pets whilst they had to attend appointments, helping prepare and check the evidence files and generally just being there to cheer them up when they felt low. They were not sure how they would have got through their terrible experience if it were not for all their support. It was such a relief to know that the nastiness and bitterness with which they had been contending should now be over.

When they visited their godchildren that weekend, one of the three-year-old triplet girls came up to Paul and sat on his lap. She smiled so innocently at him and said, 'You've got a new face.' Paul thought that summed it up perfectly.

Paul decided he and Jenna should get away for a bit to recuperate and recharge their batteries. Fortunately Easter was approaching so they could take a break from their teaching jobs. Within a couple of weeks they were travelling back to Sri Lanka to meet up with their old friends. They stayed for about three weeks and as usual enjoyed their time immensely, liaising and working with the local community. Amongst other things they went to a crocodile farm, Paul played with one of the local bands and on a number of mornings they were woken up by a troop of wild monkeys playing outside their bedroom window! It was just the tonic they needed.

Whilst there, they confided in their closest friends about the ordeal they had been through. Two of these friends had significant experience of working with mental health patients and had studied mental health disorders in a professional capacity whilst working in the UK. They immediately grasped the situation in which Paul and Jenna had found themselves and remarked how they had encountered Parental Alienation Syndrome before, although not quite so extreme. They described how easy it is for someone to fill a child's head with false memories whilst at the same time erasing genuine ones, especially during a child's formative years. They exemplified how simply it could be done, stating 'Every time Kara said something good about Paul, Phoenix could challenge her and tell her she was wrong. Every time Kara said something bad about Paul, Phoenix could reaffirm this belief and praise her for coming to such a conclusion. It would not be long before Kara would believe all the bad things said about Paul. As an absent parent, he would know nothing about it, nor could he defend himself.'

Once back in the UK, Paul met with Ashley and they discussed their next steps.

'I ultimately want to get UK law changed to stop such travesties of justice,' Ashley explained, 'with legislation possibly called "Nelson's Law". Parental alienation is awful abuse of a child and it should be recognised as a criminal offence. It will be a long process, likely taking up to ten years, but you could be a great asset in making sure this happens, sharing your knowledge. You owe it to others who may find themselves in similar awful circumstances. You can draw on your own personal experience of PAS and how it impacts parents, extended family and ultimately the child victims. You know first-hand the psychological and emotional torment of being an "alienated parent" and the nature of the pain involved. The profile of PAS within the UK needs to be raised. The long-term and potentially permanent damage it can do to families needs to be recognised, particularly the negative and self-destructive impact it can have on the children. I can formulate a long-term plan to help us achieve such a goal.'

It sounded a good idea to Paul. He knew he had to do something. To just sit back and do nothing would just allow the farcical yet appalling situation to continue. The mental and emotional abuse of children via PAS needed to be eliminated.

Paul started his campaign by writing to various authorities expressing his intense dissatisfaction at the way he had been treated. He was understandably very angry at what he considered the complete injustice of it all. He conveyed in detail how he and his family had unnecessarily suffered mentally, physically and emotionally as a consequence of the actions of the so-called family-friendly organisations Social Services and CAFCASS. On top of that, there was the significant financial burden. His letters covered the following:

✦ His dissatisfaction at the poor quality report provided to the court by the social worker. He forwarded a copy so they could see for themselves its incredibly biased nature. He highlighted the numerous incorrect statements and how he had been quoted inaccurately, resulting in him being portrayed in a negative light. Quotes he had provided in support of his good character had been excluded, despite his repeated offer of providing supporting evidence. Furthermore the totally unsubstantiated allegations of abuse that had been made against him (which he vehemently denied) were repeatedly reported as factual information rather than just allegations. He re-iterated how the report did not come across as impartial, but scandalously portrayed him as some sort of immoral, child-hating ogre who never cared for his own daughter.

+ His dissatisfaction at not receiving a copy of the report until after the first court hearing, meaning he was totally in the dark about what was happening, had no idea of his daughter's mental health issues and had very limited opportunity to defend himself. If the adoption had gone ahead at this point, the allegations would have been on his file without his knowledge.

+ Due to the biased nature of the report and because the unfounded allegations had misleadingly been reported as fact, he had no choice but to instruct a solicitor to protect his reputation. He and Jenna were teachers and allegations such as these could have had a disastrous effect on their livelihoods, for which the social worker had shown complete disregard. In order to prepare a defence, he had to spend an extraordinary amount of time preparing evidence and collecting witness statements. This had a significant detrimental impact not only on his business, but also on his and his family's health, primarily as a result of dangerously high stress and anxiety levels put upon them. In some cases, there was the need for prescribed medication. The cost of a solicitor was also a heavy financial burden.

+ Social Services and CAFCASS had both failed to see through a tissue of lies and had unfairly influenced the

Family Courts. They had missed an obvious opportunity to reconcile a loving father with his daughter and instead caused irreparable damage to a once loving family. He explained that he was not sure if this was due to the incompetence of the representatives involved, their gross negligence, or something more sinister such as collusion with the Tuckers. Regardless, he vowed to get to the bottom of it, not just for his own sake, but to make sure this did not happen to others who found themselves in the same terrible predicament.

✦ Finally he stated how he was looking for a full and honest explanation as to why the investigations, in particular that of Social Services, had been woefully inadequate, shown distinct lack of due diligence and been reported in such a heavily biased fashion.

He started by contacting Social Services directly. They were not helpful at all and appeared to show no understanding that his complaint was about the sub-standard work of the social worker, rather than the decision taken by the court. After further correspondence going back and forth, they stated, 'We cannot deal with your complaint since the issues raised were put before the court and as such were subject to the decision of the court.'

They recommended that he try the Local Government Ombudsman (LGO) if he wanted to take it further.

Paul took Social Services up on their suggestion and submitted his complaint to the Local Government Ombudsman. The initial response was that the Ombudsman could not help, giving a similar response to Social Services. However, once Paul explained that he was not challenging the decision of the court, but the conduct of the social worker, an agreement was made to investigate the matter further. In the meantime, it was suggested he submit his complaint to the General Social Services Council (GSSC) and a phone number was provided for him to ring.

About two months later Paul received a written response from the LGO stating, 'We are discontinuing consideration of your complaint on the grounds that the Ombudsman has no discretion to investigate complaints in relation to the conduct of court proceedings.' The investigator recommended Paul seek independent legal advice if he wanted to take it further.

Paul rang the GSSC as the LGO had initially suggested and got an answer message requesting that he leave his details and they would ring him back. They did ring back and requested he fill in a rather lengthy form and send it back to them. Paul did as they asked and about a month later he received the first written response from the GSCC stating, 'We cannot examine your complaint under GSCC Rules since it relates to the social worker's capability and not her conduct.'

Paul wrote back pointing out that he considered the two to be linked. Her poor capability had led to a 'standard of work well below the expected standard'. That in itself was listed as misconduct on their own Code of Conduct Guideline. They agreed to investigate it further. After another couple of months, he received a second written response stating, 'We do not seek to dispute your views or condone any of the comments made by Ms Staines, but since the Ombudsman has not criticised her, we do not have the grounds to pursue an Investigation, nor question the suitability of Ms Staines as a social worker. There is no mechanism for you to appeal on our decision to close the matter, so we suggest you take legal advice if you want to take it further.'

Not that surprisingly, the more Paul tried to progress his complaint, the more evasive and defensive the different authorities became. Some would request that further irrelevant checkbox type forms be filled in seemingly just to waste his time. Others would try to placate him and make out they were doing something, but they all invariably tried to pass the buck, recommending he try elsewhere. They all proved totally ineffectual, being of no help whatsoever.

Though exasperated, he managed to keep going, although at times he felt like David fighting 100 Goliaths. He continued to make entries in his journal, making detailed notes with respect to the responses he was getting, comforting himself that one day he would expose these bodies. In the current economic climate of austerity, he questioned their very existence. He considered them all a waste of time, space and money. From his experiences, Social Services and CAFCASS had turned a bad situation into something a lot worse and had caused a lot of unnecessary pain and suffering. To add to the sorry dilemma, supposed referee authorities were seemingly totally ineffectual, allowing it to happen.

Five months after the CAFCASS interview, the Office for Standards in Education, Children's Services and Skills (OFSTED) sent Paul an evaluation form giving him the opportunity to comment on his experiences with CAFCASS. OFSTED were collecting this type of information in preparation for an inspection of CAFCASS. They stated that if he was prepared to leave a contact telephone number, an inspector might contact him directly for his views. Paul filled in the form very candidly, criticising the CAFCASS process as constructively as he could and describing how unnecessarily painful it had been for him and his family. He gave his name and contact details in the hope they might be interested in following his case up, but he never heard anything.

Six months after the final hearing, Paul got another letter from the CSA asking for more maintenance money. He could not believe it. It wasn't just their inefficiency that astounded him; there was also the matter of gross insensitivity. He wrote a short letter in reply explaining how he had already informed them about the adoption and the surrounding circumstances. He made a point of requesting they now stop persecuting him and his family with requests of this nature.

A month later, he got a return phone call from the CSA confirming his liability for child maintenance was now no longer in force, but there was a payment of £12 outstanding. Were these people human?

He suggested they contact Phoenix. Although he was content to pay this trivial amount, he was pretty sure she would not want it. In his opinion, the CSA were just prolonging the awful nightmare everyone else was now leaving behind them. After some discussion, they agreed to his suggestion.

Three days later, he got a written response from the CSA confirming his liability for child maintenance had indeed now ended and Phoenix did not want the £12. However, there was no mention of an apology. Instead they stated, 'We reserve the right to collect this amount at a later date should we change our minds.'

Paul was hopeful that this was the last of his dealings with the CSA. In his view they had ended up being a very inefficient and unpleasant organisation to deal with. Their sole focus had been on collecting money, with very little being done in practice to help improve his relationship with his daughter. The one time they did offer to be helpful and forward on letters from him to Kara, they did not get round to it for six months! For the most part he had found their manner confrontational and he was not surprised in the slightest that their approach made fathers want to run.

Predictably Paul heard nothing from Kara or any of the Tuckers after the hearing. As time moves on he continues to buy birthday cards and Christmas cards for Kara. It's ironic that now he has an address to send them to, he's prohibited from posting them, but instead keeps them at his house. He hopes one day he will be able to give them personally to Kara in much more pleasant circumstances.

With respect to his own birthday and Father's Day, nothing much will change. They continue to be days of mixed emotions. Although he hasn't received a card from Kara in years, it will not stop him thinking about her. He is still hopeful of a joyous reconciliation, however many years in the future. For now, he devotes the paternal skills he has to his godchildren, nieces and nephews whom he loves very much. He feels most honoured to have been welcomed into the hearts of these wonderful and very loving families. The enjoyment of watching them all grow up whilst trying to be a positive influence in their lives will go a long way to making up for his loss with Kara.

On his birthday this year, his younger godchildren rang him early in the morning and all sang 'Happy Birthday' to him over the phone. It was such a fantastic and moving surprise. It exemplified to him how a good mother influences and brings up her children. Why had these characteristics apparently passed Phoenix by? He considered it tragic, arguably criminal, that a father–daughter relationship should suffer because of the vindictive behaviour of a mother, shamefully supported by supposed family-friendly organisations and the UK Family Courts. The injustice of it all!

Paul and Jenna rescued their businesses admirably considering the time they had had to take out to devote to the court case. They did suffer some financial setbacks, but overall they came out on top.

Paul has an ever-increasing number of students and has added Musical Therapist to his job title, spending one afternoon a week working with special needs adults and children. He continues to enjoy his leisure time playing saxophone with different bands.

Jenna's school goes from strength to strength and she successfully managed to put on her school's production at the town theatre. It went down an absolute storm. It was purely coincidental that the finale featured Paul playing the saxophone lead for title track of the show, Monty Python's

'Always Look on the Bright Side of Life'.

Chapter 13

Reflection on decisions and procedures followed

- ✧ Paul's views
  - Social Services, CAFCASS and overseeing authorities
  - The British judiciary system
  - Paul's solace and coping strategies
- ✧ Jenna's views
  - Phoenix's influence
  - Social Services and CAFCASS
- ✧ Grandparents' (Paul's parents') views

The whole adoption scenario over the last year had left physical and emotional scars on Paul and Jenna. Even though many months on it appeared to be at an end, it still dominated their conversation, despite their best endeavours to distract themselves from the subject. Whether alone or together, they would find themselves mulling over how the whole episode had been allowed to happen, reflecting on the incredibility of the decisions made and if there was anything they could have done differently.

Paul remained absolutely staggered that the proposed adoption went through without challenge, finding the whole affair surreal. Any confidence he might initially have had in the competence of organisations such as Social Services and CAFCASS had been totally destroyed and he felt utterly betrayed by the UK family judiciary system. Furthermore, overseeing authorities such as the Local Government Ombudsman and the General Social Care Council, who were supposed to ensure fair play in such situations, had proved themselves totally ineffective. He had lost all respect for the authorities dealing with his case.

He considered that he (and others close to him) had been put through an enormous, yet unnecessary, amount of anguish and pain, ultimately resulting in the entirely unjustifiable loss of his daughter. He knew the recommendations given by Social Services and CAFCASS were based on false information, despite his tremendous efforts to get the truth out. He had a wealth of indisputable evidence to show Kara had been poisoned against him from a young age. Kara had somehow been brainwashed into believing that he never loved or cared for her and worse still, that he was a danger to her. These were all outrageous slurs on his character and simply not true. In reality, others had been the real perpetrators of child abuse, playing with Kara's mind and ultimately destroying her relationship with her father.

He was not sure if the allegations made against him were as a result of false memories being planted into Kara's head, or whether Kara had intentionally made them up in order to discredit him in support of her mother's selfish goals. Regardless, she had been seriously misled and her actions had sadly resulted in Phoenix succeeding in her vengeful desire to distort history, trying to eliminate him from their lives.

To make matters even worse, Social Services had strongly recommended there be no future contact between him and his daughter, not even Christmas cards. This hurt him very deeply and made future reconciliation more difficult. The recommendation was based on the supposed distress caused to Kara as a result of past contact, despite there being no proven foundation whatsoever. As a consequence, he believed any chance of repairing the damage done to his relationship with Kara was now even more remote. Additionally it made him feel like some sort of dangerous criminal, which was totally unjust. The report went on to say that if there was future contact, it was to be at Kara's request and under close supervision of a third party to ensure her safety. Paul agreed that there would be merit in having a third party present to help rebuild their relationship, but certainly not for Kara's safety. The only person in danger of being further abused was him.

He found CAFCASS were slightly more empathetic to his plight after reviewing his evidence, but they were not prepared to overturn the initial recommendations of Social Services, claiming that Kara's desires, wishes and feelings must ultimately take precedence. Parental Alienation Syndrome was not given serious consideration and would not carry much weight anyway. The possibility of future mediation or counselling was quickly dismissed, despite his requests.

All information clearly pointed to the adoption application having been driven by Phoenix, despite the paperwork saying it was Ross's application. Ross himself had been very quiet throughout the whole proceedings. He appeared to be simply a means for Phoenix to get what she wanted. Paul was concerned that the adoption was not in Kara's long-term interests and any happiness on her part would only be short-lived. From Kara's perspective, nothing of much significance would change. She had been residing with Ross and Phoenix for a number of years and during that time Paul had not contacted her directly, as per her request. Furthermore, she would be eighteen in a couple of years and not a child any more, being legally recognised as an adult in her own right.

He had initially tried to maintain some sort of contact by writing regular letters to Kara six years previously, but Phoenix had shut off this last avenue when without warning she had moved house and refused to give him or his family any contact details. Why was this? She never did give him or his family an explanation and they still do not know why to this day. He found it astonishing that she could continue to demand child maintenance from him (and for that matter want to), whilst at the same time denying him any form of contact with their daughter. In one breath she was saying she wanted nothing to do with him, but in the next she wanted his money. He was only too happy to pay the child maintenance. It was the fact that the law allowed Phoenix to deny him contact with his daughter, whilst simultaneously trying to financially drain him, that irked him.

Paul found that neither the social worker nor the CAFCASS

officer appeared to work impartially. Both openly admitted their remit was to believe the child. The whole process had been excruciatingly painful. He had to cope with all sorts of emotions, spanning overwhelming anger, resentment, humiliation, disappointment, despair, rejection and a sense of bereavement. Friends and family were obviously concerned about his mental state, bearing in mind the stress and strain he was under. There were many times he was desperately crying out for help, but nowhere in the investigation was there a body prepared to support him or believe his version of events. Some sort of professional therapy, possibly in the form of counselling sessions either during or after the events, would have been useful, but nothing like this was on offer. Instead he had to rely on the services of his privately funded solicitor. He did consult volunteer organisations such as Families Need Fathers and FASO with respect to the false allegations. They were very understanding of his situation, offering their moral support and sharing useful information, but they were equally frustrated with the current system and had no real muscle to rectify his situation. In contrast, Phoenix and Kara appeared to have no end of support from many organisations who believed their story without question, arguably adding their own sick interpretations and unfairly influencing the courts.

Paul felt Social Services and CAFCASS had promoted a highly confrontational atmosphere throughout the whole process. This was not helped by their practice of interviewing each party separately. He had encountered a very 'cloak and dagger' approach to the whole investigation. He had found it frustratingly difficult to get any information about his daughter's wellbeing, her state of mind, or the nature of the allegations made against him. A lot of this information did not arrive until after the first court hearing. If he had not had his wits about him at this first hearing, the adoption would have gone ahead there and then, based on the false allegations. He would not have been able to defend himself or get the chance to exonerate his name. The allegations would have remained on file unchallenged, ready to haunt him in the future. It was only after he informed the judge that he had not seen anything in writing that a second hearing was even considered. Inexcusably, neither the Social Services nor the CAFCASS report arrived in time for him to adequately prepare himself for either of the hearings.

It was apparent to Paul that neither Social Services nor CAFCASS devoted enough time or resources to carry out their investigations thoroughly, although he admitted a better job was done by CAFCASS. Instead these organisations went for the easier option of believing the mother and child and assumed the allegations to be true, without taking sufficient time to review the evidence. Ms Staines in particular had been heavily influenced in her recommendation by the views of the consultant psychiatrist, who had stated, 'In my view adoption would be a very positive step for Kara.' Regrettably this psychiatrist had never met or spoken with Paul. The psychiatrist's opinion was based solely on the version of events given to her by Kara and Phoenix. No mention was made of the possibility of parental alienation. No attempt whatsoever was made to hear Paul's version of events and how he had desperately tried to maintain contact with Kara. The psychiatrist's position could arguably be defended in that she was abiding by patient confidentiality rules, but this did not excuse the social worker for glossing over this vital point, neglecting to mention in her report that Paul's version of events was not being taken into account. Always adopting an overly cautious stance would go some way to covering their backsides should they come up against genuine cases of child abuse, but in this case, their lack of due diligence significantly compounded the damage to a once loving father–daughter relationship.

Why did the social worker's investigation neglect to mention how Kara first required psychological treatment when Ross entered her life? Why did it not mention that she was having difficulty sharing her mother with Ross? Instead, the blame for Kara's depression was attributed solely to Paul's alleged abusive behaviour, allegations for which there was no supporting evidence whatsoever. Any possible correlation with the behaviour of her mother's previous boyfriends or Ross was totally ignored, in favour of discrediting Paul. The social worker appeared to be able to get away with such deficiencies and misleading inaccuracies, devoid of chastisement. Paul had pursued various avenues of complaint, including the Social Services grievance procedure and reporting it to the Local Government Ombudsman and the General Social Services Council, but none of these supposed referee bodies were prepared to support him, saying it was a court matter and outside their remit.

Paul was of the firm opinion that the Social Services and CAFCASS representatives involved in his case had been given a highly disproportionate amount of power compared to their capabilities. They were trying to act in the capacity of judge, psychological expert, legal advisor and mediator, to name just a few. They were hopelessly out of their depth. Decisions made regarding Kara's welfare, which would significantly and permanently impact two extended families, were going to be based on their recommendations. In his view, these people did not exhibit people skills, were poor judges of character and did not appear to have had any training or knowledge in relevant concepts such as PAS. They had been easily deceived and manipulated by devious people. Furthermore, he wondered if he should sue the social worker for reporting libellous accusations against him, having erroneously reported a number of times that he had actually carried out the abuse of which he was accused. Understandably his negative experiences so far in trying to challenge the practices of such a large organisation ultimately put him off this course of action.

Although Paul never said anything at the time for fear of being branded prejudiced, he thought both representatives came across as very anti-men and wondered whether they had experienced their own personal traumatic relationships. Had they intentionally taken jobs such as these to take their revenge on men? He recognised he was being unfair to a lot of excellent professionals who worked in this field, but unfortunately the two he had come across had seriously maligned his views of these organisations. In his opinion, they had portrayed a scandalously pitiful image.

He recalled sitting in the reception area of the CAFCASS offices waiting for his interview, reading some of their latest brochures. He was impressed with the content and they gave him hope that this organisation could help him get his relationship with his daughter back on track. In reality, however, he was extremely disappointed. Although the brochures and the associated CAFCASS website appeared impressive, the officer he encountered did not appear to be carrying out the practices that were being advertised. In his view there was a significant disconnect between what was advertised as happening and what was actually happening.

Both the social worker and the CAFCASS officer he had met were mature in years. Perhaps they were too set in their ways to take on board the new practices that their respective organisations were promoting? He was certainly not age-prejudiced, for he understood that with age comes wisdom, but in his opinion, wisdom had unfortunately passed these people by.

Paul saw first-hand how overstretched and chaotic the Family Courts were when he delivered his evidence to the courthouse offices. Everything appeared very disorganised. Additionally the judge seemed ill-prepared for both hearings.

At the first hearing, the judge turned up late and rather laboured the point of how busy the courts were and how he was keen to get the hearing over and done with as soon as possible. To add to the muddle, a copy of the social worker's report had not been made available.

During the second hearing, the judge made no mention of having reviewed any of the evidence that Paul had prepared. He may not even have known of its existence. The CAFCASS officer herself had previously admitted that the judge would be unlikely to read it. The judge appeared to simply rely on the conclusions drawn by the social worker and the CAFCASS officer, thanking them for their hard work. No mention was made of Paul's colossal efforts. Instead, the judge insensitively arranged a celebration hearing for the Tuckers. No mention was made of any counselling or therapy sessions for Paul or his family to help them cope with their loss. Where was the justice in any of this?

Paul believed that a Residence Order in favour of the Tuckers, rather than an Adoption Order, would have been far more appropriate and far less damaging to all parties. Even if there had been the slightest grain of truth in the allegations, why would it have been necessary to irreversibly break all legal ties between him and his daughter? Hypothetically, even if he were a danger to Kara, surely the fact that the Tuckers already had custody would be enough to provide Kara with the safe environment she needed? He had already agreed to share parental responsibility. Taking his legal responsibility away would change nothing in this respect. In his eyes, the authorities and Family Courts were merely pandering to the whims of a teenage girl, who had been alienated against her father by her mother. If courts simply sanctioned the recommendations of Social Services and CAFCASS without challenge, these supposed family-friendly organisations would be allowed to go about their business unchecked, arguably resulting in bad and potentially dangerous decisions.

Although Paul felt it an appalling travesty of justice that the adoption had gone ahead, he did acknowledge that the judge had gone some way to help him, particularly bearing in mind the biased nature of the information that had been provided to the court. He appreciated the judge giving him the chance of a second hearing to help clear his name and, importantly, affording him the opportunity to read his letter to Kara. Furthermore, a Court Order had been made ensuring a copy of the letter be held on file by the court indefinitely. Even if Kara never wanted to know him again, at least any potential grand-children on the horizon could get a better picture of what actually happened.

When Paul looked back, he often wondered how he had managed to cope. He could easily understand how others in his position got driven to the absolute depths of despair, suffering serious stress-related conditions, even going as far as taking their own lives. He reflected on how there appeared to be a disturbingly increasing trend of fathers taking not only their own lives, but the lives of their children too, seemingly so their ex-partner could not have everything their own way. Although he considered this totally abhorrent and inexcusable, he could understand the torment these men likely endured. It wasn't that they just missed their children, it was the fact that their ex-partners appeared to be able to easily get away with denying them their children, without chastisement. He thought about advice he could give others in his position, reflecting on his own circumstances.

22 May

First and foremost, I am so fortunate in having Jenna. She has been my rock throughout, being a major source of solace and comfort. She has always been prepared to listen and has understood what I have gone through. She has witnessed most of it first-hand and has had her own trauma to cope with, especially once her own business started to be threatened. To have to take all this on without occasionally unburdening to someone would have been unbearable.

As well as being someone to confide in, Jenna is a reminder of all the wonderful things I have in my life. She reminds me how fortunate I am to be able to fulfil my ambitions of playing the saxophone and working for myself. It may not be a lucrative means of employment, but I love being my own boss, particularly after having spent many years working for a large corporation. To focus on the positive aspects of one's life is a great source of comfort in troubled times.

We share a great network of family and friends. Throughout our ordeal, we were able to rely on these people to lift our spirits. Despite the apparent hopelessness of the situation, they knew how to tap into our sense of humour and would always share something to get us laughing again. I recall one of my best friends teasing, 'You were a wonderful loving father. It was the husband bit that needed a little refinement!' Laughter was definitely an effective counter to the trauma we went through, even if at times it may have been thought inappropriate. Regrettably we felt we could not share the full extent of our troubles with as many friends and family as we would have liked for fear of information inadvertently getting into the wrong hands, for example 'the no smoke without fire brigade'. Any 'idle gossip' or 'loose talk' could potentially have damaged our reputations and cost us our businesses. Additionally I felt a sense of shame. Although I knew this was unjustified, I still found it hard to talk about the ordeal I was going through, both at the time and even now. Although my conscience is clear, there are still odd moments when I wonder if there was anything I could have done to avert what was to transpire. When I mention this to friends and family, they are very quick to assure me that I was categorically in no way to blame for the cruelty to which I have been subjected, my only mistake being I was too trusting of Phoenix. They remain very complimentary about Jenna, reminding me of the extraordinary support she has given me. I don't really need reminding, for I know how special she is, but I love to hear others share my view all the same. Friends, family and good humour are most important to help get through difficult times.

We were fortunate in that we still experienced the joys of having young children around us. We have our nephews, nieces and godchildren who span across all ages. We are proud to be godparents and love sharing time and having fun with them all. There is absolutely no way we would allow the experience we have gone through to embitter our attitude in this respect. To allow negative experiences to bring bitterness into one's life is a sign of defeat.

Over the years we have been blessed in sharing many wonderful experiences together and we often day-dream about more amazing adventures coming our way. We strongly believe this nightmare has brought us even closer together as a couple and so far we have been proved right. Jenna often says, 'What doesn't kill you makes you stronger.'

When Paul felt low, he would purposely focus on the positive aspects of his life. It was a form of self-therapy that helped dampen some of his emotional pain. The pain never totally went away, but thankfully it could be suppressed. He found his journal a great source of comfort and a way of feeling close to Kara despite their separation. He still writes relevant details in it today. During the dark times, it was a useful vehicle to help unburden his tales of woe and help rationalise his own thoughts.

Another major factor that helped him pull through was his firm belief that good always triumphs over evil. He remains convinced that the truth will come out one day and virtue will prevail.

Jenna remained very unforgiving of Phoenix. She believed there were no excuses for deliberately and cruelly damaging Paul's father–daughter relationship. Her opinion of Phoenix had been tainted right from the beginning, when they first spoke to one another on the telephone. Jenna had found her to be cold, calculated and scheming and had been expecting trouble further down the line, but not of the magnitude that eventually unfolded. Despite her efforts to be extremely polite, she found Phoenix totally lacking in showing her any courtesy and respect in return. There was never any mention of a 'please' or a 'thank you' when she wanted anything. Jenna sadly concluded that Phoenix was just a nasty, spoilt woman, devoid of any feelings for others. She had personally witnessed the difficult times Phoenix had put Paul through, including her mind games, leaving him not knowing when he would see his daughter again. Right from the beginning she believed Phoenix had spitefully treated him like a puppet, trying to take away his dignity, since she had all the strings to pull. Jenna was surprised Paul had stayed married to her for so long. Although she did not condone his fling, she could easily understand how a woman like Phoenix could drive any man to the depths of despair.

Jenna refused to accept Phoenix's upbringing as a possible cause for her vengeful behaviour. Jenna herself had many friends who had genuinely had difficult childhoods and they had all turned out to be decent, upstanding individuals. Additionally, she had witnessed children from her own school brought up in very trying circumstances, yet they all had grown up with a sense of decency. Jenna felt Phoenix's behaviour was simply a consequence of not being able to forgive Paul for his fling with another woman. Phoenix had become so bitter and enraged that she would stoop to any depths to punish him, even if that meant using their own daughter as a weapon. Jenna had experienced elements of this type of behaviour from bitter mothers of children who attended her dance school before, but never as extreme as with Phoenix. Jenna did question if perhaps other people were spurring Phoenix on down this path, but if that were the case, she believed Phoenix should have had the moral decency to stand up to them.

Jenna and Kara got on very well when they first met and Jenna felt their close relationship would have continued indefinitely had it not been for Phoenix. Jenna was very experienced in working with girls of all ages due to her profession. They would often confide in her, knowing they could trust her judgement. She was fully aware of how young girls have a tendency to make up stories if they can't get their own way and was confident she would not have been so easily deceived or influenced as were the representatives from Social Services or CAFCASS. Ultimately she felt sorry for Kara, for she could sense right from the outset that she was being manipulated, as was evident when Kara came to visit. Particularly poignant examples for Jenna were when Kara was aged about four and Phoenix would dress her like a poor orphan girl. It was as if Phoenix was trying to make a point that the maintenance money Paul was providing was not enough. Another time was when Kara was about eight and took photographs all around their house. It felt like they were being spied upon by Phoenix, who was using Kara as her agent.

Jenna had been left equally as frustrated and disillusioned as Paul over the behaviours and working practices of Social Services and CAFCASS. She thought it disgraceful that neither the social worker nor the CAFCASS officer had made any effort to meet Paul's family in person before drawing their conclusions in their damning reports. CAFCASS had not even phoned his parents for their views. She considered it completely inexcusable that the social worker had not bothered to inform Paul of her conclusions until the day before the first court hearing. When she finally did inform him, it was absurdly by means of a quick phone call! What if he had been out at the time? She felt the social worker had treated the matter more like buying and selling a car rather than dealing with people's feelings. Kara came across as just another teenager that the social worker wanted off her books as quickly as possible, regardless of the consequences to all involved.

Jenna found the CAFCASS interview farcical. Despite the fact that she had lived with Paul for over ten years, she was not allowed in the interview room, but was made to wait outside for the first hour. This was despite everybody sitting in the waiting room being able to hear exactly what was being said. Having a closed door was absolutely pointless in that respect. Her heart sank when she clearly heard the CAFCASS officer state that 'CAFCASS policy is to always believe the child', regardless of what Paul had to say. Things just got worse when the officer added, 'The judge is unlikely to look at any of your evidence.' This made Jenna extremely angry. Surely it wasn't in the best interests of anyone to just believe a child, giving in to crazy demands without thoroughly reviewing the circumstances? It appeared that a devious child could quite easily manipulate the system if they knew how. To top it all, the CAFCASS report was indefensibly late, giving Paul inadequate preparation time for the final hearing.

She believed both Social Services and CAFCASS had ridiculously and unjustifiably treated Paul as if he were a criminal low-life, adding to the stress he was already under. She shared his opinion that the female representatives they had encountered had very big chips on their shoulders when it came to men, so much so that it badly influenced their judgement. She considered neither to be fit to make the important decisions they were taking. Could they not see the whole situation had been orchestrated by Phoenix, or had they purposely chosen to ignore this fact since it was the easier route for them to take?

During the dark times Jenna often described how she felt like she was living on tenterhooks, wondering what, if any, further accusations were going to be made against her or Paul. Despite how ludicrous and groundless any further accusations might be, the child's word was always going to take precedence. The words 'We always believe the child', as spoken by the CAFCASS officer, still haunt her today. The possibility that the child's mind could have been poisoned by an alienating parent was given very little credence.

Occasionally Jenna and Paul would watch the famous American judge on her reality TV show who often quoted the line, 'How do you know when a teenager is lying?' The judge would then answer her own question, 'Their mouths move.' Although they both felt this was a little extreme, they did understand and concur with the point being made. To them it was common knowledge that children are adept at letting out only certain bits of information, not necessarily telling the whole story, or even making up stories should it be in their favour. Surely trained representatives from organisations such as Social Services and CAFCASS were aware of this? Both Jenna and Paul were very strong believers that a child's account should never, ever be dismissed and should always be thoroughly investigated, but to just believe the account without question showed naivety and a lack of common sense. Even worse, a poorly trained professional could compound the situation by unintentionally encouraging a child to make things up.

Kara's paternal grandparents were left quite bemused by the whole affair. Following Paul and Phoenix's separation, they were initially encouraged by the fact that they still got to see Kara regularly. Paul would make a point of visiting them when Kara was staying with him for the weekend. They had always loved Kara and during these visits there was nothing shown but love and affection. As the years went by, however, they noticed Phoenix making life difficult, the pinnacle being when she moved house and refused to give their son a contact address or telephone number. At this point they felt a deep sense of betrayal. They were obviously saddened all contact had been broken, but became resigned to this loss, feeling there was nothing they could do to change the circumstances. They were well aware that grandparents had no rights under current UK legislation.

They considered Phoenix a major influence in stopping their contact, purposely brainwashing their granddaughter into believing Paul and the family were a negative influence, or worse still, a danger to her. To add to their distress, they then had the added torment of watching their son suffer emotionally as a result of the allegations Kara made against him. They knew these accusations were nonsense, being almost beyond their comprehension, but felt powerless to help. It got so bad that Paul's mum had to be prescribed medication.

Ultimately, they do not hold Kara responsible for her actions, since they believe others have had an unfair influence. They still hope that one day she will resume contact with Paul and the rest of the family.

With respect to the conduct of Social Services, they were as upset as Paul that they had not been quoted accurately in the report presented to the court. They found a number of their statements had seemingly been deliberately taken out of context, with the intention of biasing the conclusion in support of the adoption proposal.

With respect to CAFCASS, they were disappointed that they were not even given an opportunity to present their views. However, having seen the injustice that ultimately transpired, they do not believe their views would have made the slightest bit of difference to the outcome.

For now they are content to focus their love and attention on their other grandchildren, but will always be there for Kara should she ever wish to renew contact.

Chapter 14

Views and comments going forward

✧ Paul's views
  • System overhaul: the practices of Social Services, CAFCASS and the CSA
  • Improving practices within the Family Courts
  • Recognising Parental Alienation Syndrome (PAS)
  • His own future

Paul continued to write in his journal long after the final court hearing, trying to rationalise what he, Jenna and his family had been through. He used these opportunities to collect his thoughts on how matters could be taken forward.

6 November

Without doubt, there are bad fathers in this world that shirk their responsibilities and do not adequately provide for their offspring, whether emotionally, financially or both. This is justifiably regarded as child abuse. There are also a number of fathers that have been unfairly 'tarred with this brush' through no fault of their own. They would dearly love contact with their children, but mothers, supported by outdated organisations and Family Courts, have denied them this privilege. For some reason, society does not seriously treat this behaviour of mothers as child abuse. This needs to change.

Serious physical and/or mental abuse of children by a parent is an ugly, deplorable reality in our society and any parent carrying out such a barbaric abomination has to be mentally challenged in some way. The fact it happens at all needs to be addressed and children need to be protected from mental and physical abuse of this type at all costs. Regrettably media reporting has brought about such a culture of paranoia within our society on this subject, that we now immediately assume any adult accused of any type of child abuse is guilty. This can be despite overwhelming evidence to the contrary. To make matters worse, it can understandably stir very deep feelings and provoke a 'lynch mob' type mentality, where facts and common sense appear to be totally disregarded. An appropriate balance needs to be restored.

An assumption of 'guilty' appears to be the default position of organisations such as Social Services and CAFCASS, particularly if the child is making the accusations. It can even be argued that some organisations using poorly trained professionals are unfairly influencing a child to distort the truth, in the belief they are actually helping the child's situation. This can have devastating consequences for the adult that has been unfairly accused, and their family. Shamefully, there are evil people within our society who are despicably taking advantage of this culture and using it for their own immoral purposes, taking revenge and causing as much damage to an adversary as they can. Most are familiar with the scenario of the child who falsely accuses the teacher of hitting them, or the woman that falsely cries 'rape', but not so many are familiar with the scorned woman that brainwashes her child to believe and report nonsensical allegations about their father. False allegations of this nature are absolutely terrible things to deal with for two reasons. First, the accused has to deal with the nightmare scenario of being presumed guilty until proven innocent. Secondly, it takes valuable resources away from genuine cases of abuse or criminal activity. This all needs to stop.

Brainwashing of a child by one parent against the other parent has been termed by psychological experts as 'parental alienation' or 'Parental Alienation Syndrome' (PAS). The act of brainwashing or poisoning the heart and mind of a child is not necessarily anything new, but under the relatively recent heading of PAS, further studies have been carried out demonstrating just how devastating the consequences can be, particularly for the child victim. Books and papers have been published on the subject, mainly in the US to date. The UK

Family Courts and Mental Health Authorities so far do not appear to lend serious credence to this phenomenon.

Having now researched the subject of PAS myself and with the benefit of hindsight, PAS would appear to me by far the most credible explanation for Kara's extreme behaviour. Phoenix is the 'alienator', I am the 'alienated parent' and Kara is the 'child victim'. As a consequence, my relationship with Kara has been severely damaged, arguably destroyed. It seems incredible that the level of alienation was so deep that Kara was prepared to take the stand and testify against me in court. Most disturbing was that despite all evidence showing PAS to be at the root of the adoption request, Social Services and CAFCASS either chose to ignore it, or were very ignorant of it. Ms Staines in particular had been heavily influenced in her recommendation by the views of the consultant psychiatrist, who had based her diagnosis and opinion solely on the version of events given to her by Kara and Phoenix. No attempt whatsoever was made to hear my version of events and the possibility of PAS was not mentioned. This was allowed under the guise of 'patient confidentiality'. This should not be allowed to happen and the social worker should have made it clear in her report that the psychiatrist's diagnosis of Kara's mental health issues and her subsequent opinion on whether the adoption should go ahead were based on a one-sided version of events.

Additionally, there was no mention in the social worker's report that Kara required psychiatric help when Ross first came into her life and it only came to light in the CAFCASS report as a result of me pushing the CAFCASS officer to investigate matters further. Whether this oversight by the social worker was intentional or not, this example of misconduct alone should have been regarded by overseeing referee authorities as grounds for further investigation, maybe resulting in disciplinary action.

At present, it appears far too easy for a malicious and vengeful mother to brainwash her child to concoct false allegations of child abuse against the father. Once the seeds have been planted in the child's mind, there appears to be an ever increasing number of so-

called professionals willing to believe the child's version of events no matter what. This can then start a cataclysmic sequence of unchallenged injustice. Allegations made by a child appear to be believed without question by supposed family-friendly organisations, who then make their recommendations to the Family Courts. The Family Courts are very reluctant to go against their recommendations and as such lend credence to the allegations.

Such allegations can start in the school, with a supposed trained school counsellor encouraging a child to bring forward any problems they may be experiencing. Whilst this can potentially be a very effective way of ensuring children are not being abused, counsellors and other trained professionals need to also consider the possibility that the child may not always be telling the truth, for whatever reason. Such thoughts could have been planted by a vengeful child's parent for example. The credibility of any allegations should be challenged before they escalate further and it needs to be made perfectly clear that they are just allegations until proven. For professionals to just quote, 'We always believe the child' is ridiculous and opening up the system to all sorts of abuse by vicious, venomous, vengeful people simply using the child to get their own way.

Workers for organisations such as Social Services and CAFCASS need to be fully trained in dealing with cases of PAS. They need to understand alienation of this type is a serious form of child abuse in itself, akin to mental cruelty, and any perpetrator should be severely dealt with. At the moment, PAS is just given lip service and not widely understood. The current practice is to believe the brainwashed child victim, which results in the denigration and ultimate destruction of the child's relationship with the alienated parent. The prime goal of these organisations should be to preserve and nurture family ties, not break them, especially if there is no good reason. From some of the more recent literature I have read that promotes these organisations, it would appear there is agreement with my sentiments, but from my experience, the officers employed do not appear to be following their own principles and guidelines. Is this because they feel they have to err on the side of caution, for fear of missing a case of a genuinely abused child? Is it due to poor training or over-stretched resources? Whatever the reason, the disconnect needs to be addressed.

I experienced a lot of secrecy with respect to the Social Services and CAFCASS investigations. Was this a deliberate act on their part to hide their incompetence? I found it very difficult to obtain information, which only served to fuel conflict and hostility.

I believe that mediation should have been encouraged, rather than conflict between 'warring' parties. Attempts to get all parties working together, perhaps sitting around a table with a mediator present, would have been far preferable and beneficial. This would help ensure all relevant parties had access to the same information before making important decisions. These organisations should give this practice more serious consideration. Even when I did get to see a report, it was incredibly late, resulting in me always being the last to know what was happening. Furthermore, the quality of the reports was highly questionable. They contained significant inaccuracies, misquotes and a large element of bias. It would make more sense if all relevant data and facts linked to such investigations were made visible for all to see and discuss in a timely fashion. Additionally there would be significant merit in having quality checks on reports intended for submission to the court, to ensure no unfair compromise in integrity. Recordings of interviews could be useful to ensure all parties are quoted fairly and accurately.

Even now I still don't know exactly what Social Services have documented on my file, if anything. It has proved extremely arduous to obtain this information without incurring some sort of cost. Fortunately it has not stopped me or Jenna pursuing any of our teaching ambitions. A simple mechanism to check whether the allegations were actually reported on any file would be useful. If so, how do we get them removed and what are the consequences?

With respect to the adoption itself, I believe the judge's decision had been unfairly influenced by the social worker and the CAFCASS officer. To add insult to injury, the judge failed to acknowledge the evidence I had prepared, but instead commended Ms Staines and the CAFCASS officer for their reports. Had the judge been made aware of *the evidence I had so painstakingly prepared? Perhaps if he had seen the colossal efforts I had gone to for Kara, coupled with the wealth of information to support the alleged extent of PAS, the case would have been viewed differently. A mechanism for determining if all the evidence has been made available to the judge would be useful.*

I tried to pursue the various grievance procedures and avenues of complaint open to me with respect to the injustice these authorities had encouraged, but no one was prepared to take any responsibility. Organisations such as the GSCC and the LGO were of no help and declared the issue outside their remit. They could only recommend I consult a solicitor and take further legal action, which would have resulted in more expense! There should be an effective independent body that takes complaints such as mine seriously. Organisations such as Social Services and CAFCASS need to be held accountable for the quality of their decisions and recommendations. Ultimately their recommendations can have far reaching and very damaging consequences.

Paul continued to keep abreast of current affairs in the media related to cases such as his and occasionally would discuss associated issues with his family. The more he looked into it, the clearer it became that although his case could be regarded as extreme, it was by no means isolated. Problems with the UK Family Courts and organisations such as Social Services and CAFCASS were constantly in the media. It was recognised that these organisations had a tough job to do and there were a lot of excellent and dedicated professionals working in the field, but there were far too many serious mistakes being made with devastating consequences.

Another entry in his journal read:

13 December

The current political parties are very keen to address social and moral breakdown within our society, often blaming parents. Do these political parties not realise that supposedly family-friendly authori-

ties can potentially contribute to this breakdown? If society is serious about stopping fathers running away and shirking their responsibilities, the practices and procedures of organisations such as Social Services, CAFCASS and the CSA need to be given a thorough overhaul. Whilst they continue to pander to the mother and remain so biased against fathers, fathers will avoid them at all costs. Many responsible fathers who want contact with their children are forced to give up their fight because it is too draining emotionally and financially to deal with these organisations. Even if they have the time, money, evidence and know-how to go about challenging the systems, they have a very limited chance of success. As a consequence these organisations are compelling these fathers to abandon their children. This is clearly not what most fathers want and ultimately it is the children and society in general that suffer. These organisations need to ensure they are employing suitably trained, capable staff and there needs to be a paradigm shift showing clear evidence that fathers are being treated fairly. It might help if these professions were not so female-dominated.

As it was, I was made to feel like an inferior criminal by the representatives I encountered. They exuded a ludicrous air of unwarranted, self-justified superiority, which was totally absurd. There is no place for this type of arrogant behaviour in these organisations and it should be wiped out.

To further rub salt into my wounds, the judge concluded the second hearing by arranging a fifteen-minute celebration hearing for Kara to be held at the court. How could they be so insensitive? There was no support being offered for me or my loss. It's ironic that if you have an accident through no fault of your own, you get inundated with offers of support from solicitors and other such organisations offering their services on a 'no win, no fee' basis. If your child is taken away from you through no fault of your own, there is no obvious support system and no one wants to listen. The offer of some basic counselling by the court would have demonstrated that they at least had some understanding and sympathy for my circumstances, rather than just grinding me down further. Some form of counselling or *therapy should be freely available and offered to those in my position, including extended family members.*

Why was no effort whatsoever extended to try and resolve the conflict between Kara and me? Social Services, CAFCASS and the Family Courts appeared oblivious to my feelings, deeming them insignificant compared to Kara's wishes and desires. This was despite the fact I had proof that Kara's views were based on false information, likely planted into her mind by her mother. Surely the most beneficial solution for all would have been for a Residence Order to have been granted in favour of Kara's stepfather and then an effort made to get to the real heart of what was troubling Kara. Efforts of the so-called professionals within these organisations should have been focused on building bridges, rather than compounding an already desperate situation. They knew Kara was likely suffering from some sort of mental depression and they put that down to me, without question, despite watertight evidence I had prepared to the contrary. They did not appear to consider for one minute that any depression may have been caused by her mother, deviously influencing or possibly even forcing her to give up contact with me. The fact that Kara initially required counselling to accept Ross was also far too conveniently brushed aside.

These organisations have caused an unnecessary amount of pain and anguish to me and my family. In the longer term, most importantly they have let Kara down so very badly, ethically, morally and arguably criminally.

Regardless of what the future holds, we have all been deeply scarred. It's not right that this is allowed to happen in our so-called civilised society.

PAS is still a relatively controversial subject in legal and mental health professions, although it is gaining wider acceptance. There are a number of people who challenge whether Parental Alienation Syndrome is a reality, or whether it should be referred to as 'Parental Alienation' or 'Parental Alienation Disorder'.

From my experiences, parental alienation in one way or another is by far the most likely explanation I can offer at this time for Kara's unjustified hatred towards me and my family. I recognise other hypotheses can be put forward, but the evidence for PAS in Kara's case is overwhelming. Kara shows all the classic symptoms of a 'child victim' and Phoenix has acted in a manner typical of an 'alienating parent', arguably intentionally. Whether it is termed a 'disorder' or 'syndrome' is of secondary importance.

There are some that believe PAS is a myth and the term is being used out of context by parents that have genuinely abused their child, to try and absolve themselves from blame. Whilst I unfortunately accept that the latter is a possibility (and I sincerely hope and believe very much a rarity), from my personal experiences, I cannot accept that PAS is a myth. It's probably no coincidence that the majority of those that regard it to be a myth are women, and statistics show that parental alienation is most commonly carried out by the mother against the father. However, the fact that fathers can also be the perpetrators of parental alienation, effectively alienating the child victim against the mother, must not be overlooked.

Paul remains confident that the public profile of PAS will be raised over the next few years. He intends to use his time constructively, relating his experiences to help those who find themselves in a similar predicament. He would urge them not to overlook or disregard warning signals. Early warning signs shown by the potentially alienating parent or the child victim need to be addressed appropriately in a timely manner. His own experiences should be seen as testament to how serious the problem can become if left to fester. In hindsight, he considers his own case might have been helped if he had applied for contact proceedings at the earliest opportunity when his relationship with Phoenix first went sour and there was no visible sign of her cooling off. Perhaps this could have helped counter the 'poison' Kara was being fed. Regardless, he feels utterly betrayed by Phoenix after misplacing his trust in her when she said she was trying to repair his relationship with his daughter. He believes it was during the times when he had no contact with his daughter that most of the damage was inflicted. Once the alienation had taken hold, he remains at a loss as to how he could have done things differently. Nonetheless, he hopes that publicising his story will enlighten others to the consequences of particular actions they may be thinking of taking.

As the subject of PAS becomes more widely recognised, he is hopeful that an increasing number of corrective options will become available to the alienated parent, with a growing number of bodies freely accessible for advice and support. Paul has vowed to champion such a body if needs be. The purpose would be to help others avoid the same tragic circumstances he now has to deal with. He feels it imperative that more cases be publicised, to help the subject be officially recognised by the courts and mental health authorities. Until PAS gets the full acknowledgment it deserves, it will continue to be difficult for an alienated parent to know the best course of action to take. This needs resolving at the earliest opportunity, supported by a change in UK law and the processes employed by 'family-friendly' organisations.

With respect to his own predicament and his relationship with Kara, Paul feels there is not much he can do now other than wait. He remains optimistic she will one day break away from her mother's influence and start to ask, 'What really happened?' with an open mind. He still makes occasional entries in his journal should Kara ever be interested in reading it one day to get a more balanced view of past history. He has very little confidence Phoenix will ever show any remorse for her actions and have a change of heart, or show any change in her patterns of behaviour. Of particular concern to him is that since the court decided to grant an Adoption Order rather than a Residence Order, there is now no legal obligation upon Phoenix to let him know if Kara is suffering in any way, or if she needs help. He is convinced Phoenix will continue to keep him very much in the dark with respect to Kara's wellbeing. If something terrible should ever happen to Kara, he believes the only reason Phoenix would let him know would be to use it as another way of 'twisting the knife'. As a consequence he feels helpless in this respect.

Paul is still a little unclear on what the future holds. Although the adoption granted by the court is irreversible, he remains hopeful that the inhumane damage unjustly inflicted on his relationship with his daughter will not be permanent. Hopefully any unfounded allegations of child abuse have been rightly removed from his Social Services records, but if not, they are rightly recorded as unfounded allegations and nothing more. He is understandably keen to ensure his reputation has not been tarnished and there is no adverse impact on his and Jenna's future.

He is not 100 per cent certain that Phoenix, or perhaps others around her, consider matters to be finalised. For all he knows, further scheming is under way for other vengeful plans to try and make him suffer. He accepts that the fact that he even thinks along these lines means she has succeeded to some extent. He still has the odd sleepless night or nightmare. There are times when he feels he should retrospectively bring forward accusations of child abuse against Phoenix, for the way she has manipulated Kara. Additionally he could include charges of emotional and mental abuse perpetrated on him and his family. Although he and others would feel fully justified if he pursued this course of action (which could be supported by a stack more evidence if required), he's not sure it would be in Kara's best interests. He simply wants an end to all the nastiness and hopes to repair the damage to his relationship with his daughter. His conscience is clear and he feels the only way forward at this time is to wait for Kara to make the first move.

For now he is happy to focus his energies on the many positive aspects he has in his life and he remains very thankful to all his friends, family (especially Jenna) and his solicitor (Ashley), who not only handled the legalities, but helped him deal with the deeply emotional aspects of the case. Without their support, he does not know how he would have got through the horrendous nightmare. He recognises it has taken its toll on them also. He has come to terms with the circumstances and is at peace knowing that he has done all he can for now to rectify the situation. He hopes that in the foreseeable future Kara will also want to make her peace with him.

He still has unconditional love for his daughter and looks forward with optimism that one day they will have a joyful reunion before it is too late.

Take care Kara,
Love Dad, x

Reviews

Margaret Gardener. *Director, False Allegation Support Organisation (FASO)*.

Can't Explain is a very well written and gripping book, one that I could not put down. It resonates with parts of family life that we often hear about at FASO and the difficulties some families face when they decide on separation.

I believe it will go on to achieve its aim of raising public awareness of Parental Alienation Syndrome and highlights how things can easily go wrong due to misinterpretation of the situation by the state, encouraged or led by an accusing parent, whilst going through the family courts. I hope all those who read the book take the message to heart. For those who find themselves in a similar situation, I would urge you to learn from its truths and get support from the beginning of any potential conflict.

Dr Ludwig F. Lowenstein BA, MA, DipPsych, PhD, CPsychol, AFBPsS. *Clinical, Educational and Forensic Psychologist, President Elect 2010 – International Council of Psychologists, Director, Allington Manor Psychological Services.*

It is important for the reader to know who is reviewing this book. I am Dr Ludwig Lowenstein and I am one of the most well-known experts in the UK on the subject of parental alienation. I am an expert witness working in the Family Courts seeking to obtain justice for both fathers and mothers following an implacable or hostile divorce or separation between husband and wife. This frequently leads to parental alienation which indeed is well explained in this book, which is 'the vengeance of one party against the other'. In the case of Can't Explain it is the vengeance of a mother against the father of a child, thus eventually preventing good contact between the child and father where previously there was such good contact.

My aim is to find justice for either father or mother who is deprived of contact with their children due to the implacable hostility of the custodial parent against a now absent parent. I am sad to say it is an uphill struggle! Parental alienation involves the feeding of information about the other parent that is wrong, deceitful and wicked. The result is generally that the child will avoid having any contact with that parent due to the 'indoctrination' he/she has received from the hostile alienating parent.

Can't Explain is written from the heart ... a broken heart. It should be read by every parent who is in the throes of a marital dispute, even before divorce or separation occurs. Much harm is done, not only to the alienated parent by the process of alienation or brainwashing of the child against them, but to the child/children themselves. This book ably illustrates this.

As the author of a book myself on parental alienation, I have pointed out frequently the short- as well as the long-term effects of brainwashing a child against a good parent. This brainwashing process is explained in Can't Explain and shows clearly the alienation process in progress ending with the obliteration of paternity. This book is a personification of much of the parental alienation conduct which has been written about in my articles and which can be found on my website (www.parental-alienation.info).

The book is divided into 14 chapters, all of which are essential reading and lead up to the fact that the child who was once close to a loving parent eventually renounces such closeness, and in fact turns the closeness into anger and rejection against a good and loving parent. This is a form of emotional abuse that should not be countenanced by the courts, but unfortunately it frequently is. In fact justice is often not done in a Family Court to overturn such evil developments.

The book discusses the premarital relationship between the partners followed by the marital relationship and the difficulties in the marriage. This is followed by a chapter dealing with separation and the father seeking contact with his child. Issues develop over contact and in the end there is no contact. Fathers, in many cases, and sometimes mothers who are alienated take action through the courts with little positive effect. The book is written for the author's real daughter and for all those who have suffered similar depressing outcomes of having no or little contact with their children following divorce and separation. Frequently, parents are accused unjustly of abusing a child, hence the child for that reason not wishing contact. Such abuse is often false and the child has been indoctrinated by the vicious alienating parent. Unfortunately, the allegations are sometimes believed as if they were a fact.

The unjust treatment of the two characters Paul and Jenna in the book is the tip of the iceberg of many fathers and mothers who have been treated similarly by the system which includes social workers, CAFCASS officers, the courts etc. The author of this review has written many articles and books, many of which have been published, on the subject of parental alienation and has drawn attention to this injustice. Let us hope that the character Paul, who lost contact with his lovely child Kara, will one day be able to have good contact once again when Kara realises or somehow has been influenced toward the fact that she has a good father out there who wishes to love her, guide her, and have good contact with her.

Throughout the process of parental alienation the victims and the perpetrators of the evil are known. Social Services, CAFCASS and the courts must in due course change in their approach to parental alienation cases, as through their lack of positive work they make decisions that are not in the best interest of children. The accusations of abuse against a parent, be it sexual, physical or emotional, are very powerful weapons which are frequently used by alienators to destroy the contact of a loving parent with a once loving child. More must be done to prevent this.

The saddest part is that in the end Kara is adopted by her step-father and Paul has to agree to the adoption since the alienator, who has remarried, insisted that Kara should take on the name of the stepfather. The obliterating of paternity is wrong. This is a final injustice and should not be allowed to happen! Kara completely accepts the mother's decision and tells the father over the phone, *'You have never loved me. You have been a bad influence in my life and I want nothing to do with you or your family. My stepfather is the opposite. He is everything I ever wanted and is like a real dad. He makes up for all your failings and makes me feel truly wanted.'* One can only imagine how a father feels having received such a message from a loved daughter now apparently totally lost to him.

As an expert witness to the courts I have had many cases similar to this and it has always been my view that such a child is not speaking for him/herself but is being the 'echo' of the alienator and brain-washing parent. Such children should not remain with such a parent but be placed with the good parent who has never done anything wrong to deserve such treatment.

Finally, I would like to thank the authors for writing such a compre-hensive and easily understandable book on their experiences of the parental alienation process. The process of writing this book will no doubt help to alleviate some of the suffering and injustice undergone by the alienated parent, as 'a problem shared is a problem halved'.

Shaun O'Connell, BSc. PGCE. *Southern Family Aid, McKenzie friend.*

I was asked to review this book which I found to be compelling reading. It raises many issues all too common in the world of the Family Court. Social workers and CAFCASS officers have little training in their role and have almost unfettered freedom to do as they please. Many (not all) have no investigative or analytical skills and believing the child has been all too common.

There is hope on the horizon as the vested financial interest of the legal system has waned given the lack of legal aid, and the last half of 2013 saw a sea change in judicial attitudes with the process now being evaluative rather than the old discretionary basis of old. As a McKenzie friend with educational training assisting others, I can state that PAS does exist and whether it is called PAS or not is now irrelevant since the behaviours that constitute PAS are now slowly being recognised.

One father who last year had not seen his children for ten years and another who hadn't seen his son for two years now both have a loving relationship with their children, so there is hope.

I am also aware that the same pattern occurs at the hands of fathers who have main care. It is vital for anyone in such a predicament to act swiftly as the passage of time can be devastating in its effects. I am well aware of this since it happened to my own children who have been turned against the whole of my own family. It is high time for the system now to fully address the issue of PAS and make sure no more families needlessly suffer.

Sue Whitcombe, BSc, PGCE, Dip(Psychology), MA, MBPsS.
Lecturer in Psychology and Counselling Psychologist in Training, BPS Division of Counselling Psychology Trainee of the Year Award 2013.

Parental alienation is the undeserved or irrational rejection of a parent by a child, where there was previously a normal, warm, loving relationship. Can't Explain may be a fictionalised account, but sadly the themes which run through it are all too real for many children and families affected by parental alienation. Whilst each case of parental alienation is unique, these themes are often readily recognisable.

There is commonly a strong alignment with the alienating parent. A psychological splitting occurs as the child attempts to keep themselves emotionally safe. This results in the rejection of the targeted parent, and often their side of the family and even their friends. Children will often bad-mouth or verbally abuse the rejected or targeted parent, with little apparent guilt or remorse. Frequently, flippant, inconsequential reasons are given in support of their disdain and voiced wish to cease contact. Children may insist that any actions and wishes are entirely their own.

Sadly, as in this story, false or unsubstantiated allegations of domestic violence and child abuse are commonplace. Proceedings in the UK family courts are often protracted, and there seems to have been a widespread reluctance to take swift and robust action to ensure that court orders for contact are upheld. Continued separation, as in these situations, maintains and re-enforces the process of alienation. Once alienation has become entrenched, as in Kara's case, it is particularly resistant to intervention.

In the short term, children who reject their parent through the alienation process may appear to function well in their day-to-day lives. However, the medium and long-term effects can be significant and distressing with evidence of depression, substance abuse, damaged self-esteem and enduring relationship issues. Adults who experienced parental alienation as a child have been found to have a greater incidence of divorce and alienation from their own children.

As I read through *Can't Explain*, the lives of many of the parents I have met in my clinical work and research jumped out from the page. The behaviours of alienating parents, children, legal and social work professionals, as well as the disbelief and scepticism expressed by many people, were clearly apparent. This book is a representative portrayal of one family's encounter with parental alienation. I commend it, especially to those who work with young people and their families, so that the dynamics and features of parental alienation are better recognised and acknowledged. My sincerest hope is that a greater awareness and understanding will enable professionals to offer early, robust and appropriate interventions to the benefit of all concerned.

James Williams. *Mens Matters Radio,*
http://www.youtube.com/user/Menmatters/videos,
jameswilliamsgb@aol.com

Can't Explain is written in the third person; Paul Nelson is the central character. The story is laced with diary entries that lend authenticity to the plot. Paul is a normal, nice guy and becomes a proud father to a daughter, Kara. Like most parents, he seeks to ensure her welfare and happiness. Unfortunately, for father and daughter, the mother, Phoenix, has other ideas.

The book wastes little time in describing places or physical appearances, helping to demonstrate that what happens could happen to anyone.

Can't Explain is a thoroughly engaging true-to-life drama that sets out to describe Parental Alienation Syndrome (PAS). This is a form of child abuse where an abusing parent exploits a child's vulnerability and conditions their mind into hating and despising the other parent and all those associated with that parent. However, the book goes further than perhaps intended as it actually describes the most dangerous of human psychological disorders, for the mother displays many of the traits of a psychopath.

The abuse that unfolds is a classic example of the destructive nature of emotional abuse which is officially recognised as a definition of Interpersonal/Domestic Violence.

Phoenix uses Paul's confession of having had a 'fling' as an excuse to engage in a dehumanising campaign. However, his abuse had started long before. Unbeknown to him, Phoenix had been steadily isolating Paul from his friends and family right from the start and it was her escalating hostility that eventually destroyed their relationship.

The narrative progresses as an unfolding tragedy that engages the emotions and carries the reader along with the father's hopes of a happy outcome. Unfortunately, Phoenix uses his devotion to Kara to perniciously destroy the mutual love that once existed between father and daughter and twists everything to maximise harm.

Each encounter with Phoenix shows her to be narcissistic, sadistic, remorseless, lying, controlling and manipulative, demanding, inconsistent in her behaviour and hostile when she does not get her own way. She never accepts any responsibility for wrongs and yet will heap self-praise on herself for her own perfection. These traits correlate with those of a psychopath.

For a psychopath, love is a weakness and Phoenix exploits Paul's love for Kara to fashion an emotional hell. Given that 1% of the population have psychopathic tendencies, this book is a must read for anyone who is suffering relationship breakdown. Remorseless and driven by an urge to control and dominate, the rules of civilised behaviour do not apply to psychopaths.

Not appreciating what he is dealing with, Paul adds to his own woes by self blaming, a typical response for many normal people. Throughout, Paul tries to act in an appeasing manner, but this consistently plays into Phoenix's hands. Every concession encourages her to impose greater control. Paul sends letters to Kara expressing how much he misses her, but everything is sent through Phoenix with no guarantee that Kara ever receives it.

By the time Paul realises what he is dealing with it is already too late. Kara is receiving psychiatric therapy and her mother's control is complete. Phoenix, perhaps tired of Paul's presence and with a new man in her life to exploit, decides to twist the knife one more time. Her fully programmed daughter has become psychotically alienated. With all the venom that has been indoctrinated into her, Kara blames

Paul for everything and seeks to purge every aspect of him from her life by making vexatious and malicious allegations against him. It is gut wrenching stuff where the truth is crucified and Paul is stripped of his dignity as a father.

Paul learns that parental alienation is a common experience, especially for fathers, but he also finds out there is an almost complete lack of support available. Even pro-father organisations tend to offer little more than advice and sympathy.

To top things, Social Services (aptly referred to as the 'SS') and CAFCASS, who are supposed to act in the 'best interest of the child', prove to be the opposite of what they purport. They demonstrate a shocking lack of sensitivity that can only be described as misandric. Their mantra of 'always believe the child' is as breathtakingly flawed as it is stupid and dangerous. Paul faces ruinous false allegations which these organisations are prepared to accept in spite of the wealth of evidence against the claims. The reader is left with serious doubts over whether these organisations are fit for purpose.

Towards the end of the book, Paul reflects on how many men are pushed into total despair. He was fortunate to have a supportive family and friends and a modest income to help him cope, but his story exposes the callous disregard that society has for men. Many are driven to commit suicide and a smaller number even carry out murder-suicides.

At the conclusion, the reader is left unhappy with the seeming triumph of evil over love. Paul is left with a living bereavement, but there are loose ends. Will Phoenix's latest man, Ross, ultimately be subjected to Phoenix's destructive nature when she tires of him? The prospects for Kara, too, seem bleak with the mind-poisoning effects potentially inflicting permanent mental scarring on what should have been a loving, normal girl.

Hindsight is a wonderful thing. There were warning signs that

Phoenix had psychopathic tendencies early on in their relationship but, as with most people, the realisation came too late.

Paul makes suggestions that the SS and CAFCASS need badly to be reformed and trained to appreciate parental alienation, but this has been suggested by others. I believe it will not work whilst they employ individuals who are incapable of objective report writing and who carry deeply prejudicial views about men. Additionally, these services and the family courts seem to be completely incapable of dealing with psychopathic mothers. Unfortunately, such ignorance, bigotry and ineptitude means the unnecessary suffering goes on. Thousands of lives will continue to be lost and children will continue to be exposed to untold abuse on a daily basis.

Can't Explain is very good value for money and could save a lot of misery, but is a disturbing reflection of early 21st Century society. It also shows that the lack of support for male victims of domestic abuse is a disgrace.

www.ingramcontent.com/pod-product-compliance
Lightning Source LLC
Chambersburg PA
CBHW07084325O626
47159CB00003B/913